SHATTERED
TRUST

SHATTERED TRUST

THE SHATTERED SERIES #2

.

MAGDA
ALEXANDER

Montlake
Romance

Published by Montlake Romance, Seattle.

www.apub.com

Amazon, the Amazon logo, and Montlake Romance are trademarks of Amazon.com Inc., or its affiliates.

ISBN-13: 9781477817353
ISBN-10: 1477817352

Cover design by Eileen Carey

Printed in the United States of America

For Teresa
For being there

Chapter 1

Trenton

"I've been arrested." Those three words had thrown me into a tailspin.

A minute ago, my cell phone had rung with the strident peal I've programmed for unknown callers. I'd debated letting it go to voice mail. But a premonition told me to answer the call. Might have been a prospective client, after all. A lost soul who'd found himself in the slammer for something he allegedly didn't do. So I'd clicked on the phone. "Trenton Steele."

"Hello." Mitch Brooks. My former mentor and current friend. He sounded . . . shaky. Had he been hitting the booze again? Hoped not. He'd been clean and sober for the last ten years.

"You sound like hell."

And then came the three words that would shatter my dreams of a future with Madrigal. "I've been arrested."

It takes me a couple of seconds to come to grips with that devastation. This is the man I view as a savior, the one who saved me from an abominable life. When I was fourteen, he vouched for me in front of a judge, keeping me out of juvie hell. Later on, he taught me how to be a man. Any modicum of success I've achieved, I owe in large part to him. Taking a deep breath, I ask, "What for?"

"The murder of Holden Gardiner."

My heart slams into my throat. "What are you talking about? Holden committed suicide."

"No, he didn't, Trenton. He was murdered with my gun."

Sweet Jesus. I rake my hand through my hair. I need to see him now. Find out what this is about. "Where are you?"

"Loudoun County Detention Center in—"

"Leesburg. Yes, I know." I'm familiar with the jail. Over the years, a couple of my former clients had been arrested by the Loudoun County police. It's after eight, and the detention center closes at nine. If I hurry, I might just make it. I don't have a minute to lose if I'm to see him tonight. "I'll be there as soon as I can."

I make it to the front door just as Madrigal appears at the top of the stairs of her family home. A little over a month ago, she'd come to work as a summer intern at my law firm. Her beauty, innocence, and passion had torn down my defenses, and I'd been enough of a bastard to pursue a sexual relationship with her. After that, there'd been no going back. I'd come to her home tonight to propose we move in together. But now, that plan is clearly in shambles.

"You're leaving?" Madrigal asks as her younger sister, Madison, joins her at the top of the maple staircase.

Torn between wanting to stay and needing to leave, I clutch the edge of the door. "Something came up. I have to go. I'm sorry."

Her brow furrows. "What happened?"

"I got a call. Someone's been arrested." I can't tell her who it is. At least not yet. It'll only worry her. "Have to get to the Loudoun County Detention Center before visiting hours are over."

Her lips slash into a white line. "I see." She's upset about my desertion.

I climb up the steps and kiss her on the cheek in deference to her sister, who has no inkling as to the nature of our relationship. "I'm sorry. Truly. I'll be back as soon as I can."

She braves a smile. "All right."

"Can I go back to my room now?" Madison's petulant. She's only sixteen and probably wondering about my connection to her sister. Unfortunately, that explanation will have to wait.

"Yes," Madrigal says in a wistful tone.

Madison stomps away to her room, leaving Madrigal and me alone. She'd been so happy a few minutes ago when I proposed a future together for the two of us. But now? "I'm sorry. I have to go."

"I know, Steele." She presses my hand. "Go."

I'm sorrier than I can say about the sadness in her voice. I can't leave her like this, so I kiss her the way she wants. The way I want too. She whimpers as I cup her ass and nibble the sweet honey of her lips. "God, I want to fuck you."

"I want that too." She trembles as I knead her luscious bottom and devour her mouth.

But much as I'd prefer to stay and do just that, I can't. Easing out of the kiss, I whisper to her, "I'll be back as soon as I can."

She nods, but doesn't say a word. No wonder. I've stolen her breath.

Praying no cop's lying in wait to catch an unsuspecting speeder, I race up Route 50. I'll barely make it to the jail by nine o'clock. Half an hour later, I pull into the parking lot.

"Visiting hours are over," the beefy front desk officer says after I tell him I'm here to see Mitchell Brooks.

"Please. I'm his lawyer. He just got arrested." I show him my bar card and driver's license.

He blows out a breath that reeks of onions and mustard and clicks on his computer keyboard. "He's in a holding cell waiting to be processed. I'll bring him to the interview room." Lifting sausage-sized fingers, he says, "Five minutes. That's all you get."

It won't be enough, but I'll take it.

Wobbling toward the door that separates the reception area from the cells, he nods to his compadre. "Process him, will you?"

I've been through this before. So knowing the drill, I hand over everything in my pockets, including my phone and car keys. After he slips everything into a manila envelope and puts it in a locker, he gives me a ticket with the number 23 so I can claim my possessions when I leave. Once he's done, he escorts me to interview room no. 1.

Mitchell's brought in handcuffed. His usually groomed gold mane is mussed up, as if he's been combing his fingers through it.

The cop unlocks his cuffs and chains him to a metal ring on the table. "Five minutes," he says before he leaves. As if I need reminding.

When Mitch stares at me, the agony in his eyes is too much for me to take.

But there's no time to reminisce. Five minutes will go by in a blink. "What happened?"

"They showed up at work."

Work meaning the United States Securities and Exchange Commission in DC, where Mitch is the head of the Investment Management Division.

"Who are *they?*"

"Detective Broynihan and three other officers."

The detective who'd come to the house the night Holden Gardiner died—by his own hand, we had all thought. But apparently the evidence points toward murder.

"They read me my Miranda rights, told me I was being arrested for the murder of Holden Gardiner. And then Detective Broynihan said it was my gun that was used to kill him."

"What gun?"

He shakes his head. "I don't know. He didn't explain. The only thing I can think of is it must be the gun I gave Marlena."

"Madrigal's mother?"

"Yes. During her second year in college, there'd been assaults on campus. She was taking a night class and was afraid something would happen to her. I had a .22-caliber pistol. So after training her how to use it, I gave it to her."

"Maybe there's been a mistake? Maybe it's Holden's gun?" He was a gun enthusiast. Or so I'd heard.

He spears me with his glare. "Do you think they would have arrested me if they weren't sure?"

The door behind me opens. I turn around, even though I know damn well who it is. Sure enough, the stocky guard who let me in taps his watch. "Time's up."

"I'll find out who's been assigned to your case. I'll be back tomorrow."

His shoulders droop. "Tomorrow's Saturday. You won't be able to get that information until Monday."

Damn it. Broynihan did this on purpose, the bastard. He arrested Mitch on a Friday so he'd have to cool his heels in jail for an entire weekend. Although the law states that he must be arraigned within forty-eight hours, weekends don't count. I see nothing but trouble because of the delay. A high-ranking SEC official arrested for the murder of a well-known figure in the state of Virginia who was also a revered patriarch and head of his own law firm is like catnip to the media. The newspapers will have a field day with this as soon as word leaks out.

"Tick-tock," the officer says.

"You hang in there, Mitch."

"I will." He sounds despondent. But why wouldn't he? He's in jail, for Christ's sake. As I stand up, he pleads, "When you tell the girls, please break it to them gently."

The girls, Madrigal and Madison. They've always referred to him as Uncle Mitch, but now? He'll be known as their grandfather's murderer.

5

Chapter 2

Madrigal

As soon as Steele's car pulls into the moonlit driveway, I rush to greet him. It's after midnight. I've been waiting for hours, pacing the floor.

"Madrigal." Stepping out, he retrieves an overnight bag from the backseat of the car. He looks more tired than I've ever seen him. There are shadows under his eyes that weren't there before. Although he usually dresses like he stepped out of *GQ*, his jacket's rumpled and his tie's askew. What on earth happened to him?

"Where did you go? I expected you a couple of hours ago."

Curling his arm around my shoulders, he rushes me toward the front door of my grandfather's mansion. No. Not his. Not anymore. The house has belonged to my family for centuries, and now it belongs to Madison and me.

"Let's get inside. The night's turned chilly, and I don't want you catching a cold."

It's not the least bit chilly. Muggy, yes. Chilly, no. But rather than argue with him, I do as he says. "What's with the bag?"

"I'm spending the night."

Even though we're lovers, he wouldn't make such a move, unless . . . "Something's happened."

Once we step inside, he closes the front door and snaps the bolt. "Where's Madison?"

His furtive actions make me nervous. He needs to get on with whatever he has to say. "Upstairs in her room. Stop stalling and tell me what's going on."

He parks the bag in the foyer closet before turning to me. "Is there somewhere where we can talk?"

Going by the downturn of his lips and his bunched-up brow, I'm not going to like what he has to say. "The morning room." The space my grandmother used to write her thank-you notes, meet with her house-keeper, and plan events. I have a feeling its purpose is about to change.

Steele embraces me, and the scent that is uniquely his surrounds me. I love his strength, his intelligence, the ways he shows that he cares for me. But there's more than that to him and me. Even though he's years older than me, I crave him with every cell in my body. Despite all his sexual expertise, it was me who propositioned him our first time. He tried to turn me down, but I insisted. And after that? Well, we couldn't exactly resume our roles of boss and intern as if nothing had happened. But now something's come up. I don't know what it is, but suddenly I'm afraid.

I pull away from his arms to glance at him. The worry in his eyes is so clear, it sets off alarms. "What's wrong?"

He pulls me down on the flowered chintz settee. I've always taken pleasure in this room with its classic curves, curlicues, and floral fabrics. It reminds me of my grandmother, who'd sneaked sweets to me when I was young. But now the air's charged with tension, and the room no longer provides the ease it once did. "Just tell me, Steele."

A resigned look rolls over his face. "That phone call I got? It was from Mitch."

"Did a friend of his get arrested?"

"No. He did."

My breath catches in my throat. Uncle Mitch has been a fixture in my life since I was little. He's one of the finest men I know. "What for?"

Steele rubs his hands up and down my arms to warm me. "Your grandfather didn't commit suicide."

I shudder at the memory of my grandfather sprawled over his desk, his brains scattered across the ink blotter, the weapon he'd used clasped in his hand. "What do you mean? I saw the gun with my own eyes."

"He was killed." He pauses and gulps, as if what he's about to say is too painful. "The police arrested Mitch for the murder."

His words are like a punch to the stomach. "No. That can't be." All of a sudden I can't breathe. Fighting for air, I gasp, but my throat's closed up, and no oxygen gets through. I clutch him as the edges of my vision start to waver.

"Madrigal." He shakes me, but that doesn't do any good.

Sobs struggle to get out, but I need air to cry. No matter how much I try, I can't seem to take any in.

Steele stops shaking me and slaps my face.

As my body jerks from the shock, my throat opens up. I hold my hand to my cheek to soften the sting. I want to ask him why he did such a thing, but I can't seem to hold any thoughts together other than anger, outrage, confusion.

He brushes a hand down my ponytail, rubs my back while I gulp in great big honking mouthfuls of air. "That can't be. That just can't be," I say when I can finally speak.

"God damn it. You need a drink." Standing up, he looks around the room. He's not going to find one here.

"Gr-Gramps's study," I stutter. My body's gone cold. Cold as the grave.

While I try to hold myself together, he races away and returns with a glass half-filled with an amber-colored drink. "Here."

"What i-is it?" My teeth are chattering.

"Scotch."

"I d-don't like it."

"Drink it, or I swear I'll pour it down your throat."

He holds my shaky hand as I bring the tumbler to my lips and sip. The liquor burns on the way down, and I hate the way it tastes. I try to stop, but he tips the glass until all of it is gone. I cough and wipe my mouth with the back of my hand, trying to swipe away the vile taste.

In one move, he turns me and rests my legs on the settee's arms before yanking the blanket off the back of the small sofa and draping it over me. Once I'm settled to his satisfaction, he pulls a chair next to me, tucks my hands in his, and chafes them until they warm up. Then he turns his attention to my arms, my stomach, my legs.

A minute or so goes by before he asks, "Better?"

"Yes. I'm sorry." I attempt to sit up, but his hands urge me to remain lying down. "I shouldn't have gone to pieces like that."

He cups my cheek, and his warm hand feels like heaven. "You've been a trooper through your grandfather's death, the funeral, and now this. It's no wonder you had that reaction to the news. You've been so busy taking care of everything and everyone, you haven't given yourself a chance to fall apart."

"I had to h-hold it together. For Madison's sake."

"She's not here. And you don't need to pretend with me. So cry if you need to cry."

A wave of grief rolls over me. Thoughts of my grandfather on that last day. The awful argument we had. Me accusing him of knowing about my father's abuse of my mother. And now to find out he didn't commit suicide but was murdered. It's all too much. As my shoulders shake and the tears come hot and furious, I collapse against Steele. Even though I've known him for hardly more than six weeks, he's become my lover, my refuge, my rock.

For several minutes he lets my sorrow pour over him while he mutters words of comfort into my hair and rubs my back. When the paroxysm of grief abates, I pull back, painfully aware of how I've ruined his shirt with my tears. "I'm sorry." I pat his chest in a futile attempt to minimize the damage.

"It'll wash."

Eager to move his focus to something other than me, I ask, "Are you really spending the night?"

"Yes. It's not safe for you to be alone in the house. We'll need to arrange for security."

"We have a security service that monitors the estate."

The corners of his mouth turn down as his eyes narrow. "Which didn't work the night of your grandfather's death. We need to figure out what happened."

It's the *we* in the sentence that gets to me. "'We' don't need to figure anything out. I do. It's my home."

Going by the jerk of his chin, he's taken aback by my reaction, but his reply is kindness itself. "I'm sorry. You're absolutely right."

"Stop trying to pacify me." I shouldn't be yelling at him. But the tears released the anger I still feel at my grandfather's death, at the unfairness of it all. I'm in charge of everything. The house, the estate, Madison. Everyone's depending on me. I need to be strong, get a handle on things. Not depend on Steele to manage me.

"I'm not. I'm trying to help."

"Then stop being so damn bossy." He likes to control every situation, but I'll be damned if I let him this time.

"Sweetheart, I'm not." He tries to embrace me, but I fight him off.

"Leave me alone, Steele."

"I can't."

I stand and turn my back to him. "I think you should go."

"The hell I will." He storms to his feet and steps in front of me. His eyes spark with emotion. Probably annoyance. "You're in danger," he says. "Someone murdered your grandfather. Whoever did it could come back, or, even worse, it could be someone right here in this house."

My head ticks up at that. "Do you honestly believe one of the staff killed Gramps?"

"Someone killed him, and right now we have no clue as to who."

"I don't believe it was anyone in this house. Our staff has worked with us forever."

"Most were here that night. We'll need to question them. Make sure we know where everyone was at the time of the murder."

"We can't do that. It'll make them look like suspects."

He slices his hand through the air. "Of course they're suspects. Everyone in this house is. Stop acting like a petulant child."

I glare at him. "A child, am I? You didn't think so when you had sex with me."

"Madrigal, be reasonable. You're in danger. You need someone here."

"Not you. Not tonight. Please leave."

Someone knocks on the door, interrupting our argument.

"Come in," I yell.

Olivia steps into the room, her brow wrinkled. After our parents' deaths, she helped raise Madison and me while acting as Gramps's housekeeper. "Is everything okay?" Her voice is filled with concern. We'd closed the door, but our argument had probably carried into the foyer.

"Everything's fine," I say, wrapping my arms around my middle. "Steele's just leaving."

His jaw clenches. "I'm not going anywhere until you have someone watching over you. Where's that horse trainer of yours?"

"Hartley?" I ask.

"Yes."

"He's in the stable, nursing a sick foal."

"Get him," Steele says to Olivia. "Please."

Once Olivia leaves, I say, "His job is to take care of the horses, not us."

"Someone killed your grandfather, and we don't know who. It could be anybody. A friend, an acquaintance, a servant in this house. You and Madison need protection. By tomorrow, I can get a security team here. But tonight someone must stand guard."

Somehow his logic gets through to me. And for the first time, I'm afraid for our safety.

A few minutes later, there's a knock on the door. "Come in."

"You wanted me, Ms. Berkeley?" Hartley stands at the door with his ever-present cap in hand.

I breathe out a hard sigh. I really have no recourse. Steele is right. We must have someone here guarding us. "Mr. Steele suggested we need protection, and he thought of you. I told him you were busy with the foal."

"She's doing better, Ms. Berkeley." He nods. "The medicine the vet prescribed fixed her right up. I was just about to head home."

"Could you stand watch over the house tonight?" Steele asks.

Hartley's gaze bounces from Steele to me. "Anything wrong, miss?"

"Mr. Steele's worried that the house is vulnerable." It's not the right time to tell any of the staff that Gramps was murdered. I'll do that in the morning.

"Can you make sure the alarm's set and all the doors and windows have been secured?" Steele asks.

"Yes, sir."

"Once you've checked everything, I need you to stand guard in the foyer. With your shotgun."

Hartley's eyes widen, but he doesn't question Steele's command. Squaring his shoulders, he says firmly, "Yes, Mr. Steele. Don't worry. I'll keep Ms. Berkeley and her sister safe."

Steele turns to me. "Make sure the windows in your room and Madison's are locked up tight before you go to bed."

I nod, unable to say a word to him. It's beginning to dawn on me how wrong my behavior has been. I should apologize, but I'm too proud to do so now.

"I'll help her, Mr. Steele," Hartley says.

"Thank you. If you don't mind, could you secure the place now? I need to talk to Ms. Berkeley before I leave."

Once Hartley is gone, Steele's hard gaze drills into me. "You're not shutting me out, Madrigal. I'm in your life now, and I won't allow you to push me away. I'll be back in the morning, and then we'll talk."

"Fine," I whisper. When he tries to kiss my lips, I turn my head so the kiss lands on my cheek instead. If I allow him to kiss me, I'll beg him to stay, something I can't afford to do. With everything that's happened, I need to mull things over, and I can't think straight when he's around.

After he leaves, the place is silent, too silent. I shouldn't have yelled at him, but I resented like hell his assumption of command. I hate it when he does that. This house and everyone in it are my responsibility now. He has to understand he can't come in and issue orders, especially to me.

After Hartley helps me check all the windows in the house to ensure they're locked tight, I change into my nightclothes and crawl beneath the sheets. Thoughts of Steele loving me, caring for me, pop into my head, making it almost impossible to fall asleep. I'd been wrong when I asked him to leave. But I hated his presumption that he's responsible for the welfare of my sister and me. I can take care of Maddy, of myself, as well as manage the house and the servants. Maybe I'll make mistakes. No maybe about it. I probably will. But I don't need him to save the day. Thing is with Gramps's death being ruled a murder, life has gotten infinitely more complicated. So even though I resent his take-charge attitude, I'll have to accept his help. I'll just have to set down some rules, some lines he cannot cross.

Chapter 3

Trenton

Worried as I am about Madrigal, I barely sleep. Doesn't she realize the danger she's in? Somebody killed her grandfather, and it sure as hell wasn't Mitch.

He's been a close friend of the family since he was in prep school with Marlena, Madrigal and Madison's mother. When Holden created trusts for his granddaughters, Marlena insisted Mitch be appointed as co-trustee. He's showered Madrigal and Madison with birthday and Christmas presents and attended plenty of family functions.

On the night Holden died, Mitch and I were trying to rescue Madrigal and Madison. Holden had put Madison in a mental institution and locked Madrigal in her room. I'd been concerned about how Holden would react to our interfering with his granddaughters, but Mitch had assured me he had an ace up his sleeve as far as Holden was concerned. He never revealed what it was, but that's something I need to find out if I'm to keep Mitch out of prison.

Detective Broynihan knew about our rescue attempt. But somehow he'd added two and two and come up with five instead of four and arrested Mitch for Holden's murder. But he's dead wrong. Mitch is not the culprit, and it's up to me to prove his innocence. There's a killer loose out there. And Madrigal and her sister are vulnerable.

A foolproof security system needs to be set up. The night of Holden's death, someone disabled the alarm, because it didn't go off when I climbed over the fence to rescue Madrigal. The company that installed the security system is one of the best in the area, so if it was tampered with, it had to have been someone with expert knowledge of alarms or who lives or works in the house. And I'll need to figure out which.

I can't hold out any hope that the person I saw running across the grounds that night killed Holden. The shot went off inside the house a mere second before I saw him. But who was the bastard? And what was he doing there?

So many questions with no answers. But I'll find out if it's the last thing I do.

***

As soon as dawn rolls around, I call Charlie White, the guy I employ to investigate criminal matters. Charlie had been a detective since his early twenties and, after retiring from the force, set up his own agency. He's done his share of investigating adulterous spouses, missing property, and the like. But his specialty, and the one thing he loves, is investigating criminal cases. Twelve years ago, Madrigal's parents had been killed. Earlier this summer, Madrigal set out on a quest to discover the truth about their murders, so I'd asked Charlie to look into it.

But now I'll need him to shift gears and help me with Mitch's case. Hopefully, he can get some information before Mitch's arraignment, which will probably take place on Tuesday.

"Chief." Charlie's voice is groggy as all get-out when he answers the phone. "What the hell are you doing calling me this early?"

"It's six thirty."

"On a Saturday morning. The only damn day I get to sleep in."
Hard as it is for me to believe, Charlie goes to church every Sunday, a
habit ingrained in him by his mother. I think he does it more to honor
her memory than anything else.

"Sorry. It can't wait." I take a deep breath before I break the news.
"Mitch's been arrested for the murder of Holden Gardiner."

"Son of a—"

"Yeah, that pretty much sums up the way I feel about it. I need
you to—"

"Hold on, Chief. I gotta take care of business."

While I wait impatiently for him to return, I make a list of the
things I want him to do.

"Okay, I'm back. Damn bladder."

"Yeah."

"Oh, like this shit happens to you." Charlie's in his early sixties. I
feel for the guy, but he's a smoker and drinker and hasn't led the life of
a saint. Maybe a word of advice would do him good.

"Well—"

"Yeah, don't go there. So what do you want me to do?"

"I need you to call your contact at Loudoun County police. Have
her find out everything she can about Mitch's arrest."

"When did it happen?"

"Yesterday. The bastards showed up at the SEC."

"Hey, don't get pissed off at them. They got a job to do." Figures
he'd take the side of the police.

But he's wrong. They could have made it easier on Mitch. "They
could have damn well arrested him at home, and you know it. No. They
intended to make it as public as possible." I run a hand through my hair.
"I don't know how much damage control I can do before it gets leaked
to the press. At the very least I'll ask Madrigal, her sister, and their staff
not to answer any media questions. If anyone comes to the house, they
can be referred to me."

"You sure that's a good idea?" Going by the phlegm in his voice, he hasn't lit his first cigarette of the day.

But then we all have our bad habits. In need of a caffeine fix myself, I head toward the kitchen. "What do you mean?"

"You're representing the man who's been arrested for Holden's murder, and you want the media to talk to you rather than Ms. Berkeley or her staff. Someone might cry conflict of interest."

"Not if Madrigal appoints me as her spokesperson," I say, dropping a Keurig coffee pod into my single-server machine. Not as good as espresso, but darn close.

"What about Mitchell Brooks? You think he'd be okay with you acting as their adviser?"

"I not only think he'd approve, I think he would strongly encourage it. He loves Madrigal and Madison and wants the best for them."

"And that would be you?"

Of course it would be me. Who else would it be? Certainly not that idiot ex-boyfriend of Madrigal's. Brad Holcomb's as weak as they come, depending on his father's nonexistent money to bankroll his way through life. "I'd like to think so, yes. After all, I have their best interests in mind." Eager to get the hit of java in me, I grab the cup off the coffeemaker as soon as it's done.

His silence tells me he doubts the wisdom of my reasoning.

"So, about Mitch. What's your next step?" he asks.

I'm glad for the change of subject. Trying to talk me out of anything that affects Madrigal is futile. "Do my best to get him out on bail," I say, blowing on the steaming coffee to cool it down.

"I don't know about that, Chief. If he's charged with first degree murder, the judge won't cut him loose."

"I won't know the charge until the arraignment."

"Anything else you want me to do?"

"Yeah, I need you to contact that private security firm you've worked with in the past. What was it?"

"Stone Protection Services."

"That's the one. I need round-the-clock protection for Madrigal and her sister as well as the house. Have them send me the bill."

"Have they been threatened?"

"No. But somebody killed their grandfather. Until we find out who, I'd rather have someone around who knows the business end of a gun."

"How soon do you need someone?"

"Yesterday."

A phlegmy chortle rings out. "That soon, huh? I'll talk to him. See if he can get someone there by this afternoon." After a pause on Charlie's end, he says, "You have cleared this with Ms. Berkeley?"

"We talked about it last night." Of course, she hadn't agreed, but I'll convince her to do the right thing by playing on her weakness—Madison. "Oh, we'll need at least one person who knows how to ride horses."

"Chief, that's not a skill the typical bodyguard possesses."

"Well, see what you can do. Thank you for the file from Detective Collins. Strange he sent it to you and not me."

"You really didn't want that delivered to your office, did you? If your assistant read that file, it could have gotten back to Holden in a flash."

And that would have caused Madrigal a world of hurt, since Holden would have gone ballistic over his darling granddaughter's covert investigation into her parents' murders. "You're right. Thanks for looking out for Madrigal. We'll need to go over the file at some point, but that can wait for now." Collins had been the police detective in charge of investigating the murder of Madrigal's parents. He'd kept a secret file on the case that I'd paid to have sent to me. But we'll need to take a break from that investigation while we deal with the charges against Mitch. As much as I sympathize with Madrigal's need to discover the truth, Mitch's case takes precedence.

"Have you told Ms. Berkeley about that file?"

"No. And I'm not going to tell her either."

He grunts. "Steele, that's not right."

"What she doesn't know won't hurt her." She can't stand another shock. Not after the way she reacted last night to the news of Mitch's arrest for her grandfather's murder. I will bring it up. In time.

After hanging up, I shower, get dressed, and grab a quick breakfast before heading back to Madrigal's house. The drive to Loudoun County, Virginia, takes me north to the George Washington Parkway, then west to the Beltway and I-66 before heading to Route 50. The weather is typically hot and humid, one of those sultry summer days that Washington, DC, is famous for. But the AC in the Jag keeps me comfortable. One of the things I'm infinitely grateful for is air-conditioning. When I was little, we couldn't afford it, so my brother, Reece, and I broiled in the heat of the hellish DC summers. If we were lucky, someone would crack open a fire hydrant. We'd rush out into the street to play in the water spray until some utility worker showed up to end our fun. Even though I was only five, I'd looked out for my three-year-old brother to make sure he didn't get injured by a passing car. Protecting my brother came naturally to me. God knew nobody else would.

I shake my head to rid myself of those thoughts. Not that they will be gone for long. Memories of the brother I couldn't save will haunt me for the rest of my days.

An hour later I arrive at Madrigal's home. It's barely eight, but she's inside waiting for me. After her grandfather's murder, she gave me the code to the front gate so I could let myself into the estate, but of course the system alerted her to my arrival.

After the way we left things last night, I don't know what to expect. But before I have a chance to do much more than walk into the house, she wraps her arms around me and kisses me. Her lips are soft and hint of tears. Her scent, her taste, set me ablaze as they always do. But we're standing in the foyer where anyone could walk in on us, so I attempt to pull away from her.

Refusing to let me go, she curls her arms around the back of my neck and whispers, "I'm sorry," against my mouth.

I glance into her flushed face. Her dark-haired beauty and blue-purple pansy eyes have drawn me in from the first day we met. I'm willing to forgive her just about anything. "What for?"

"Last night. I shouldn't have yelled at you."

"Madrigal. It was a lot to take in. How are you feeling? Did you sleep well?"

"I'm fine, now that you're here. I couldn't sleep last night. Missed you so much." She brushes her soft lips against mine once more. "I shouldn't have kicked you out."

I push back a lock of her hair, which has fallen across her face. "I missed you too." I burn to kiss her, to savor the sweetness of her, but it's something we can't do out in the open. Grasping her hand, I lead her into the morning room. After closing the door, I take her into my arms and crush my mouth against hers.

A soft sigh escapes her as I devour her. Clamping my hand on her ass, I lift her and grind against her. I'm thinking about taking this vertical when, just like last night, a knock sounds on the door. "Mad?"

Madrigal wriggles free. "It's Madison."

"Have you told her about us?" She would have had time last night after I left.

"No. It didn't feel right to tell her without you standing next to me."

She hasn't made our relationship public yet. Not a surprise. Madison is not keen on me. It's not anything I've said or done. She just resents the hell out of anybody taking her sister's attention away from her. Like the teenager she is, she wants Madrigal's focus solely on her.

"I didn't tell her about Mitch either. I wanted you here. She's bound to be upset, and you can answer questions about his case better than I could."

"I don't know much more than what I told you last night."

"Mad?" The rat-a-tat becomes even more urgent.

"Come in," Madrigal yells.

I try to step away, but she pulls me right back to her. From her shoulder to my hips, we're glued to each other.

With the energy of youth, Madison bounces into the room, but stops cold when she sees me. Her gaze pings back and forth between us before it settles on me. "You're here again."

I don't know what to say other than, "Yes."

Her eyes grow wary. "Why?"

"I have some news for your sister."

"News?"

"It concerns you as well, Maddy. Please take a seat," Madrigal says.

"You don't need to explain things. I know you hooked up. I got eyes in my head. I can tell."

Madrigal frowns. "Maddy, please. Don't be so crass."

"It's the truth, isn't it? You and him. He's not moving in, is he? Is that what you wanted to talk to me about last night?"

Madrigal points to the settee we occupied the night before. In a no-nonsense tone, she orders, "Please sit."

The sixteen-year-old flounces to the small sofa and plops down on it. "Just for the record, I don't approve."

"Of what?"

"Of him moving in."

"If we decide to live together, that's none of your business."

"What about me then? You gonna leave me behind, the way you did when I was four?"

"I didn't leave you behind. Gramps put me in the Meadowlark Mental Health Facility, the same place he put you in two weeks ago."

Madison fists her hands, worries them against her stomach. "You didn't come home for a year. I was all alone. With Gramps and Olivia. No mother, no father, no sister." She lances Madrigal with her glare. "You all abandoned me."

Madrigal blinks as her mouth pinches into a tight, white line. "Did they abuse you, Madison?" she asks.

"No. They treated me right enough. But I missed my big sister. I missed Mom and Dad. And I only had Blue for company."

"Her stuffed teddy bear," Madrigal says by way of explanation to me. "Sweetheart, something happened yesterday." Her voice quivers.

"What?" A shadow rolls over Madison's eyes. I don't think she can take much more tragedy.

"Gramps." Madrigal clears her throat. "Gramps didn't commit suicide."

"He didn't? But you said—"

"That's what we all thought. But the police believe he was murdered." Madrigal's lips tremble as she says that last word.

Bending from the waist, Madison drops her elbows on her thighs. "Who would kill him? Who?"

Madrigal takes a seat next to her on the settee. Much like I did last night when I broke the news, she sweeps a hand down Madison's amber-colored hair. "I don't know, sweetheart, but someone's been arrested."

Madison jerks up. The look of desperation on her face as her gaze bounces from Madrigal to me is heartbreaking. "Who?"

"Uncle Mitch."

"Noooooo!" She jumps up, points at me. "Is that what he came here to tell you?"

"Yes."

She rushes at me, fists flying, and pounds on my chest. "Take it back. You take it back!"

Madrigal rises from the settee and embraces her sister from behind. "Maddy, please."

I gently clasp Madison's wrists to stop her from hurting herself. She struggles in my hold, pushing and pulling, until she realizes I'm too strong for her. "Let me go."

I instantly free her. "I'm so sorry, Madison."

The look of hate she shoots at me would put a lesser man in the ground.

"He didn't do it. I don't care what they say. He didn't do it."

"I know," I say as kindly as I can. "And I'm going to do my very best to prove just that."

.

Chapter 4

Madrigal

In tears, Madison races for the door, but before she gets there, I step in front of her. "Where are you going?"

"Riding." A hiccup escapes her, a clear sign of her distress.

"You're upset. You shouldn't be on a horse right now. You could get hurt or injure Marigold. I'd prefer it if you went up to your room."

Madison tosses her head. "You're just like Gramps. I won't be kept a prisoner. I won't."

"Maddy, please." I place my hand on her arm. She's vibrating from the emotion coursing through her. "It's just until you calm down."

"I hate you." She flounces out. But instead of heading for the stables, she stomps up the stairs, making enough racket to wake the dead.

After Maddy's outburst, I drop my face in my hands. When Steele puts his arms around me, I bury my head in his chest. "I'm sorry you had to witness that."

"She's a teenager. The drama comes with the territory." He drops a kiss on my head before he stands back to study me. "So what do you need to do next?"

I laugh bitterly. "I don't know. There's so much to take in. So much to do."

"Let me help. Please. I can move in temporarily. As long as you need me to stay."

"Are you sure? Don't you have enough to handle with Mitch's defense?" Clamping my hands together, I turn away from him. "I know we talked about moving in together, but now I don't know if that's the right thing."

His breath stutters before it takes on a hurried rhythm. I've upset him. That much is clear. "Why?" he bites out.

"Because of Madison. You see how she is. She has a hard time controlling her emotions. Either she acts like she doesn't care or she goes off like a rocket. There's no in between. I'm taking her to see a doctor. Someone different than the one she's been seeing. I want to know what's going on with her."

"Is she on any medication?"

Flabbergasted by the question, I can only stare at him. "I don't know. God. How could I not know that?"

"Olivia would know. Find out from her."

"Of course." I breathe easier once more. He's good for me, and not just because I crave him with every bit of my soul. He centers me, helps me think logically. I should be processing things for myself, I know. But with so much being thrown at me in such a short span, I'm having a hard time keeping my head above water.

Stepping up to me, he rests his hands on my shoulders. "Madrigal, I want you to listen to me. Very carefully."

"Okay."

"You have more than enough on your plate. Madison, your grandfather's murder, Mitch's arrest, the investigation into your parents' murders, the estate, plus studying for the bar. You *are* still planning on taking it?"

"Yes, of course."

"Let me help. You will make all the decisions and delegate whatever you want to me. I'll be your *consigliere*."

"What's that?"

"Didn't you ever see *The Godfather*?"

"No."

The corners of his lips hitch up. "One of the best movies ever made. We'll have to watch it someday. A *consigliere* is an adviser, usually to a mafia crime boss. In our situation, I can advise you as to the best course of action, be your sounding board. You're the boss. I'll just provide you with my best counsel."

"And how would that work? Would I hire you?"

"No. I'd do it free of charge. It's what I've been doing with the investigation into your parents' murders, after all. I suggest we extend my counsel to other parts of your life."

I tense for a moment. "I wouldn't want you to call the shots."

"I won't. But I can't say I won't argue my point of view. If I think you're making a mistake, I'll call you on it."

I rub my chin. "I don't know, Steele."

"You can't do this all alone, Madrigal. It's too much."

I let out a sad laugh.

"What's so funny?" he asks.

"I'd been planning on asking Mitch to advise me. After all, he's the co-trustee of Madison's and my trusts. But now that can't happen."

I pace around the room thinking about the ramifications of such an arrangement. I would have preferred to keep my personal relationship with Steele separate from the issues sure to arise in the handling of Gramps's estate. But I do need help. And since I can't very well ask Mitch, Steele is the logical choice. "All right, *consigliere*, let's give it a whirl." In the time-honored tradition of a business transaction, I walk up to him and extend my hand.

Recognizing the gesture for what it is, a meeting of two minds, he shakes it. "Along those lines, as my first bit of advice—"

"I already know. Charlie called."

"Oh?"

"He asked me if I had a preference for female or male bodyguards. Apparently, I've hired the services of one . . . or two."

"In my defense, I did bring it up last night."

"And requested him to obtain a bodyguard without my consent."

"That's why I just brought it up."

"And what would you have done if I'd said no?" Tilting my head, I wait for his answer.

"Tried my darndest to talk you into it. Seriously, Madrigal, you need one. We don't know who killed your grandfather, and the night of his death the alarm system did not go off. Somebody needs to look into that and find out what's going on here."

"You're right. I thought about it last night and came to the same conclusion."

"So what was the verdict? Man or woman?"

"I told him to hire the best person for the job."

"Wise as well as beautiful." He cups my chin and strokes the edge of my jaw, and I shiver in response.

Unable to think when he's touching me, I pry myself free and step away.

With a small smile, he tucks his hands into his pockets. I'm not hiding a thing from him. He knows what he does to me.

"One more thing, if I may," he says.

"Yes?"

"Once the media get wind of the change in circumstances surrounding your grandfather's death, they're bound to storm the estate. I suggest you leave them to me. If somebody calls or tries to intrude into your world, give them my name and phone number. I'll talk to them."

"You don't think—"

He strolls to my side and grasps my shoulders. "Yes, I do. At the very least, they'll harass you on the phone. At the very worst, they'll start climbing fences, which is one more reason why you need security. So leave them to me."

"Ugh." That's one task I'll be glad to delegate to him. Last thing I want is to deal with the press. "All right."

He squeezes my arms, which tells me he's pleased with my decision. "When are you going to let the staff know?" he asks.

"No time like the present." I find Olivia and ask her to gather everyone in the living room. Fifteen minutes later, when all are present, I open my mouth to speak. But nothing comes out.

It's only when Steele rests his hand on the small of my back that I gather the courage to tell them what I have to say. I clear my throat and square my shoulders. "Good morning."

A chorus of "Good morning, Miss Berkeley" echoes through the room.

"I'm afraid I have some distressing news." The wariness and fear in the eyes of some of them warn me that the faster I get the words out, the faster they'll get over the upset. I take a deep breath. "The police have determined my grandfather's death was not a suicide."

Olivia clutches her throat. Even from where I'm standing several feet away, I can see her trembling.

"Begging your pardon, miss," Hartley asks, "but if it's not suicide, what is it?"

"Murder. Cold-blooded murder." Technically that's not correct. But right now I want to make them realize the seriousness of the matter.

"Oh, my!" one of the maids cries out while another collapses into a chair. Without making a sound, Olivia folds into herself. Steele rushes over and leads her to one of the couches. Helga, our cook, wrings her hands while her husband, Hans, comforts her. Hartley, who had to have some sort of inkling after last night, stands with his cap in his hand worrying his lip.

"I know how upsetting this must be to you. It certainly was to me. We have some difficult times ahead. So I ask that you support each other as well as my sister and me."

"Who could have done it, miss?" Helga asks.

Now comes the second most difficult part of my announcement. "I don't know. But the police have arrested Mitchell Brooks."

"No," Olivia exclaims. "He couldn't have done it."

"I agree. Uncle Mitch could never have done such a thing. But given the circumstances, we'll need to bolster our safety. Mr. Steele suggested we hire a security firm to watch over us. All of us. They will be here hopefully today."

"One more thing before you go," Steele says. He cautions them against talking to the media and requests that they refer any inquiries from the press to him. With a word of encouragement, he hands out his business card. All of them nod and grin back. Even in this tense situation, he can make people feel at ease.

Before they leave, each and every one of them pledges their support. I'm grateful, I truly am, but a part of me wonders if there is one among them I cannot trust.

When I dismiss them, I ask Olivia to stay back. I'm worried about her.

"Are you all right?" I ask.

"Yes, of course." No *of course* about it. She's trembling, and her face is deathly white.

"Would you like something to drink?" Steele asks.

She looks at him with a lost expression on her face. "Perhaps a glass of sherry."

"Of course," Steele says and heads for the liquor cart in the corner of the room. He returns with a glass, and after Olivia sips at it, her color returns.

Sitting next to her on the couch, I rub her hand to get some blood flowing into it. "I'm sorry, Olivia. I should have told you first. So much has happened in the last twenty-four hours." I should have pulled her aside and told her privately. I don't think of her as just a member of the staff. She helped raise Madison from the time she was four years old. After my parents' deaths and my release from the Meadowlark, when all I wanted to do was cry, she dragged me out of bed, made me study, and forced me to rejoin the living. I owe her a lot.

"No. It's fine, Madrigal. It was just the shock." She takes another sip. "So Mr. Brooks is in jail?"

"For the time being," Steele says. "I'll try to get him out on bail."

"He didn't do it," she says.

"Of course not. The police got it wrong. I'll straighten it out," Steele says.

"Good. Good." A swift bob of the chin accompanies each word.

"Olivia. I want to ask you something about Madison."

"Where is she?"

"Upstairs in her room." After I'm done here, I'll go check on her.

"You need to watch over her now."

"Are you afraid something will happen to her?"

Gone is the lost look as her gaze snaps to me. "Aren't you? There's a mad killer on the loose. She could get hurt."

"We don't know what happened, Olivia. As I mentioned, we're taking steps to protect ourselves. A bodyguard will arrive either today or tomorrow. He—"

"Or she," Steele interrupts.

"Or she will make sure all of us are safe, especially Madison."

Finished with the sherry, Olivia rests the glass on the coffee table in front of her. "Very well. Can I go? I think I'd like to lie down and rest."

I can't let her go. Not just yet. "Can you tell me first what medications Madison's taking?"

Olivia clamps her hands on her lap. She's not trembling as much, although there's still a slight tremor. "Oh, there's quite a list, dear."

When she rattles them off, I'm appalled. "Why so many?"

Olivia's wide-eyed gaze finds me. "I don't know. They're the ones the doctor prescribed."

"What doctor?"

"Dr. Holcomb."

I get a sinking sensation in my stomach. Dr. Holcomb was the doctor Gramps called the day Madison ran away. And he's the one who admitted Madison to the Meadowlark facility. I'd thought his involvement in Madison's life was a onetime thing. But it seems to have gone on for years.

"He was your mother's physician as well. She suffered from quite a nervous disposition. Madison must have inherited it from her."

"But my mother didn't—"

Steele interrupts. "Thank you, Olivia. That will be all."

Olivia struggles to stand, but after coming to her feet, she takes a deep breath, straightens her shoulders, and marches out like a soldier.

"My mother didn't take any pills," I say once she's gone.

"As far as you knew. Maybe she hid them from you," Steele says, ever the voice of reason. "So, should I stay or should I go?" Even though he throws out the question with a casual air, I know how much the answer means to him. Truth is I want him around. Not because he's my *consigliere*, but because I need him from the bottom of my soul.

"Stay. I'll have one of the maids prepare the room next to the study for you. It's nothing fancy. Gramps used to sleep there sometimes." In the next second, it occurs to me he might not want the room next to the study where my grandfather was killed. "You don't mind, do you?"

"No, I don't mind." A muscle twitches in his jaw, and his voice no longer carries that vibrant warmth he exhibited seconds ago. He clearly objects to being placed in the small room. But I can't bring him upstairs where I'd be tempted to get into bed with him. And with Madison as upset as she is, I don't think we ought to flaunt our relationship in front of her. So for now, that's where he'll need to sleep.

Chapter 5

Madrigal

But after I crawl into bed that night, sleep eludes me again. My decision to assign Steele to a room downstairs was the right thing to do. We can't share my room. Besides the fact that Madison would be upset, the bed's too narrow for the both of us. We'd need a bigger one if we're to sleep together. Not that we'd be doing any sleeping.

After two hours of lying awake, I give up and wander downstairs in search of Steele. It feels weird but strangely comforting knowing he's here. But before I reach his room, I spot light seeping from beneath the door to Gramps's study.

Without knocking, I throw open the door. When I see him, my wildly beating heart settles into a saner rhythm. "It's you."

His glance finds me. There's no emotion there. None. "Why are you up? It's past two. You should be tucked away and fast asleep."

"I couldn't. So I thought I'd . . . come down and get a glass of milk. But then I saw the light. What are you doing in Gramps's study?"

Without glancing up, he says, "Looking for information, clues."

"We had the room cleaned." The detective in charge of the case had referred me to a service that specializes in crime scene cleanup.

Who knew such a thing existed? After the police finished collecting evidence, they'd gone through the room and left it spotless. But ever since I haven't been able to enter Gramps's study. It still feels like my grandfather is here somehow.

"Not that kind of evidence. I'm looking through his papers to see if anything jumps out at me. Somebody killed him. Do you know of anyone who had a grudge against him? Any servants, friends, acquaintances?"

"He had a property dispute with one of our neighbors over water rights, but they settled that. And he also had disagreements with one or two of the partners at the firm."

"I can get the partners' names on my own or from Mitch. But I'll need the name of the individual who argued with him over the water rights."

"I'll get it for you in the morning, if that's okay."

"That's fine. Anyone else you can think of? Staff members, for example." He drills me as if I were on a witness stand, except he's not meeting my gaze. He's furious. Not hard to see why. He wants to be with me, rather than exiled to the small room next to Gramps's study.

"No. He left the running of the house to Olivia. As far as I know, they never fired anybody. If people left, it was of their own accord."

He slides open the right bottom drawer, rifles through its contents. "What about the stables?"

"Hartley manages the stables. The afternoon Madison ran away, he told Hartley to fire the groom who allowed her to saddle her horse. I doubt Hartley did it, though."

"I'll check with him." He finally looks up, and his brow wrinkles. "Come in and close the door. I don't want anyone to know I'm investigating."

I glance at him, at the desk where my grandfather's shattered body had lain. "I can't."

His brow scrunches as he stares at me. "Why not?"

"You know why. This is where—" I can't finish.

Keeping his eyes pinned on me, he prowls closer. Once he arrives by my side, he crooks two fingers and raises my chin so our gazes collide. "It's just a room with four walls."

"His room. His study." I try to pry my jaw from his grasp, but he won't allow it.

"Not anymore. Now it's yours. Come." Letting go of me, he holds out his hand.

"I can't," I say in a strained voice.

"You can and you will, Madrigal." I hate the command in his voice.

In the next second, he clasps my forearm and pulls. Having no recourse but to follow, I focus on his broad shoulders while he heads for the desk.

And then it dawns on me. What he's planning to do.

When we get to the desk, in front of the very spot where my grandfather was shot, he winds a hand around my loose hair and pulls. Lowering his head, he nibbles my neck and licks his way down to the top of my breasts.

I should push him away, run screaming from the room. But I don't. Wanting more, I wriggle against him. His breath hisses as he takes a long, hard look at me. I'm wearing a demure white nightgown with spaghetti straps, nothing fancy.

"Kiss me, Madrigal."

I stand up on my tippy-toes while he kneads my ass and grinds that body I love against me. "I need to fuck you. Right here. Right now."

My breath hitches, and I shake my head. "I can't, Steele. Not on his desk."

"He's not here. It's only you and me. And this." He pulls off the nightgown and tosses it to the floor.

With one hand, I cover my breasts; the other crosses my groin. "Steele, please. Not here," I beg.

But there's no mercy in him. He winces as he picks me up by my ass and drops me on the desk.

No wonder. The night my grandfather was killed, somebody shot Steele too. His shoulder has to be tender. Deaf to my protests, he pries my hand from my breast and allows his gaze to roam over me. When he bends to suckle my nipple, a streak of heat races through me. Just like that, I'm lost. Everything fades: my objections, my grandfather's essence. All that's left is Steele and me and our consuming hunger for each other. He nudges my legs apart. No doubt where he's going. Burning to have his hot shaft in me, I encircle his nape and clamp him to me. He pulls something out of his pocket, yanks down his sweats, kicks them off, and climbs on the desk with a condom in his hand.

How does he plan this far ahead? Was he that sure I wouldn't turn him down?

There's no doubt in my mind that he desires me. His big, thick cock, curled practically all the way to his navel, bobs up and down. He tears open the foil packet and rolls the condom over his erection.

"Did you lock the door?" I ask now, when it's much too late.

His mouth quirks into that wicked grin of his. "No."

My breath shorts. "What if somebody walks in?"

"No one will."

In one small move, he lifts my ass, finds my opening, and thrusts into me. I grunt, and so does he. "Are you okay?" he asks.

"Yes." I'm stretched, stuffed to capacity by his hard length, exactly how I want to be. He swivels back his hips and pounds into me. It almost hurts, this invasion. But not enough to ask him to stop. All I want is more. More of his hard cock, more of his hard loving. More of him. "Harder. Faster."

Grabbing my ass with one hand, he thrusts deeper while I clutch the edge of the desk to keep from slipping off. "Yes, Steele, yes." He does something with his hips, which touches something inside. I explode and start to scream, but he clamps his mouth over mine so barely a peep escapes.

For barely a second he rests on me. Then he climbs off, grabs his sweats, and steps into the bathroom that abuts the study. When he returns, he helps me to stand. Good thing, because my legs won't hold me up. I'm still trembling from the aftermath of our lovemaking when he slides the nightgown over me and says, "There. You won't be afraid of that desk anymore."

I glance at the desk. He's right. Although the memory of my grandfather lingers, it's the remembrance of what we just did that will prevail. I toss a half-indignant glance in his direction. "Is that why you did it?"

"No. I did it because I wanted to fuck you more than my next breath." He cups my cheeks and ravishes my mouth. I have enough experience with him to know he's ready to go again. I'm debating whether to take him up to my room or make love in his when something outside the window catches my eye.

"Steele, there's somebody out there." I point to the window.

"Where?"

"The oak tree. Someone's climbing it, and it leads directly to Madison's room."

Chapter 6

Trenton

We race up the stairs to the second floor where the bedrooms are located. I don't know the location of Madison's room, so by necessity Madrigal leads the way.

As it turns out, her sister's room is only a couple of doors away from hers on the opposite side of the hallway. Madrigal frantically knocks on the door. "Madison. Are you awake?"

When silence greets us, Madrigal jiggles the knob, but it's locked. "Open the door, Maddy. Right now." An edge of hysteria rides her voice.

Several agonizing seconds pass before her sister yells, "Hold on, I'm coming."

A full half minute later, Madison swings open the door. She's dressed in a sweatshirt and sweatpants. Maybe that's typical pajama wear for a teenager. But what do I know?

The window behind her is open a crack. Whoever broke into the room didn't close it all the way. Suddenly it becomes clear who the tree climber must be.

"Where is he, Madison?" I ask in the voice I use to interrogate hostile witnesses in court.

Her eyes widen in feigned innocence. "Where is who?"

"The person who climbed in your window."

"I don't know what you're talking about." She sounds outraged, but her gaze has turned wary.

"We were downstairs in Gramps's study and saw someone climbing the tree outside your window. That branch reaches close enough for someone to use if they want to get into your room," Madrigal says.

Madison shrugs. "No one came in that way."

Not believing her for a second, I go for the most obvious place—the closet. If it's anything like Madrigal's, it's large enough for somebody to hide in.

When I walk in that direction, Madison freaks out. "What are you doing? You can't go in there!"

Ignoring her, I fling open the door. Sure enough, a man is inside. He's young, about eighteen, looks Nordic with blond hair, and is dressed all in black. Was he the one I saw running across the lawn the night when Holden was killed?

"Who are you?" I ask.

His Adam's apple bobs, but he's man enough to meet my gaze. "Philippe Dupin. I'm Madison's boyfriend."

"Maddy!" Madrigal screams. "You sneaked a boy into your room?"

The mulish look on Madison's face tells me we're going to get nowhere with her. "If you can do it, so can I. Just look at you."

Nothing like being hoisted with our own petard. Not only is Madrigal wearing a nightgown, but all I've got on is a pair of sweats. Clearly, we've been doing more than talking.

But Madison is made of stern stuff and waves her sister's objections aside. "I'm of legal age. Whatever I do with Trenton is none of your business."

"It is my business if it happens in this house."

Philippe Dupin's been quiet through this sisterly confrontation, but now he speaks up. "I wanted to introduce myself and date her the proper way." His speech is slightly accented. "But Madison said her grandfather would not approve of us dating."

Madison stamps her foot. "And he wouldn't have. You know how he was. He wasn't happy unless we were kept prisoners in this house."

"We were not prisoners. You went to school. I went to work."

"Yeah, during the day, but at night I couldn't go anywhere that was not preapproved by him."

We'll need to get the story out of them. If there's something I've learned as a criminal law attorney, it is to put people in separate rooms while they spin their tales. "Madrigal, why don't you talk with your sister? I'll take Philippe downstairs." Catching the young man's attention, I wave my hand in the direction of the door. "After you."

Madison crosses her arms across her chest. "It's so not fair."

Philippe and I descend the stairs in silence. I can't take him into the study. The room probably reeks of sex, so I head into the morning room. My masculine bulk seems out of place among the feminine, delicate furniture. Philippe, on the other hand, blends in with the room's aesthetics. Even though he's around six feet tall, his build is leaner than mine.

"Please take a seat. My name's Trenton Steele. I'm a friend of Madrigal Berkeley, Madison's sister." That's all this whelp needs to know, so I don't go into any of the details as to my relationship with Madrigal.

Parked as he is on the edge of the seat, he appears ready to bolt. "I'm sorry. I shouldn't have come to her room. I know how wrong this must look." Obviously, the young man is contrite, but that doesn't mitigate how wrong his actions were. Before I get to the hard questions, I start with something easy.

"So where did you meet Madison?"

"At a steeplechase race a couple of months back. It was the last one of the spring season."

"So you race horses for a living?" Some owners employ riders rather than race the horses themselves.

"No. They're my horses. Been doing it since I was a child."

"And you live around here?"

"Yes. About five miles away. My stepfather owns Pierpont Stables."

"I see." I stroll across the carpet to the bookcase where perfectly matched books fill the shelves. Curious, I choose one and pop it open. To my surprise, it's a diary. The delicate handwriting tells me it belonged to a woman. Returning it to its home, I make a mental note to ask Madrigal about it before turning back to Philippe. "You have an accent."

He squirms on the delicate settee. Don't know why. I haven't gotten to the hard questions yet. "Yes. I was born in France. After my father died, my mother moved to the States. She worked as a translator at the United Nations. That's where she met my stepfather. He was a UN diplomat. They fell in love, married."

Propping my arm on the mantel over the dormant fireplace, I examine a Dresden figurine. "How old are you, Philippe?"

"Nineteen."

"Are you in college?"

"Yes. University of Virginia. I'm prelaw." A bead of perspiration rolls down his temple. I'm making him nervous.

A bar cart that hadn't been here before has been rolled into the morning room. Madrigal must have added it to the decor. Its gold-plated finish matches the room, which tells me it must have been part of the furnishings at some point. "Would you like some water?"

"Yes, please."

I hand him a water bottle, keep one for myself. He guzzles half the container in one swig. Breaking and entering is thirsty work.

But then so is fucking. I swallow the contents of my bottle before I continue my interrogation. "So how did you get here tonight?"

"I rode Valiant, my horse."

"At night?" Seems dangerous to me.

"There's a full moon. It's bright enough to see the ground."

I pace back and forth while I settle on a surefire question to put him at ease. "You know about Madison's grandfather?"

"Yes. I read it in the paper. We've been texting each other as well. Madison's really upset about it."

"I think you know more than that, Philippe. The night he died, I saw a figure dressed in black racing across the lawn." At the time, I couldn't tell if it was a man or a woman, but the person had been dressed the same way Philippe is tonight. "I think that person was you."

He glances down, perhaps wrestling with his conscience. I let him. If he lies, I know my course of action. I'll out him to the police. If he tells me the truth, I'll ask him to go to the authorities himself. If he's serious about Madison, he'll do the right thing. Finally, he looks up. "Yes, that was me. We were supposed to meet that night. I climbed the tree like I did tonight, entered her room, but she wasn't there. I heard voices, so I hightailed it out before I could be caught. I didn't want to get her in trouble."

"Did you hear the shot?"

"There were two. I'd just touched the ground when I heard the first one. Took off running away from the house toward the wall where I'd left my gear. The second came when I was halfway there."

The first shot injured me. The second killed Holden. The bullet that hit me had gone right through. Although the police searched the lawn, the bullet was never found, so there's no way of knowing if the same gun that killed Holden was used to shoot me. "Didn't you think about coming back?"

"No. I knew she wasn't in her room, and I didn't belong here. I might have been blamed for whatever happened. So I just ran." He hangs his head. "I was a coward. I know."

He's very young. I probably would have made the same choice at his age, so I can't blame him.

"You didn't ride that night?"

"It was dark, so I drove."

"Where did you leave your car?"

"I parked about a quarter mile away on a dirt road that leads to the property." I'll investigate that to find out if he's telling the truth. But something tells me he is. Regardless, he must report his presence to the authorities. Sooner or later, they're bound to find out, and he might be charged with fleeing the scene of the crime, which will weigh against him if he ever sits for the bar.

"You'll need to go to the police and explain what you saw."

"But I didn't *see* anything," he protests.

"But you heard something. You were here that night. That makes you a witness. You need to report your impressions to the police."

"My parents will find out what I've been doing."

"Maybe not. Maybe the detective will keep it to himself." Although I highly doubt it. At the very least Broynihan will probably drag him into court to testify as to what he heard. So he's fucked whatever he does.

"It's not that I don't want to cooperate, but what does it matter?" he argues.

"Holden Gardiner did not take his own life. He was murdered."

"My God." He stares at the floor, shakes his head. "No wonder Madison's so upset."

"She didn't tell you?" I would have expected her to share the news with him.

"No. She texted me and asked me to come over. Maybe she wanted to tell me in person."

"You have a problem, Philippe." Actually he has several, but I'll start with the one likely to get him into the most trouble.

"What?"

"Madison is sixteen years old."

His eyes widen as panic rolls over his face. "She told me she was eighteen. She showed me her ID with her name and age and everything."

"It was a fake ID. She's not eighteen. Which means you broke into the room of a sixteen-year-old." I stop pacing and confront him. "Did you have relations with her?"

"Relations? You mean sex? No! We didn't! We haven't."

"You better hope Madison says the same thing, because if she doesn't, you can pretty much kiss your law career good-bye." At the very least he could be charged with delinquency of a minor. If they had sex, he could be charged with something much worse.

"*Mon* Dieu." He drops his head on his hands and pulls at his hair. "Why did she lie to me?"

"Because she likes you and didn't realize what the consequences would be."

He rushes to his feet. "I need to talk to her."

I shake my head. "Not tonight. Madrigal's upset with her. With you. My advice is that you tell your parents what happened. Get yourself a lawyer. Then go to the police and give them your statement."

He doesn't look too happy with my words of wisdom, but I'm giving him the best advice I can.

"You'll need to stay away from Madison. At least until things clear up."

"That won't be a problem. We're going on vacation in three days. I don't want to leave things like this with her, though. Can't I at least say good-bye? Please."

I feel for the guy. Yes, he's done some stupid things, but I sense underneath he's a decent young man. "It will have to be quick." If her sister allows it at all, which I'm not sure she will.

"All right."

"Let me see what I can do." I leave him in the sitting room and take the stairs to the second floor. As I approach Madison's room, I can hear them going at it hammer and tongs.

"I don't understand why I can't have a boyfriend."

"You're sixteen."

"That's old enough."

"To have a boyfriend, yes. To have him in your bedroom, no."

"Why not? You have your boyfriend in your room. I saw him the day of the picnic."

At the firm picnic two weeks ago, Madrigal and I argued. Unwilling to leave without making peace with her, I'd knocked on her bedroom door. Afraid somebody would see us, she'd pulled me into her room. We'd done more than talk, of course, and somehow Madison must have seen us.

"Madison, I'm eight years older than you."

"And that gives you the right to invite a man into your room?"

My knock on the door interrupts their argument.

"Come in." Madrigal's voice. She sounds exhausted.

Stepping in, I close the door behind me. Don't know how much anyone else has overhead, but I'd just as soon keep this private. "Philippe would like to say good night to Madison."

Madrigal appears torn between wanting to say no and approving the request, so I help her out. "I don't see the harm in it. He's going on vacation with his family. I advised him not to communicate with Madison before he leaves."

Madison pipes in, "That's why he came tonight, so we could say good-bye. Please, Mad."

Madrigal huffs out a sigh. "Fine, but I'll be in the room."

"Okay," Madison says.

The three of us walk downstairs. As soon as we enter the sitting room, Philippe stands up.

Madison runs to him, throws her arms around his waist, and rests her head on his shoulder. Well matched in height and in coloring, even in build, they make a beautiful couple. But they're so young, especially Madison. I doubt their relationship will outlast her adolescence, given her volatile temperament.

Philippe hugs her, but then pulls away. "You lied to me, *ma petite*. You told me you were eighteen."

Worrying her lip, Madison glances down at the rug before looking up at him again. "I'm sorry. It's just that I liked you so much and you were in college. I knew if I told you I was only sixteen, you wouldn't have liked me."

His frown reveals what he thinks of her excuse. "We won't be able to see each other again before I leave."

"Why not?" Tears tremble in her eyes.

"Because there are things I must do. Once I return, if your sister approves, we can see each other again." He gazes at Madrigal. Her stone face does not reveal how she feels about this pronouncement. "May I kiss her good-bye?"

While Madrigal mulls over his request, Madison begs, "Please, Mad."

Madrigal tosses her head. "Fine. One kiss."

The look Philippe bestows on Madison before he kisses her tells me he's truly in love with her. He's too young to understand the ramifications of giving his heart to a volatile sixteen-year-old. But then who am I to judge? I'm in love with a woman who's thirteen years my junior. There's no arguing with what the heart wants even if it spells ruin.

Chapter 7

Trenton

Between the night's drama and Madrigal crawling into bed with me after Philippe leaves, we do not get much sleep. Sunday morning we don't rise until eleven. A subdued Madison and an anxious-looking Olivia join us for brunch, which consists of mounds of eggs, bacon, sausages, pancakes, and pitchers of coffee, hot water for tea, and orange juice.

For someone who often went without food during his childhood, it's a veritable feast. "Do you always eat like this?"

"On Sundays, yes," Madrigal explains. "With everyone coming and going during the week, we often don't get a chance to connect as a family, so this is a way to share our adventures."

The conversation among those present starts off stilted, but soon Madrigal's asking Madison about the newest foal in the stable and Olivia about her latest knitting project. By the end of the meal, the tension in the room has, if not vanished, eased quite a bit. And it's all thanks to Madrigal's efforts. She's quite good at making people comfortable.

After brunch, Madison wanders to the stables while Madrigal adjourns to the sitting room with Olivia, probably to get more information about Madison's medication. I head to the bedroom Madrigal assigned to me, the one in which we fucked half the night. To my surprise, the room's been straightened up and the trash taken away. A maid's been here. Damn. I'm not used to having someone pick up after me. At my Crystal City apartment, I take care of my needs, and a cleaning lady comes in once a week. I'll let Madrigal know I'd just as soon look after myself. Don't want someone snooping about in my things. Not when I'm in the middle of a murder investigation.

I park my posterior on the studded leather chair in the corner of the room and pull out my cell. There's someone I need to talk to—Joss Stanton. The news has hit the media, so she's bound to know Holden's death has been ruled a murder and not a suicide. She and Madrigal's grandfather had been lovers since his wife died from cancer more than a decade ago. Not only that, she's a partner at my law firm, the one Holden founded. So I feel a certain obligation to check in with her.

"Joss."

"Trenton." Her voice lacks her usual vigor.

I cut to the chase. "Can I come over? There's something I need to discuss with you."

"I already know about Holden. It's all over the news."

I curse softly under my breath. "I'm sorry you had to discover it that way. I should have called you as soon as I found out."

"I imagine you're quite busy with Madrigal and her sister."

"Yes, I am." From the day Madrigal came to work as an intern at her grandfather's law firm, I'd been attracted to her. During a trip to interview a prisoner on death row in North Carolina, we'd been forced to take shelter at a fleabag motel in Virginia when a hurricane forced us off the road. One thing led to another, and Madrigal and I ended up in bed. When Madrigal's expense report raised a red flag, Joss deduced we'd shared one room. Even though she strongly suspected our mutual attraction, she never breathed a word to Holden. This is the first confirmation that she knew about our liaison.

"Mitch asked you to represent him?" A logical deduction on her part. She's aware of Mitch's role in my life. If it hadn't been for him, God only knows what would have happened to me. I'd probably be dead, just like my brother.

"Yes, he did." As an attorney, she's familiar with client confidentiality, so she doesn't bother to ask questions I can't answer. "He didn't do it, of course."

"I'm not so sure about that, Trenton."

"What do you mean?"

"Haven't you ever wondered why Mitch left the law firm?" Three years before, Mitch had severed his partnership with Gardiner, Ashburn & Strickland. Even though I questioned his decision, he never explained. "Ask him about that."

"Do you know?"

"If I did, I wouldn't tell you. I'd never betray Holden's confidence." Which means she knows the answer. "It can't hurt him now."

"It can hurt Holden's legacy, and that's something I'm going to do my best to protect. If you want to get to the truth, ask Mitch. I'll tell you one thing: it had nothing to do with the law firm." So, in other words, it was personal.

As soon as I finish my conversation with Joss, Charlie buzzes me. "Called in a favor at the Loudoun County Police Department."

"And?"

"My sources tell me there was no gunshot residue on Holden's hands. That's what clued them to the fact it wasn't a suicide."

There's no doubt it was murder, then. The gun that fired the fatal bullet belonged to Mitch. And, if Joss is to be believed, there's something Mitch is hiding. Some bad blood between him and Holden that the prosecutor will use as a motive. But what could it have been? Given sufficient provocation, anyone is capable of committing murder—that much I've learned as a criminal attorney. But what could Holden have done to drive Mitch to murder? He's a closed-mouth bastard most of the time, but if I'm to have any hope of getting the charges against him dismissed, I'll need to force it out of him.

"We're going to have to set up an evidence room to put all the pieces together. I'll start one at the office. Once that's done, I'll give you a call." This is not the first time we've run an investigation. Far from it. Charlie is the best at gathering evidence, but it's the visual clues that usually help us figure out the best defense for our clients.

"I'll organize my notes so we can hit the ground running, but you'll need Mitch's input to mount a credible defense."

"I'll talk to him after I'm done at the office. See you tomorrow, Charlie." I'll have to transfer a couple of clients to other partners in the criminal law practice group. Larceny and assault and battery, although felony offenses, don't compare to the murder charge that lies in Mitch's future. I'll need to talk not only to Mitch but also to the Loudoun County Commonwealth's Attorney assigned to the case, to get a bead on things. With any luck I can get the charges dismissed before the preliminary hearing.

Someone knocks on the door to my room. Madrigal. "What are you up to?"

"Calling Joss. She already knows. Heard it on the news."

Madrigal's face crumples with emotion, and her gaze turns watery. Joss is not only a partner at her grandfather's law firm but a friend. "I'm sorry she had to find out that way. How is she?"

I walk up to her. I'll never get over how beautiful she is. And how much I want her. Even now, in the middle of this tragedy, I'd love to lay her down, cover her body with mine, and make love to her. "Sad. Not talking." Unable to keep from touching her, I cup her cheek.

She tilts her head as if she yearns for me too. "About?"

"The reason Mitch left the firm."

"You should ask him."

"That's what she suggested. I'll do that when I see him tomorrow."

"I'm going up to my room to study for the bar exam. That darn thing is only a couple of weeks away."

Pulling her into my arms, I kiss her the way I've been burning to do. She doesn't struggle. "You'll do fine, Madrigal."

"I still have to hit the books," she mumbles into my chest. "What are you going to do to entertain yourself?" she asks, looking up.

"Jot down all the details I remember about that night. Do you mind if I talk to a couple of the staff?"

Her gaze turns wary. "Who?"

"Hartley for one, Olivia for another."

"She couldn't have done it. Grandfather locked her in her room, just like he did me."

"I know, but she could have seen something."

"Do it soon. This has been too much for her, and she's decided to take some time off."

That makes sense. The woman was Holden's housekeeper and Madison's nanny. I'd be surprised if she didn't need a break after everything that has happened. "Where is she going?"

"To visit her sister in New York. She hates planes, so she'll travel by train. It'll take her a couple of days to arrange everything, so she'll be around until Tuesday or Wednesday."

I spend the rest of the afternoon jotting down notes on the case, pinpointing avenues to investigate. My conversation with Olivia is painfully brief. The woman's a bundle of nerves. Hopefully the time with her sister will do her good. But Hartley's made of stronger mettle.

"Mr. Gardiner could be a hard one. He sometimes punished the girls, but I expect you know that."

"Yes, Hartley, I do. And you manage the stables?"

"Yes, sir. I make sure everyone toes the line. Of course"—he clears his throat—"horses are another thing."

"What do you mean?"

"We had a filly, Rosebud. A real beauty. But she disappointed Mr. Gardiner when she stumbled and lost a steeplechase race. Turned out she got hurt on the course. I could have fixed her, but he insisted she was done for and no good to him. So he had her put down."

Son of a bitch. "He killed a horse because she lost a race?"

"He could be a hard one if someone or something didn't live up to his expectations."

God. I knew Holden was a demanding bastard, but to kill a horse over a lost race seems deranged.

By the end of my conversation with Hartley, it's dinnertime. The mood at the table is much lighter, and Madrigal does not have to keep the conversation going. While we're enjoying coffee and dessert in the living room, one of the maids interrupts. "Pardon me, miss, but there's a gentleman at the front door."

"Who could it be this late?" Madrigal asks.

Even more important, how did he get in? The front gates are locked, or should be. Anyone trying to gain access to the estate would have to be buzzed in or know the password.

We find a dark-haired stranger in the foyer. I'm six three, but this man has a couple of inches and at least twenty pounds of hard muscle on me.

Even though her brow furrows at the sight of him, she extends her hand. "I'm Madrigal Berkeley. What can I do for you?"

"I'm Hunter Stone from Stone Security."

Her brow clears up. "Oh, yes. Charlie White told me to expect someone from your company."

A sense of déjà vu rolls over me. I've seen him before, but darn if I can remember where or when.

She points to me. "This is Trenton Steele. A friend. He's living here for the moment."

His blue-eyed gaze would drill a hole in a guilty man. Good thing I'm not guilty.

"Stone," I say, shaking his hand. "I'm sorry. Have we met? You look familiar."

"Not that I recall." He turns back to Madrigal. "There's been a slight change of plans. The operative I assigned to your detail has been delayed en route. She'll be here first thing in the morning. In the meantime, I will provide protection tonight. I'm dedicating a team of three operatives—one woman, two men. Each will be on an eight-hour shift. Alicia will handle the day shift. She rides, so she'll be able to accompany your younger sister"—he peers into his phone—"Madison, when she goes riding. In the meantime, I'll need to go over your security setup. I will be changing the security code for the estate."

"But our staff need the code to get in," Madrigal says.

"As of right now, nobody gets in without our approval. They'll have to buzz to get on the property. I'll need a list of all your staff, plus their photos."

Going by the twist of her lips, she's not on board with that plan. "That seems cumbersome. They're used to coming and going."

"Which is exactly why you need a security company. With all due respect, Ms. Berkeley, your grandfather could have been killed by anyone. The culprit could just as easily be someone within the estate as someone who gained illicit access, so I'll be running security checks on your staff."

"Some have been here forever. They will object," she warns him.

"I'll explain it's absolutely necessary in order to provide you and your sister with the best security."

Madrigal folds her arms across her chest. A defensive maneuver I've seen before. "Fine. The house will be protected, but what will you do about the rest of the property? There's thirty acres of land."

"Although our main objective is to protect the inhabitants of your home, we will, with your permission, of course, post security cameras throughout the property." His eyes assess the foyer and move up the curving staircase before snapping back to Madrigal. "Unless you already have them?"

"No, we don't." She tosses her head. "My grandfather wasn't keen on technology."

Stone's phone buzzes, and he excuses himself. While he's gone, I try to allay Madrigal's concerns. "He's only doing what you hired him to do."

She shoots me a dirty look. "*I* didn't hire him. *You* did."

"You want him to leave? Say the word, and he'll be gone."

"No," she says, gritting her teeth. "We need the service he's providing. I just wish it was less intrusive."

"You can't go on the way you have been. Look at how easily Madison's boyfriend broke in last night."

She stamps her foot. "That's because Madison turned off the alarm!"

"Well, with him around"—I nod in the direction of Hunter Stone—"that won't happen again."

Finished with his conversation, Stone tucks his cell into his jacket and strides back toward us. "My tech guy will be here in the morning. By sundown tomorrow, he'll have you all set up."

"Thank you. Have you had dinner, Mr. Stone?"

"Yes, thank you. There's no need to treat me like a guest. I will eat in the kitchen with the rest of the staff, but first I'd like to be introduced to them and your sister. And then I'll need to check out your alarm system. If you could arrange it, we'll also need a command room for our staff so we can set up some equipment—laptops and such—to keep track of things."

"Yes, of course." She's doing her very best to be polite, but even so, her resentment slips through.

Stone's gaze narrows as he studies Madrigal. "This seems pretty intrusive to you."

"Yes, it does."

"I understand. My staff is well trained, Ms. Berkeley. We'll try to make our presence as invisible as possible. If we do our job right, you'll hardly know we're here."

His charm gets to her, and she laughs. "Somehow I doubt that."

Madrigal smiles at him, and the green-eyed monster within me surfaces. Stone's at least a couple of years younger than me. And that dimple on his chin? That's something many women like. Maybe Madrigal's one of them.

After we introduce Stone to the staff, Hartley shows him the security system. Last night, Madison confessed she'd been the one to turn it off shortly before her grandfather was murdered. She'd been expecting Philippe and didn't want him tripping it. It's a sad state of affairs that no staff member noticed the alarm had been disabled that night.

As Stone becomes acquainted with the system, Madrigal glances over her shoulder at him. "He seems quite . . . competent, don't you think?"

"*Seems* competent? That man is staring at competent in the rearview mirror. He's an ex–Navy SEAL, for God's sake." Charlie had e-mailed me Stone's résumé as well as a write-up of his company.

"Will you need me for anything else, Mr. Stone?" she asks.

"Not tonight. I'll just familiarize myself with the equipment. But we'll need that room as soon as possible."

"I'll take care of it first thing in the morning. Or do you need it tonight?"

"No. Tomorrow will be soon enough."

"Good night, then."

"Night." And with that he turns his attention back to the alarm equipment. It's hard to get a bead on him. His expression gives nothing away.

When she takes the curving staircase up to her room, I follow her. I'm about to say good-night and head back to my own space downstairs when she tugs on my tie and lowers my head so she can nibble my lower lip.

"You're not jealous of Hunter Stone, are you?" There's a spark in her eyes, the witch.

How did she pick up on that? "Of course not."

"Why don't you come in for a minute?" As soon as I do, she walks to the window and draws the curtains. "Nobody will bother us here."

Tucking my hands into my pockets, I nod at the door. "Maybe we should hang my tie from the knob?"

"I doubt Olivia will understand."

"Maddy will. She seems pretty savvy. And she's trying to stay in your good graces."

She wrinkles her nose as if she finds the maneuver distasteful. "That would be a bit obvious, don't you think?"

"Isn't that the whole point?"

Chapter 8

Madrigal

Giggling, I fall back on the bed. "You're jealous of Hunter Stone."

"I'm not."

"Yes, you are." I glance at my fingernails before peering up through my eyelashes at him. "He is quite yummy, I must admit. But honestly, Steele, he doesn't do a thing for me. I can't stand men who issue commands right and left. I had enough of that with my grandfather."

Sitting up, I tug on his tie and lower his head so I can kiss him. "I may like Mr. Stone. I may even find him attractive in a primitive male sort of way."

He growls and pulls me toward him, a maneuver I just adore.

"But you're the one who gets me wet. Now what are you going to do about it, Mr. Steele?"

"I'm going to get you naked and lick every inch of you, Ms. Berkeley, that's what I'm going to do."

Dressed for success as he is, it takes him a while to lose his clothes, but finally he's standing in front of me in his Skivvies and nothing else, with all that lovely, lovely skin on display.

I'm wearing a T-shirt and jeans, and it takes him no time at all to rid me of them. All that's left are my bra and panties.

"Mmm, I love this bed," he says after making himself at home on it.

"I know you do. You're such a perv. Making out with the school cheerleader."

His eyebrows take a hike. "You were a cheerleader?"

"We're making believe, silly."

"Are we?"

"Yes. That's what you wanted to do in this room, isn't it? Imagine you're a teenager in another teenager's room? Maybe you're the star quarterback who sneaked into my room, and I'm the high school cheerleader. We have to be real quiet in case somebody hears us."

His mouth curls up in that wolfish grin that turns me on. "You'd do that for me. Make believe?"

"Yes. If that's what you want."

"No. What I want is you, my beautiful Madrigal, just as you are." He threads his hand through my hair and tilts my head to the side so he can nibble his way down my throat.

Breathless, I ask, "But what if that's what I want?"

He stops tasting me only to stare at me. "You want to be the cheerleader making out with the football captain?"

I shake my head. "No. I used to dream about one of the NSYNC boys sneaking into my room, though."

His hand circles my jaw while his thumb presses against my bottom lip as if he wants me to open for him. "Which one?"

Sucking his thumb into my mouth, I nip the tip. "Lance, of course."

He climbs full on the bed, pushes me down, and plants his massive arms on either side of me. "You do know he's gay."

Loving this power play, I brush my hand across his abs, tweak one of his nipples. "I do *now*. I didn't know it then."

His eyes flash with heat. "How about we do away with fantasy and go for the real thing?"

I turn serious. "That's important to you, isn't it? That I want you and no one else."

"Yes."

"I do. I want you and only you. I've only had one serious boyfriend, and he was a weenie." I hold up my little finger and giggle.

"What's gotten into you? You're normally not this giddy." Turning me over, he playfully slaps my bottom.

"Ouch," I say, even though it doesn't hurt. Twisting back, I toss my hands around his neck. "I'm happy, I guess."

He playfully nibbles my breasts through my bra. "Why?"

"Because I really, really like you being here with me."

"And I really, really like being here with you." The heat in his eyes tells me he's ready to drive this up another notch.

"Turn off the light, Steele."

"Why?"

"Because it's better in the dark." Somehow I feel less inhibited, more powerful in the shadows.

He rises and flicks off the light switch. While he's gone, I ditch my bra and panties.

When he starts to crawl back into bed with me, I remind him about a condom.

"Right." He digs around in the dark, curses.

Even though I'd tossed my playfulness to the side, I can't help but giggle.

"What's so funny?" he asks when he returns to the bed.

"Reminds me of our first time. You stumbled over something in that hotel room on your way to retrieve a condom."

"I banged my shin on the corner of that blasted sofa. It hurt like a son of a bitch." When he slides me under him, his cock brands itself on my skin. "Now, Ms. Berkeley, shall we get down to business?"

"Yes, please."

"Kiss me."

"You want me to kiss you?"

"I just asked, didn't I?"

"Very well." I pull down his head and peck at his lip. He tastes of something sweet, like licorice. Strange. I didn't know he liked such a thing. I only have a second's warning before he devours my mouth. I knew he wouldn't wait long to take control of the kiss.

He kisses his way down my body, pausing to worship my breasts. "I love your tits, your nipples." He licks the sides, and they grow heavy with need as he nips and nibbles the tips. Craving attention, my core heats. I wiggle under his assault and tug on his hair. "Lower, Steele."

"Your wish is my command, sweetheart."

He pursues his eager exploration until he arrives at my clit. When his wanton tongue rasps at my pearl, I moan.

"Ambrosia." Not wasting time, he slides a finger into my sheath and finger-fucks me. When I arch, he presses down on my midriff to keep me just where he wants me. I squirm as the sound of his erotic assault and the perfume of my need waft around us.

Eager to be impaled by him, I demand: "Steele, now."

"No. Not until you're mindless with passion. Not until you beg me to fuck you."

I'm ready to beg right now, but I sense it's not a regular supplication he's after. He wants me to turn over every inch of me to his keeping so he can do what he will with me.

When he slides a second and third finger into me, I buck under him while his mouth devours my core.

He then flips me so I'm facedown on the bed and raises my head. "Look at us." The floor-length mirror that stands on the other side of the room bears silent witness to our passion. I gasp at the picture we make.

"You want me, Madrigal?" he asks as he strokes his massive cock between my cheeks.

"You know I do."

He teases my opening a bare inch. I buck back to take more of him, but he's a wily bastard and retreats.

"Beg me."

"Please fuck me."

"Hard and fast?"

"Yes, please."

He notches his cock in me and thrusts. Then he pulls back and thrusts again, deeper, faster, and infinitely harder. In and out while he clutches my ass. I love it when he does that. It's like he can't get deep enough inside me.

Finally we come. Him first, me second. We're drenched in sweat. He rises and goes to the bathroom to toss away the used condom, wash up, and slip back into bed with me. "This bed is really, really small."

"I know. We'll need to find a bigger one if we're to sleep together."

"Are we?"

"Are we what?"

"Going to sleep in one together?"

I brush my hand across the stubble on his chin. "Wouldn't you like that?"

"I would."

"Well, there you go. And we've certainly got enough beds in this house. Finding one won't be a problem."

For a few minutes, we breathe in unison. Happy that we are together, I clutch him to me while he rests his head on my breasts.

"Do you believe they haven't had sex?" I ask, running my hand through his hair.

"Your sister and Philippe?" His voice rumbles from my chest.

"Yes."

"Well, he's nineteen and believed she was eighteen, the age of consent. So . . ."

"God. I hope they used protection. He should have asked for her ID."

"He did."

I come up on my elbows. "You mean she has a fake ID?"

"Apparently. You'll have to take it away from her. She can't be allowed to use it. Aside from the fact it's illegal, she can get into a world of trouble flashing false identification."

I plop back on the bed. "God. I was never this much work."

"When you visit the doctor with her, you might want him to draw blood and do a pregnancy test."

"You don't think—oh, God, what if she is?"

"Don't jump off that bridge unless you have to, sweetheart. If she is, we'll handle it. Together."

In future days, I would look back fondly on this night. Because it took no time at all for things to turn bad.

Chapter 9

Trenton

Monday morning comes too soon. Much as I hate to leave her, I must. Duty calls me back to the law firm. As we stand in the foyer, I hold her close to me. "I have to go to the office."

"I know." The corners of her lips twist. Perhaps she resents our separation as much as I do.

Needing to touch her, I brush the back of my hand across the satin softness of her cheek. "How will you spend your day?"

She curls her arms around my waist, rests her head against my chest. "Studying for the bar exam, after I make a doctor's appointment for Madison. Hopefully, I can get one for tomorrow or Wednesday at the latest."

"Do you have a lead on a doctor?"

"Yes. I know someone whose sister is a doctor at Georgetown University Hospital. I'll start there."

"If you need help, let me know."

She gets that mulish look on her face. "I can handle this, Steele."

I kiss her lips, squeeze her arm. "I know you can. Don't study too hard for the exam. Chances are you already know most of it and only need a refresher course."

"I never studied domestic law, and that's one of the topics we'll be tested on."

"You want me to put you in touch with someone from the Virginia bar?"

"No, I can do this."

The urge to help her burns right through me. But she resents my offer, so I dial it back. "Okay."

During the drive to the office, I think about the best approach to take with her. Maybe the best thing I can do is just be there for her instead of constantly offering my assistance. I laugh. Easier said than done given my type A personality. I crank up the hip-hop station, hoping to drown out the control freak in me.

When I get to the office, a message waits for me. A management meeting is scheduled for nine o'clock, and my presence is requested. Since Mitch's arraignment is tomorrow, I fill in the time by dialing the Loudoun County Commonwealth's Attorney's office to find who's been assigned to Mitch's case. The receptionist takes down my information and promises that someone will get back to me.

When nine o'clock rolls around I make my way up the elevator to the west conference room on the ninth floor. With its view of the mall and the monuments, the room is one of the loveliest in the firm and just big enough for the ten or so members of the management committee. When I step in, a sense of foreboding rolls over me. I don't know what the hell's going on, but my nemesis, Dick Slayton, is seated at the head of the table, which tells me nothing good can come from this.

"Good morning," I say.

A few of the partners mumble greetings in return, but no one meets my gaze, not even Joss Stanton.

"Please, Trenton, take a seat," Dick says.

Unbuttoning my jacket, I sit near the foot of the table, as far away from Slayton as I can get.

Dick clears his throat and combs back the little hair he's got left on his head. "We understand Holden's death was ruled a murder and not a suicide."

"That's right." I relax into the seat. Maybe all they want is a sit report from me. Understandable given the circumstances.

"And Mitchell Brooks has been arrested in connection with the murder and asked you to represent him."

I nod. "Yes, he has."

"You'll need to decline representation."

I snap upright. Didn't see that one coming. "Why the hell should I do that?"

"Holden Gardiner was the founding member of this firm. You can't represent his accused murderer. It's morally incomprehensible you'd even consider such a thing."

"Isn't the accused presumed innocent until proven guilty? Besides, there's no conflict of interest."

He shrugs, a clear dismissal of my argument. "Maybe not legally, but morally there is. It's very simple, Trenton. If you want to represent Mitchell Brooks, you can no longer be a member of this firm."

Disgust pours out of my every pore. "And this is the decision of the management committee?"

"It is. We took a vote this morning. It was unanimous."

It's a power play, plain and simple. Dick never wanted me in the firm and has always resented the hell out of me for being made partner. Rising to my feet, I drill my closed fists into the conference table. "If you expect me to drop Mitch's representation, you're sadly mistaken."

The son of a bitch smirks. "I expect you'll represent him no matter the harm to your career. You never were able to look out for yourself. Always trying to save those poor souls who couldn't afford representation. You refused to look out for the bottom line."

How he can make that argument is beyond me. He's the one who insisted on hiring high-priced lawyers for his practice group who contribute very little to the financial welfare of the firm. "You do realize that many of my clients will follow me? The moment I hang out my shingle somewhere else, they'll flock to my new firm en masse."

He waves his hand as if the thought does not bother him one whit. "So be it. I don't really care."

"You will when their money flows my way. This firm is already on shaky ground. When my clients turn to me, you won't have enough money to run it."

Leaning forward, he steeples his hands over the conference table. "So you're leaving?" He voices the question as if the answer means less than nothing to him.

"You know damn well I'm not going to turn down representing Mitch."

"I thought that would be your decision. Good-bye, Trenton." He thinks he's won. Son of a bitch.

On the way back to my floor, I wrestle my emotions under control. I'll be damned if I allow my temper to show. I walk into my office to discover my computer has already been disconnected as well as my phone. Someone from support services helps me pack. Even after all these years in the firm, I have few mementos. My law school diploma, a photo of Mitch and me, a Montblanc pen he gave me when I passed the bar. It takes no time at all to stuff everything into a file box. Someone from Human Resources shows up to take my office key card. I walk out of the place where I've worked for eight years with my head held high. Not one person meets my gaze. Nobody wants to witness my walk of shame, but I know there are plenty of eyes peering out their glass-enclosed offices while I wait for the elevator that will take me away from this fucking place.

Once I reach the garage, I drop my pitiful box of belongings in the backseat of my Jag. Driving up to street level, I hand my parking pass to the attendant. I most certainly will never use it again, and he can sell it to someone else for the remainder of the month.

"You're not coming back, Mr. Steele?"

"No. I'm not."

"Good luck, then."

"Same to you, Harry. Same to you."

I pull into the E Street traffic, hang a left on 15th, and head on home to my Crystal City condo. There I'll plan my next move, but only after I get good and drunk.

***

Hours later, a strident buzzing wakes me. "What the hell?" Somebody's calling from downstairs. Sitting up, I press the button that connects me with the concierge on the first floor.

"Mr. Steele, there's a Madrigal Berkeley here to see you, sir." It's Tommy. One of the guards at the front desk.

After drinking two bottles of wine and falling headfirst into bed, I look like shit and stink worse, but I can't leave her hanging downstairs while I clean up. "Send her up, will you, Tommy?"

"Yes, sir."

I meet her by the elevator. Her eyes look crushed. As soon as the door opens, she walks forward and embraces me. "I'm sorry you're no longer at Gardiner."

Her kindness touches something deep within me. I've had so little of it in my life. Dropping my chin on top of her head, I say, "How did you know?"

"I dialed your cell. When you didn't answer, I called Joss. She told me what happened."

In the state I'd been in I had no wish to talk to anybody. "I turned it off." A thought occurs to me. "You didn't come by yourself?"

"No. One of the Stone Security guards drove me here. I sent him home after he dropped me off."

Which means she intends to stay. A slow fire starts in my belly. "You're spending the night," I rasp out.

"Yes. Have you had dinner?"

"No."

"You need to eat. Should we order in?"

I love how concerned for me she is. "No. I'll make something. Have to shower first. I reek." She, on the other hand, smells of lavender and rose.

"Okay."

After emerging from the bathroom a lot fresher than before, I head for the kitchen, where I find her perched on one of the stools. Before I fix dinner, I decant a bottle of wine and allow it to breathe. In less than thirty minutes I have chicken roasting in the oven and pasta bubbling on the stove. I scoop up a portion with a wooden spoon and offer it to her. "You want some?"

"I already ate."

"So that whole order-in suggestion . . . ?" Rather than toss the morsel back in the pan, I gobble it. Predictably, my stomach rumbles with gratitude.

The corners of her lips turn up. "I wanted you to eat. I know how much you value food."

She's picked up on that, has she? And here I thought I'd hidden my food obsession so well. "Where's Madison?"

"At home. There are two guards there—Hunter Stone and another operative. She's well protected. Right now, you need me more than she does."

I do need her. She just doesn't know the extent of it.

"So Joss didn't explain much. She only mentioned you left the firm." Propping her elbows on the counter, she drops her chin on her hands. "What happened?"

"Dick Slayton sandbagged me. He called me into a management committee meeting this morning and gave me an ultimatum—either I drop Mitch as a client or my services are no longer needed at Gardiner, Ashburn & Strickland."

"And you chose Mitch."

"Of course. If it hadn't been for him, I would probably have been killed in the mean streets of DC, the victim of gang violence."

After the chicken browns nicely, I fold it into the drained pasta, pour two glasses from the bottle I'd decanted, and pull up a stool next to her. As I do, she climbs down from hers. Soon she's washing the pans and cleaning up the kitchen. "You don't have to do that," I say.

"I want to." She points to my plate. "Eat. You need it."

Used to eating fast, it takes me no time at all to devour the meal.

I toss the dish and the cutlery into the dishwasher, grab her hand and the bottle of wine, and head for the living room. "It's too warm to get a cozy fire going."

"I don't need a cozy fire," she says, dropping next to me.

"What do you need, *bella*?" The low fire in my belly has become a roaring furnace. I ache for her more than my next breath.

She rests her hand on my chest. "You."

I wrap my hand around her nape and pull her toward me, but soon kissing her is not enough. I lift her off the couch and drop her into my lap, and then I push my cock into her belly so she can feel every inch of me. With open mouths we devour each other, stealing each other's breath, tasting one another.

"Take off your shirt," she commands.

She doesn't have to ask me twice. One-handed, I strip off the Henley. As soon as I do, she nibbles her way down my chest to the ring that adorns my right nipple.

"When did you have this done?"

"In college." I lie back on the couch and straddle her legs over my cock. In that position, she can suckle my nipple to her heart's content and pleasure herself by riding my erection.

"Why?" When she curls her tongue around the ring and tugs, I hiss in a breath.

God almighty. "A friend of mine worked at a tattoo parlor. He needed the practice."

As she palms my right pec, she shivers. "And you offered yourself as a guinea pig?"

"Yes." My gaze follows her every move, wondering what she'll do next.

"Did it hurt?" She trails her hand down my flank.

"A little." Not wanting her to reach the Promised Land just yet, I clamp my hands on her hips and roll mine beneath her.

I know I've sparked her sweet spot when she gasps. "And the winged tattoo?" With a trembling finger, she traces the symbol branded on my chest.

The answer tamps down the heat blazing between us. "That's in memory of my brother."

"When did he die?"

Hoping to avoid the subject, I sit up and kiss her hard. "Do we have to talk about this right now?"

"No. But I'd like to know."

I have no defenses against her honest curiosity. And it's not a surprise. I knew she'd ask about it one day. "We were taken away from our father when I was eight and he was six. I begged Social Services to keep us together, but they put us in separate foster homes. I tried to keep tabs on him, but it was hard. We kept getting transferred from one home to another. When he was ten, he was arrested for selling drugs. Promising to keep him safe, the authorities talked him into turning state's evidence against his gang. After he testified, they returned him to juvie. Before they could relocate him, he was killed. They never found out who did it." The pain of that memory, vivid as it ever was, cuts me to the core.

"I'm so sorry, Steele." Fast and furious tears flow down her face.

"Hey." I brush the moisture away. "I don't want you crying over me."

"I'm not. I'm crying over your brother."

She probably is, but her tender heart's also bleeding for me. I take her mouth, suckle her lips, taste the sweetness that is Madrigal Berkeley. The combination of the wine and her salty tears stirs something in me. Nobody has ever cried for me. And I certainly don't deserve her tears, not with my wicked past.

"Are you going to make love to me?" she asks.

"I don't make love, sweet girl, I fu—"

She lays a finger over my lips. "Don't."

I nibble her fingertip before sucking it into my mouth. My hand skims down her panties to find her wet. "Don't what?"

"Don't say that word. I know the difference between fucking and making love, and what we do is make love."

Chapter 10

Madrigal

He picks me up by my ass and in one smooth move comes to his feet. I love it when he does that. He's so big and strong and so very, very male. When we get to his bedroom, he slowly peels off my blouse, stopping to kiss every inch that he reveals. My old boyfriend had always been in so much of a hurry that sometimes he didn't even stop to take off my clothes. It was like I was a duty to him.

But Steele? With him, I feel precious, like something to be cherished. As soon as my bra comes off, he suckles the tip of my breast, and I wiggle beneath him.

"You like that?"

"You know I do."

"You're going to like this even more." He shimmies off my skirt and my panties. I'm lying naked while he's still wearing his silk pajama bottoms.

He pulls something from his night drawer.

"What's that?"

"A silk scarf."

Unsure about his intentions, I ask, "You're going to tie me up?"

"Yes. Unless you have an objection."

"No." I trust him not to hurt me, not to take more than I can give.

"Place your hands above your head."

"What if I want to touch you?"

"You can't." There is no softness in his voice. It's as hard as the rest of him.

"Doesn't seem fair that you can touch me, but I can't reciprocate." I want to feel the hills and valleys, the virile heat of him.

"We can stop if you like."

"No. Do it." I raise my hands above my head. In the next second, he secures them to the bedpost.

Hunting in his drawer again, he retrieves a second item. A mask. I bite down on my lip. I'll be helpless. Do I really want this? "I won't be able to see."

"Yes, I know. I won't fasten your legs. We'll do that another time."

"Oh?" After the mask is in place, I will my breath to saw in and out while I wait for him to take the next step. Some rustling occurs. "What are you doing?"

"Getting ready."

"Ready for what?"

"To fuck you."

Too late I realize I shouldn't have said what I did. He has two ways of fucking. One is what he's done with me all this time. The other? Whatever he's getting ready to do, which I imagine is what he does with other women. My heart takes up a wild rhythm. What is he going to do to me?

He climbs back on the bed, clasps one of my tied hands, and curls it around his thick, hard cock. "Feel me."

The musk of him surrounds me. More than anything I want to taste him, to put him in my mouth, but that's not what he wants. At least not right now. I pump him the way he likes, and he groans.

"All the way down to the root."

When my fingers brush against him, I find something there. A cold, metal object wrapped around him right at the base of his shaft. "What is that?"

"A cock ring."

"What does it do?"

"Makes me hard so I can keep you coming all night long."

My breathing goes staccato as he leans over me to suck my nipple into his mouth. "Don't stop pumping."

When I continue, his cock grows thicker, longer, and he groans.

I jerk away my hand. "I'm hurting you."

"No, you're not." He curls my fingers back around him and moves them up and down his shaft. With his hand over mine, we're both stroking him, something I find strangely erotic. I lick my lips, and he comes closer. "You want to taste me, don't you?"

"Yes." My voice wavers.

"Here. It's all yours." He teases my lips open, and I take him in, at first just the head. I lick him, and he groans.

Filled by him, I can't talk. I can only let him know with my tongue, my teeth, how much I'm enjoying him. As he slowly slides and retreats, I rake them over him.

"Fuck." For the next few seconds, he gently surges in and out. But then when I lick the rim, his breathing grows harsh, and he pops out. "That's enough."

"I want you to come in my mouth."

"No. Not tonight."

"Fuck me, then. Please."

He slides down my body, kissing my skin every inch of the way until he gets to the very heart of me. I wish I could wrap my hand around him, guide him to me, but it's not to be.

When he parts my folds and licks and suckles my pearl, I shudder. "Please, Steele." One hand climbs up and clamps over my mouth. How much control does he want? I can't touch, can't see, and now he wants to silence me. He teases his cock against my folds, and I moan beneath his open palm. When he finally gives me what I want and slips an inch into me, the feel of him is exquisite. I want him deep in me, so deep he'll touch my heart. I clamp my legs around him, communicating my need with the only avenue left to me. Grunting, he thrusts. He's so hot, so big, so thick, I can't help but buck beneath him. Unhinging his hips, he pounds in and out until he hits rock bottom. When he does, I whimper. The girth of his rigid length is almost more than I can stand. I tense from the sweet ache.

"Relax."

"I can't," I mumble beneath his hand.

"Yes, you can. Trust me, Madrigal."

Taking a deep breath, I will every cell in my body to ease, to let his body claim mine in the most primeval of ways. Somehow I do. When he thrusts again, my body flushes with pleasure. I've gone totally liquid. Everything is heat and ache down below. I lick my lips, thrash my head. I want to touch him, but I can't. He's holding my hands captive above. Jerking up my hips, I murmur, "Faster, harder."

He grabs my ass, and his pace goes to double time. I arch, but he forces me down so he can do what he wants with me. His hand finds my clit, and I go from urgent to downright desperate. I jolt up toward him, but his strength holds me down.

"Stop moving. You will lie there and take what I give you, take me."

Sliding his hands under my thighs, he opens me wide so he can sink farther and then lets it rip, pumping hard and fast into me until I don't know where I begin and he ends. I scream with mindless pleasure as he lets loose the punishing strokes of his cock. Sweat, pungent with his lust, drips on me and mixes with my own, creating a unique cocktail of our scents. We're one in this world he's created. There is no him and me, just us, two sexual creatures intent on nothing but this dark, mindless paradise.

Heat streaks through me. Everything about me trembles—my legs, my arms, my breath. "I'm coming!" I scream. No words slip out from beneath his hand.

He comes with a curse. I'm so out of it, I barely register his collapse on the bed next to me. A minute goes by before he unties my hands, takes off the mask. He's wrecked, but then so am I. My gaze finds his cock. The ring's not there; he took it off.

While I'm still experiencing the aftershocks of what he did to me, of what we did together, he says, "There. We fucked."

Why did he do this? To prove a point? It doesn't take long for me to find an answer. Because I got too close. And because I felt sorry for him after the firm severed their partnership. This is his way of telling me I never should feel pity for him. He doesn't need or want that emotion from me. And he just made it clear what he does want. Mind-blowing sex. The kind I will never, ever forget and will crave for the rest of my life. But is there another reason for him to behave this way? Is he trying to pull us apart? If he thinks I'm going to run away because he showed me this side of him, he's got another think coming.

Still lost in the aftermath of our lovemaking, I trace my hand through his scruff. "Yes, we did, and I loved it."

His eyes widen as his right brow hikes.

Pulling him to me, I nibble his sensual lips. "I hope we do it again soon, except next time I'll tie *you* up."

He throws back his head and laughs before he flips me over, grabs another condom from the night table, and slips it on. And this time when we join, it's not another fuck. It's plain and simple making love.

Chapter 11

Trenton

After rising at my usual time of five thirty, I brew a cup of Italian roast in my Keurig before jumping into the shower. Half an hour later, I've shaved and dressed, while Madrigal sleeps. She's got to be exhausted after last night's marathon sex session. I'd made good on my promise to keep her coming, if not all night long, then at least until two in the morning. When after a final orgasm she'd fallen asleep, I'd dropped off into a dreamless state myself. This morning I was tempted to wake her in the best way possible, but she has to be sore, so I let her rest.

I'm knotting my tie in front of the bathroom mirror, tossing the occasional glance toward her glorious body, naked and spread out on my bed, when she slowly awakes. She blinks at me, at the clock on the night table, and back at me. "You're dressed already? It's not even six thirty."

"Mitch's arraignment is today," I say. "But first I want to swing by the Commonwealth's Attorney office to talk about the case and their thoughts on setting bail."

With her breasts jiggling, she climbs out of bed, walks toward me, and pushes my hands out of the way. "Here, let me. You're making a mess of it."

No wonder. I'm too busy ogling her tits to focus on what I'm doing. She tugs and pulls on my tie until it's arranged to her satisfaction. "There." She pats the tie. "It's perfect."

"Just like you." I smack her ass. She's naked, and I'm fully dressed. Something's wrong with this picture.

"Is the Commonwealth's Attorney handling the case himself?" she asks, picking up the clothes I'd tossed on the floor last night.

Her butt wiggles in the air, and my cock gets ideas. As much as I'd like to sink balls deep into her, I won't abuse the privilege. The rude bastard will have to wait until tonight. "Yes, he is. Your grandfather was a pillar of the community, too important to let someone else prosecute."

She lays out her clothes on the bed and smooths the wrinkles before turning to me. "Wish I could help."

"Me too." As much as I'd love her assistance, it can't happen. Holden was her grandfather, after all. I can't discuss the case with her, not only because I must maintain lawyer-client confidentiality but also because she's bound to be called in as a witness since she was present the night Holden died. The thought that Holden's murderer is running loose brings me back to the present. "How is the security detail working out?"

She scoots into the bathroom and, standing in front of the mirror, wrangles her hair into her ubiquitous ponytail. "Fine. They seem to have sorted themselves out. Alicia Carson is on duty during daytime hours."

"She seems competent."

"She is. Madison went riding with her. She's very patient, something Madison needs. She was an excellent choice." Bouncing back to my side, she stands on her tiptoes and kisses me. "Thank you."

"Don't thank me. Thank Hunter Stone. He chose her."

"Yes, but it was your idea to hire security in the first place. I'm not anxious about Madison going riding anymore. Mind if I shower?"

"Of course not."

"Got more towels?"

"In the hall closet."

She dances her way into the hall, grabs a couple of towels, and sashays back.

My cock's so hard, walking's going to be a challenge. "How are you going to get home?"

She tosses the towels on the clothes hamper in the bathroom before, all swaying hips, she turns to me. "I'll call Stone."

My eyes narrow at the mention of his name.

"I thought we settled the Hunter Stone issue," she says with a teasing smile.

She thinks this is a fucking game. I pull her to me. "You're mine. And mine alone." I plunder her mouth while my hand finds the seam of her ass and kneads her cheeks. Finally, when she's whimpering with need, I walk away.

I leave her wobbling on the carpet. No doubt her pussy's dripping as much as my cock's throbbing. Serves her right for torturing me.

***

It takes the entire trip to the Commonwealth's Attorney's office for me to get my head in the game. I've made an appointment, but they keep me and my heels cooling in the reception area for a good half hour before Beauregard Jefferson's assistant leads me to his office.

In his late forties, Jefferson's been a fixture in the Loudoun County Commonwealth's Attorney office since he graduated from law school. Rumor has it he's got his sights set on a congressional seat and that he'll announce his candidacy in the next year. A victory in the courtroom would provide him with plenty of publicity, and Holden Gardiner's murder case will certainly gain him plenty of ink in the papers and notice in social media.

"Trenton! Sorry to keep you waiting." He extends his hand while showing every one of his pearly, perfectly aligned teeth. They're nice and shiny, and not one of them is chipped.

"Beau."

"Take a seat, please." He waves at the leather chair in front of his desk. Probably an antique passed down from an ancestor. Just like Madrigal's, his family dates back to colonial times, so Virginia blue blood runs in his veins as well. Makes sense. Who else would saddle a son with a name like Beauregard? He smooths down his tie before dropping into his chair. "So what can I do for you?"

"Mitchell Brooks."

"Oh, yes. Interesting case. Very interesting. Anything in particular you want to know?"

"What are you looking at for bail?"

"I'm afraid, old boy, we won't be recommending a bail amount. We'll need to keep Mitchell Brooks in jail."

I'd been afraid of that. "May I ask why?"

"Well, the charge will be murder."

"First or second?"

"Murder in the first degree."

I stop breathing. "Why? The evidence does not support such a charge." Special material facts need to exist before a defendant can be found guilty of first degree murder. And the circumstances surrounding Holden's death don't even come close.

He sways back in his chair and folds his hands over his stomach. "You don't know the whole of it, Trenton. We do."

"You're required by law to reveal whatever evidence you have."

"We will during the discovery phase. In the meantime, we'll ask Judge Sutton to deny bail."

"Unless I can convince the judge otherwise," I mutter under my breath on the way out. I'll have to dig deep to discover what evidence the Commonwealth's Attorney's office has that supports the charge of capital murder.

I stop at the Loudoun County Detention Center to give Mitch the news so he won't be surprised at the arraignment.

Once I tell him, he almost shrinks into himself. "I didn't do it."

"I know that, Mitch. But they say they have evidence that would warrant a capital murder charge." I run through the ten factors that would provide grounds for such an indictment. None of them seem to fit the crime. Except for one. "Did you stand to gain financially from Holden's death?"

"No. You were there when the will was read. He left all his money to Madison and Madrigal and made small bequests to his staff."

"Why did you leave the firm, Mitch?"

"I had my reasons."

"They'll use that against you."

"I don't see how they would know."

"They'll bring Joss into it. She'll testify."

"It'll be hearsay. She doesn't know why I quit. I never shared my reason with her or anyone else. The only one who knew was Holden, and he's dead."

"You know damn well there are many exceptions to the hearsay rule. They'll find a way around it." I smack my hand on the table. "You have to level with me."

He doesn't even blink at my show of emotion. "I can't."

"You can't or you won't?"

"Isn't it the same thing?"

Stubborn and closemouthed to the core. As always. He's not stupid. He has to realize the danger he's in. There's a reason why he refuses to talk. I just have to find out what it is. "You're protecting someone."

He stares at me stone-faced. Mitch isn't going to tell me anything he doesn't want me to know.

"See you in court." I pound on the door and storm out of the detention center. Only when I'm safely inside my car do I let loose a string of curses. If he doesn't cooperate, if he doesn't tell me the truth, he may very well end up with a lethal injection in his veins.

Chapter 12

Madrigal

"Madison Berkeley?" the nurse at Georgetown Physicians Associates calls out. I'd contacted several friends from high school to get a referral to a doctor. One of them recommended a psychiatrist in this practice, saying she was one of the best in the area. Dr. Durham was booked solid, and her next available appointment was in two weeks. Explaining my sister's condition and my worry over her current drug regimen, I'd pleaded for an emergency appointment. The shameless begging worked, and they'd squeezed Madison in today.

Coming to her feet, Madison heaves out a sigh. "Do I really have to do this, Mad?"

The ungrateful brat. And after all my groveling too. "Yes, you do," I spit out. Aside from the fact that I'm honestly worried about her mental health, I need to know the effects of the medication she's taking.

After the nurse leads us to a room and takes Madison's vitals, she asks, "What medications are you taking?"

I hand her a Ziploc bag filled with Madison's prescriptions. As she jots them down on the laptop, her left brow rises, but she doesn't comment on them.

After she leaves, Madrigal fidgets on the examination table while waiting for the doctor. We don't have to wait long. Five minutes later, Dr. Durham steps into the room and offers a friendly smile to Madison and me. She's in her midforties, with glasses and copper hair tucked into a bun.

"I'm Dr. Durham. And how are you today?" She directs her question at Madison. Good. She needs to gain Madison's confidence.

"I'm fine. More than fine." I don't miss the aggressive tone. My heart goes out to her. Last night when we talked about the appointment, she'd shared her fear that something is truly wrong with her.

"Good. I'm glad to hear that," Dr. Durham says. "Now let's take a listen to your heart and your lungs, shall we?" She conducts the routine examination, including Madison's eyes, nose, and mouth. After she enters the results in the laptop, she spends some time looking over the list of medications before swiveling her chair back to Madison. "All right, now, how long have you been taking these medications?"

Madison shrugs. "A while."

"All of them or just some of them?"

"I've been taking the blue one for about four years and that little white one for the last two. The rest longer than that. But I don't take them all the time." She thrusts up her chin.

"Why aren't you taking all of them?" Dr. Durham's tone is gentle but firm.

"Because some of them make me stupid. That little white one? I feel like a zombie after I take it. So I don't swallow it most of the time."

"So why *are* you taking them? Do you know?"

Madison fiddles with her clasped hands. "When I turned twelve, I ran away."

I'm learning this for the first time. Nobody told me, not Gramps, not Olivia.

"Why did you run away, Maddy?" I ask.

"Gramps wanted me to go to some stupid firm event where they were going to have hayrides and apple bobbing and I'd have to deal with runny-nosed kids. I refused. So he punished me by locking me in my room."

No wonder she never attended the firm's picnics.

"So I packed a bag, climbed down the tree outside my window, and took off on Marigold."

"Who's Marigold?" Dr. Durham asks.

"My horse. I didn't get far. Hartley found me and brought me back. Gramps called Dr. Holcomb, and he came by and gave me a shot. He prescribed the blue pill then. And then two years ago, I had a meltdown, so that's when he prescribed the white one."

"What kind of a meltdown?" Dr. Durham asks.

"I went shopping with my friends after school. When I got home, Gramps locked me in my room. Again. He wouldn't even allow Olivia to bring me any food. They'd gotten smart and nailed shut my window so I couldn't escape. So I screamed the place down until they brought me dinner."

"I see," Dr. Durham says, pushing back her glasses. "Well, we'll need to get your medical records from Dr. Holcomb. Your sister will have to sign some paperwork."

"Of course," I say.

"We'll also need to draw blood to check your liver and kidney function as well as other things. How are you with needles?"

"Fine," Madison says.

"I want to see you again in about a week. By then we should have the lab results and your medical records from Dr. Holcomb. And then we'll take it from there."

Madison pushes out her lip the way she used to when she was little. "I don't want to take all those pills anymore."

Dr. Durham rests her hand on Madison's shoulder. "I understand. I really do. You think the medicine is not doing you any good and hate the way it makes you feel."

"How do you know?"

"Well, you just told me. Plus, you're not the first patient to come through that door and tell me the same thing. But for now? Please continue taking the medication. It was prescribed for a reason, and it's not good to quit taking it cold turkey. It can cause more harm than good if you do."

"Okay." I can see Madison doesn't really mean it. I'll have to talk some sense into her.

"Now, once I get your records and look over your lab results, I'll assess your drug regimen. We might be able to adjust your meds at that time. Is that fair?"

Madison shrugs. "I guess."

"Good." Dr. Durham pats her shoulder. "I'll have the nurse come back in and draw your blood. While she's doing that, I'll talk to your sister in my office. Once the nurse's done, she'll bring you to us. Is that okay with you?"

I love the way she gets Madison's okay every step of the way. No wonder she's got such a great reputation.

"Sure. I can listen to my tunes while I wait," she says, gesturing to her iPhone.

"Good." She sticks out her hand. "Good to meet you, Madison."

"Thank you, Dr. Durham."

Once we arrive at Dr. Durham's office, her smile vanishes. "She's taking some very serious drugs, Ms. Berkeley."

"Do you know what conditions would warrant prescribing those pills for her?"

"She's taking antipsychotic medication. That regimen is usually pre-scribed for individuals suffering from delusional disorders."

"What does that mean?"

"A person with a delusional disorder can't tell reality from fantasy."

"So she might be making up all those stories?"

"Maybe. And maybe she's telling the truth. I understand your grandfather passed away recently."

Of course she knows he was murdered. It's been all over the news. "Yes."

"Is there somebody else who can verify her grandfather locked her up after running away? She mentioned an Olivia and a Hartley."

"Our housekeeper and horse trainer. I'll ask them."

"Good. Find out the truth. I'll need their take on things to see if they jibe with Madison's."

Once we say good-bye to Dr. Durham and make an appointment for the following week, I treat Madison to a round of shopping. And then we get a bite to eat at a restaurant in the mall where we can talk.

"I really hate taking all those pills," Madison says once we've been shown to our table.

"I know, sweetheart, but can you please take them for another week or so? Once Dr. Durham gets your medical records, she might be able to adjust them."

"I'll take all of them except the little white one."

"Okay." That's the best I can hope for, I guess. This coming week I'll watch her carefully to make sure she doesn't start acting strange. I reach over the table to her. "I'm so sorry I didn't know about any of this, Maddy."

She shrugs. "It's okay. Gramps didn't want you to know. That's why I didn't tell you. But I don't need those pills, Mad. I don't."

"I know you feel that way, sweetheart, but maybe they do some good. Were you taking them the day Gramps died? You blew up at Gramps that afternoon."

"No. I refused to take them when Olivia brought them to me. But I had a right to be mad. He knew about our father torturing our mother, and he hid it from us." Her lips tremble as she mentions the last two things.

Of course she'd been upset that day. So was I after reading our mother's diary. Anyone would feel that way after learning what their father had done to their mother and the torture she'd suffered. After reading it, I'd run right into Steele's arms. And he'd helped me deal with my pain and misery. But I hadn't been there for Madison. After reading the journal, she'd had a screaming match with our grandfather and taken off on Marigold. But I plan to be there for her in the future.

"Well, you won't have to worry about being alone anymore. I'll be right here, Maddy. If you need to talk, just let me know, and we'll talk. Okay?"

"Okay."

"Now, about Philippe?"

"I know I shouldn't have lied to him about my age. But have you seen him? He's gorgeous." She gets a faraway look in her eyes. "He says the sweetest things. In French."

My sister's first crush. I can't take that from her, but there are some limits to what I can allow. "I need your fake ID, Madison."

Making a face, she fishes it out of her purse and hands it to me. "It won't do any good, you know. As soon as school starts back up, I can get a new one." Yeah, she probably can. But at least until September, she won't be able to use it.

On the way home, my cell rings. It's Steele. I press the "Talk" button on my steering wheel. "Hi."

"Hi, gorgeous. I miss you." I flush a little at the term of endearment.

"I miss you too."

"I can't wait until—"

Before he can say something entirely inappropriate, I cut him off. "I'm in the car with Maddy and Alicia Carson. We're headed home."

His tone veers from hot and sultry to a more businesslike approach. "So you're done with the doctor's appointment?"

"Yes."

"When you get a chance, call and tell me about it."

"Will do. Bye."

I hate to give our discussion short shrift, but with my sister and the security guard in the car, I can't very well carry on an intimate conversation with him.

From the corner of my eye I catch Maddy's expression. Her mouth is scrunched up, and she's chewing on her bottom lip. I wish she'd get over her dislike of Steele. Somehow I have to find a way to help her make peace with his role in my life, because I'm not kicking him out.

Once we arrive home, Madison heads up to her room, and Alicia goes to check in with her boss. I find Olivia and ask her if she has time to talk.

"Of course," she says.

Stepping into the living room, I close the French doors behind us. Even if we're interrupted, someone has to knock first. She takes a seat on the couch and glances expectantly at me.

I'm restless. So rather than sit, I take to pacing the floor. "You know about Madison's doctor's appointment."

"Of course." She folds her hands on her lap, not a hint of trembling in them. For her sake, I'm glad she's calm again.

"I'll need to keep track of Madison's medication so I can report to the doctor. So from now on, I'll monitor her meds."

Her shoulders ease. "Makes sense." Her relief is obvious. It had to have been quite a burden. One she probably resented, but now she won't have to be responsible for Madison's well-being. From now on, that job is mine.

"I do have several questions, though." I retrieve the Ziploc bag filled to the brim with Maddy's pills from my purse. "Do you think she needs to take all this medicine, Olivia?"

"I don't know. I did as the doctor ordered. And your grandfather demanded."

She might doubt the efficacy of Madison's drug regimen, but it's something she had to do, not only for Madison's health but also to keep her job. Gramps would have fired her in an instant if she'd refused. "Do you think Madison's delusional?"

"I think she has a tendency to exaggerate things, but no, I don't."

"At the doctor's office, Madison mentioned Gramps locking her in her room twice: when she ran away at twelve and again when she went on an unauthorized shopping trip with friends. Is that true?"

"Yes. It happened just as she said."

"Why do you think Dr. Holcomb prescribed such medications?"

"I have no idea. But the medicines made her sleep, which kept the drama down. Frankly, that's something your grandfather preferred. He never knew how to deal with Madison when she became agitated."

"What do you mean?"

"She'd have bad dreams, wake up screaming. The pills helped her get a good night's sleep. They calmed her down."

She'd also had nightmares after she discovered the crime scene pictures of our parents' murders at the newspaper where she'd interned. But she'd stopped taking the pills by then, so having bad dreams made sense.

"I've been meaning to ask you about my mother's journals. The one I fetched from the attic disappeared from my room."

Her eyes fill with tears.

"What's wrong?"

"After Madison read it, she raced into your grandfather's office and accused him of condoning your father's abuse of your mother."

"You heard?"

"The whole household heard. After she rode off on Marigold, he asked me to fetch the journal from your room. His face turned quite ruddy while he read it. I thought he'd have another heart attack. He asked if there were more of them. What else could I do but say yes." She wrings her hands and looks at me with worried eyes.

Fearing the worst, I ask, "What did he do, Olivia?"

"He burned them."

"All of them?"

"Yes."

My stomach plummets. I'd counted on reading those journals, not only to reconnect with my beautiful mother but also to find out how her marriage had gone so wrong that my father had taken to torturing her. But now all that evidence is gone.

"I'm sorry, Madrigal. I would have stopped him if I could have."

"There was no stopping him. Ever." I take a deep breath, then let it out. Olivia was so calm when she stepped into the room, and now she's agitated again. I'm sorry my questions have caused this change in her, even if they had to be asked. "Have you finished making your plans to visit your sister?"

"Yes. I'll be leaving in the morning. Hans will drive me to Union Station."

She needs the break. God knows she's been through enough. But then we all have. "I hope you have a nice time with your sister."

"Thank you, Madrigal." When she stands, we embrace. She's so very dear to me. I hate to see her upset.

Once she leaves the room, I dial Steele's number and give him a rundown of the doctor's visit. "She's taking all these antipsychotic drugs. No wonder she acts so differently from one day to the next. And I don't know if it's because she's not taking all her medicine or because she is."

"It wouldn't hurt to get a third opinion," he suggests.

"I'll wait and see what Dr. Durham says before I do that. I feel I can trust her. In the meantime, I'll keep an eye on Madison. There's something else." I gulp in air before I proceed. "Gramps burned my mother's journals."

He doesn't respond right away; he's probably as surprised as I am. "I'm sorry."

"Me too," I say, wiping a tear from my eye. Those journals were the last link to my beautiful mother, and now they're gone. No sense getting upset about it, though. I'll handle it, just like I've handled everything else. "When are you coming home?"

Chapter 13

Trenton

Home? It's her home, not mine. I'd much prefer for her to move into my Crystal City apartment with me. We'd have privacy there, and I could enjoy her anytime I pleased without the fear of someone walking in on us. But that can't happen. Not with everything that's going on with Madison. Her sister needs the comfort of her home, the escape of horseback riding. So for now, I have no choice. If I want Madrigal in my life, I must live at her estate. Problem is there's always someone watching us. The servants, Olivia, the operatives from Stone Security. We need a weekend away from everyone, but that's not happening anytime soon.

There is an upside to living at the mansion, however. It's the place where Holden was killed, so I'll be able to search the premises and question the servants.

Yesterday, I decided to open up my own firm. It's a risk, but one I'm willing to take. For some time, I'd been dissatisfied with choices made by Gardiner, Ashburn & Strickland as well as the direction of the management committee. I have enough of a reputation in this town to draw in high-profile clients who pay well. So, yes, it's time to start my own practice. Having made that decision, I've gotten the ball rolling, and the first step is to find office space.

I glance at my watch. "I have a three o'clock appointment with a Crystal City Realtor to go over my space requirements. That should take a couple of hours. I'll head home after that."

"So seven?"

"Definitely."

"I'll hold dinner until you get home then."

"Okay." I can't help but smile. Nobody's held dinner for me. Ever. After my mother walked out on us, abandoning Reece and me to our abusive father, I was the one in charge of preparing dinner. Half the time my father forgot to go grocery shopping, preferring to spend his money on booze. Many days all that remained in the cupboards were a couple of cans of soup. My brother and I would pay the price for that. I tried to take the beatings so my younger brother wouldn't suffer, but more often than not, the bastard knew what I was up to and would go after him. We got whipped with his belt and punched with his fists at least twice a week until the time I turned eight, when Social Services finally wised up and took us away from him. The bastard died a few years after that from liver failure. Didn't shed one tear for the son of a bitch, not after all the pain he caused.

The Crystal City Realtor is smart and knowledgeable about the real estate market. She spends half an hour asking about my requirements and expectations. After crunching the numbers, she determines I'll need at least five thousand square feet. At a rate of $36 per square foot, the yearly lease would come to $180,000. That seems like a lot, so we settle on three thousand square feet, which would make the rent a much more reasonable $100,000 a year. That would provide enough space for a couple of partners besides me, two associates, various staff members, plus room for the common areas.

The buildings she suggests have plenty of square footage to expand. So we could relocate within the same address to slightly larger spaces if the need arises. I want to set up the office as soon as possible and have Charlie establish the evidence room. I agree to inspect her prospective sites on Friday.

The drive to Loudoun County and Madrigal's home is hellish as usual. With the traffic bumper to bumper on I-66, I move at a snail's pace. They really need to convert the HOV lanes to express lanes. In the meantime, I'll just have to deal with this insanity if I want Madrigal in my life. And I do.

My phone rings, so I push the button on my steering wheel to connect the call. "Trenton Steele."

"Trenton, it's Marcus Waverly." A criminal law partner at Gardiner, Ashburn & Strickland.

"Marcus." Maybe he's calling to get some intel on a client I've handled.

"Thought I'd touch base with you."

"What's up?"

"A few of us from the criminal law group got together. After hours, of course."

Interesting. "Of course." Makes sense if they wanted to discuss something they didn't want the rest of the firm to know about.

"We don't like how you got railroaded out of the firm. Or the decisions Dick Slayton has made. He's laid down some new rules that are rubbing people the wrong way and made his crony, Harry Shiner, the head of the criminal law practice."

"Oh?" Harry Shiner is seventy years old. Although in his day he was quite an attorney, his faculties are not what they used to be. Not only that, he hasn't stepped into a courtroom for the last ten years. The firm kept him on more out of respect for his seniority than anything else.

"A few of us are looking to jump ship. So I was asked to get in touch with you and see if you had plans to open your own office."

"As a matter of fact, I am."

"Great." The relief in his voice is palpable. Things must have really taken a turn for the worse at the firm. And in only a day or two.

"How soon can you cash out?" I ask.

"Two weeks for most of us."

"Who exactly is us?"

He rattles off the names of two partners and three associates. That would make six attorneys who would need private offices, including me. We'd also require space for a receptionist, a couple of administrative assistants, and copy and lunchrooms, plus at least one conference area. Maybe I'll need those five thousand square feet after all.

"There's a paralegal who'd be interested as well if you can guarantee her health insurance and child care."

"Of course. Monica?"

"Yes." Her requirements don't surprise me. Monica is a single mother with two school-age kids.

"I think we can work something out. I'm looking at space this Friday. But chances are we'll have to rough it for a week or two."

"Anything's better than what's going on here. The place is falling apart."

"Let's get together for dinner. My place in Crystal City on Friday night at seven?"

"I'll let everyone know."

"Thanks, Marcus. I'll e-mail you the address."

"We have it, Trenton."

"See you Friday, then."

I arrive home in time for dinner. Madrigal's family tradition calls for cocktails, with a few nonalcoholic beverages for Madison, before the meal is served.

Madrigal takes one look at me and smiles. "Something's made you happy."

"Yes. You," I say, taking her into my arms and dropping a kiss on her smiling mouth.

Her eyes sparkle at me. "Well, thank you. But I think it's more than that."

"I—"

Madison bounces into the room, interrupting me. "When's dinner?"

"Seven. Say hello to Trenton, Maddy, please."

"Hello," Madison says over her shoulder as she heads for the drink cart and pours a glass of iced tea.

"Hi," I say.

"So you were saying?" Madrigal asks, pulling me down onto one of the three sofas in the room.

I glance at Madison and back at Madrigal. "Later. I'll tell you later."

Madison freezes up, but then she says, "I can leave, if you have something private to say."

"You don't have to."

"That would be good."

Madrigal and I speak simultaneously.

"I'll go grab a snack," Madison says. "Excuse me." She walks out, closing the door behind her.

Madrigal lets out a heavy breath. "You can't make her feel unwelcome. She's my sister. If you want me in your life, you have to make room for her as well."

"I'm fine with her, but the nature of what I have to share with you is confidential. I don't want it to leak out just yet."

"Very well." She folds her hands on her lap, which tells me she's not entirely convinced by my argument. "What is it?"

I tell her about Marcus's phone call, and the mulish look disappears from her face as she warms to the idea. "That's great. Really great. And just like that you have your own law firm."

"Well, it's going to take more than office space and staff. We need clients too. But it's a beginning."

"My grandmother used to say that when a door closes, a window opens somewhere."

"Holden's wife?"

"Yes. She was a gentle Southern woman. Loved my mother. Loved me. She never got to meet Maddy, but she would have loved her as well."

"I think you have a lot of her in you." I'd read some of Madrigal's grandmother's journals in the sitting room. From the pages she'd written, I learned that she'd loved her volatile husband but often had to step in and smooth out Holden's hard edges.

Just as I bend down to kiss her, Madison returns with a bowl in her hands. "You through talking?"

No, I want to say, but I don't. I'll have to make allowances for her popping up at inconvenient times. It's her home, after all.

"Is that chocolate pudding?" Madrigal asks.

"Yes." Madison curls a protective hand around the bowl. "You can't have any."

"I don't want any, squirt. But it's likely to ruin your appetite."

"Don't worry. I've saved plenty of room." She pats her stomach. "Helga says dinner's ready." And with that she dances out of the room.

"She can be such a child at times," Madrigal says.

I tweak her chin. "She's a teenager, which means she's a child one moment, an adult the next."

The corners of her lips turn up. "How would you know?"

"I've heard enough people at work talk about them." I stand and hold out my hand. "Let's go have dinner."

"Yes, let's."

During the meal, the give-and-take of the sisters and the cozy atmosphere provide me with a sense of peace. This is what it means to have a family. This is what it means to have a home. Maybe, just maybe, things with Madrigal will work out after all.

Chapter 14

Madrigal

"Please take a seat, Charlie. Would you like something to eat or drink?" On this scorching hot summer day, he's been kind enough to travel to Leesburg to provide me with his report. At the beginning of his investigation into my parents' murders, we'd met in Steele's office. That, of course, is no longer an option. And to tell the truth, I'd rather conduct the investigation from my house. So I hope he's amenable to dropping in now and then.

"Some lemonade or iced tea would be nice."

Standing up, I smooth down my skirt. "Of course. Excuse me. I'll go attend to it. In the meantime, make yourself at home."

When I come back with a glass of iced tea and a plate of biscuits fresh from the oven, he's studying one of the paintings on the wall. "That's Mount Vernon."

"Yes, it is."

"Looks old."

"It's an original drawing. From 1757, I believe. Our ancestors were great friends with George Washington. Here you go, Charlie." I place the tea and biscuits on a table within his reach. "Thank you for coming."

"It's a nice drive. Pretty country out here. Lot of green space."

"Where did you grow up?"

"In DC. Lived there my whole life. Not too much green around where I grew up." Trenton has gone to him time and again whenever he needs something or someone investigated. So I fully trust him to help me with the investigation into my parents' murders.

"I'm glad you enjoyed the drive. So you say you have the file from Detective Collins?"

"Yes." He reaches into his battered briefcase and hands it to me. "He kept his own notes on your parents' case. Of course, it's not as good as the official files. Photos are missing."

"We have photos of the crime scene."

"Steele told me."

It occurs to me I could use his expertise with the photos. "Would you like to see them?"

"Of course."

I stand and turn to leave, but before I do, a thought occurs to me. "Does Steele know about the file?"

"Yes."

"And he asked you to let me know?"

"Not in so many words, no."

"What words did he use, Charlie?"

"He thought it might be better to wait."

"Until when?"

"I don't know." He takes a sip of the tea. "You might want to ask him."

That bastard. He kept the file from me. The file from the detective who investigated my parents' murders. Why? To protect me? I don't want to be protected, damn it. I want to know the truth.

"Charlie?"

"Yes, ma'am."

"From now on, you report only to me, not Steele."

"You will have to clue him in on that fact, ma'am. He may have a different opinion about it."

Right now, I don't give a damn what Steele thinks. "I will. Please bill me, not him, and let me know how much he's already paid you. I'll need to reimburse him."

"I thought you might want to know, so I prepared a summary." He digs into his briefcase and comes up with a folder. Inside is a detailed list of his time and expenses.

"Thank you, Charlie. I'll go get those photos. In the meantime, enjoy the tea and biscuits."

His eyes light up. They say food's the way to a man's heart. I have a feeling Helga's flaky biscuits are the way to his.

When I return with the photos, he says, "We'll need to set up an evidence board where we can create a timeline and jot down any pertinent information about the case."

"Where exactly can we find one?"

"Any office supply store should have them. Oh, and you'll need pushpins, loose-leaf paper, and markers as well."

After I write down everything he needs, I go on the hunt for Hans and ask him to buy the items from the Staples store in Leesburg.

On my return to the room, I discover he's polished off the biscuits. I clamp down on my lips to keep a smile from breaking out. "Okay, that's taken care of. While we wait for Hans to return, would you care for lunch? I believe Helga prepared barbecue chicken, potato salad, and some cantaloupe sherbet for dessert."

Before I finish my recitation, he stands and eagerly follows me into the dining room. As soon as we're seated at the table, Ms. Doesn't-miss-a-meal-if-she-can-help-it shows up. Madison asks him a million questions about his experiences as a detective. By the end of the meal, the seasoned investigator and the budding reporter have struck up an odd friendship.

Charlie and I return to the evidence room to find Hans putting the boards together. "I bought three," he says.

"Good."

Charlie and I spend the rest of the afternoon taking apart Detective Collins's file. An hour into it, we've drawn a pretty tight timeline as to the sequence of events. The break-in, when 911 was called, when the police arrived, plus the approximate times of my parents' deaths. Detective Collins even went so far as to draw a map of everything in the room where my parents were found. We can get most of that information from the photos as well, but unfortunately some of the details are fuzzy.

"So my father was found shot in the stomach at the foot of the bed?" I fight to control my emotions, but even so, my voice trembles.

"Going by the blood that pooled beneath him, that's a logical conclusion."

"But my mother." I struggle against rising nausea. "My mother did not die there." She'd been found lying on the bed, sightless eyes staring up, a mass of wounds on her back, her stomach, her legs. Clearly, she'd been whipped.

"No. There's no blood beneath her body. Given the extensive damage she suffered, there should have been, especially when her throat was slit."

"Excuse me." I take off running toward the closest bathroom and barely make it in time to spew my lunch. Barbecue and a murder investigation clearly do not mix. I head to my bedroom where I brush my teeth, gargle, and lie down for a couple of minutes until my stomach's settled. And then I head back down to the evidence room.

"How are you feeling?" Charlie asks. His soft brown eyes glow with kindness.

I force out a laugh. "I've had better days."

"Why don't we stop for now and take this up again over the weekend?"

"That might be a good idea." I don't think I can continue today, not the way I feel. "Thank you, Charlie. I really appreciate everything you're doing. See you Saturday?"

He nods. "What time?"

"Let's say ten o'clock."

"I'll be here," he says, standing up.

"I'll have some of Helga's biscuits waiting for you."

His smile tells me he approves.

When Steele arrives home a half hour later, I want to ask him why he withheld the file from me, but in my current condition I'm simply not up to an argument.

"What's wrong?" he asks.

My pale complexion must have given me away. "Tummy trouble."

"Oh?"

"I think my period's coming." It's a few days off, but close enough for me to make that claim.

"Oh!" I expect him to change the subject, but he surprises me. "Is there anything I can do to make you feel better?"

"A massage would be good."

He points to the stairs. "Lead the way."

After stripping, I hand him the massage oil I use on my legs. "Um, lavender-rose. Is this where your scent comes from?"

"Yes. I have several products with that fragrance."

He folds his jacket over a chair and rolls up his shirtsleeves. The dark hair on his forearms gets my motor running. But before I spend too much time admiring him, he has me lie down on a towel, and his hands work their magic. The knots in my back disappear as he kneads my flesh.

"Where did you learn to do this?" I ask in a state of bliss.

"In college."

"You sure were a busy boy in college, getting piercings and tats and learning how to massage."

"The tattoo parlor where my friend worked? There was a massage parlor next door. I struck up a friendship with the owner. She taught me."

"She?" Jealousy rears its ugly head, and I sit up. I can only imagine on whom he practiced.

He pushes me back on the bed so he can continue his task. Ignoring my obvious state of mind, he kneads the heck out of my right leg, and soon I'm in nirvana again.

"Sela was my first investor," he says.

I turn my head to the side and look at him. "Investor?"

"I majored in business. With Mitch's help, I spent the first two years in college learning about trading. Once I had the basics, I dipped my toes in the stock market. But with little money to play with, I couldn't make much headway. I talked about it one night while Sela and I were—"

"Doing it."

"Yes. Well. When Sela found out, she asked me to invest her savings. Within six months, I'd doubled that sum. So I started a small fund. Friends asked me to invest their extra beer money and then cashed out for spring break trips. As word spread, more serious money started pouring in. By the time I graduated, I was a millionaire several times over."

"Whoa!" I sit up again. "How come I didn't know that?"

"I don't spread it around."

"So why are you still working as an attorney?"

"Because I like what I do. I like making a difference in people's lives."

A knock sounds on the door. "Mad? Dinner's on the table." Madison. God forbid anything interferes with a meal. I have no idea where she puts it all.

"Okay, we'll be right there," I yell.

"Hurry. It's chicken-fried steak and mashed potatoes night."

I groan. "No wonder I can't lose any weight."

"I like your curves." He curls his hand around a breast, squeezes, and I melt.

But there's no time for that. I jump out of bed, head for my closet, and pick out a fresh dress to wear. And with the tension rubbed out of me, I head down with Steele to the dining room.

Chapter 15

Trenton

The Friday night dinner at my Crystal City apartment is everything I hoped it would be. I'd reviewed my wine collection and popped open several bottles of red and white. With the Pentagon City Costco so close, I'd also stopped there and picked up a few of my favorites as well as some new artisan beers. Rather than cook, which I'd have been more than happy to do, I'd chosen to have Pietro's, my favorite Italian restaurant, cater the meal. I'd also hired some of his staff to serve and handle the kitchen duties.

I'd talked Madrigal into attending the dinner. Having her here means a lot to me, as does the presence of my hopefully future employees and partners. Marcus Waverly is in attendance, and so are Rob Dwelling, Rayne Adams, Susan Bush, and the paralegal, Monica Watkins.

"Thank you for coming," I say once we're all enjoying Pietro's delicious cuisine.

"Thank you for inviting us," Marcus says.

Over the course of the meal, we hash out plans for the law firm. I assure each and every one of them that he or she will have a chance to shine.

"You will have health insurance, including dental?" Monica asks.

"Of course." I have no idea how I'll manage it, but you can't run a law firm without basic benefits. "As well as a 401(k) plan."

"So what's the focus of the firm, Trenton?" Rob asks.

"Criminal law. At least to start. Once the firm grows, we'll probably open additional areas of practice, such as trusts and estates and taxes."

"God knows there are enough prospective clients in this town."

A wave of laughter travels around the room.

After we toast our new venture, someone asks, "So what should we name the firm?"

"Trenton Steele and Associates, of course," Madrigal says. So far she's been quiet, but on this issue she's very sure.

A chorus of agreements circles the room.

"Makes sense."

"Absolutely."

"Of course."

Whether it's from the excitement of our new venture or their trust in me, a flush rises in my cheeks. And then again, maybe it's just the wine. "Thank you for your vote of confidence. I'll try my hardest to make sure we all succeed."

"You'd better," Marcus says with a laugh in his voice. He doesn't appear too worried.

Attaching my name to the new law firm does make sense. After all, I'm well known about town as the criminal law attorney who can get you out of trouble. Later on we can rethink the firm name as more of them make partners. Their attendance and interest in my new venture is more than I hoped for. Everyone's excited about the opportunity to be part of it.

"So what about clients?" someone asks.

"I've gotten calls," Marcus says.

"So have I," Rob echoes.

Marcus laughs and turns to me. "I don't think you have anything to worry about, Trenton. Clients are being fed the party line—that you left against everyone's wishes because you wanted to start your own firm. More than a few of them are concerned about their cases. Those who contacted me are very interested in finding out where you've gone. As soon as word gets out you've opened your doors, I'm pretty sure they'll camp on your doorstep, begging you to represent them."

"Let's hope," I say, raising my glass.

After everyone toasts to our clients, Marcus says, "You'll need to set up a communications network."

"I'll have a phone line installed as soon as I can and hire a receptionist as well. I know someone who can set up computers and such."

"I can help you with staffing, Mr. Steele," Monica, the paralegal, pipes up. "I used to work in Human Resources."

"Perfect. If you want that job, it's yours."

"I can do both until you get everything sorted out. But you'd be better off hiring an administrator. I really prefer the paralegal work."

"Whatever she can't handle, I'll be glad to pitch in too," Rayne Adams, one of the supersmart associates, offers. She used to work in Dick Slayton's group, but bored out of her mind with the lack of work, she'd asked to transfer to the criminal law practice, which she'd taken to like a duck to water. Her help had been invaluable in the hockey player's case. She'd been the one to wheedle out of the so-called victim the admission that she was more interested in fleecing the eighteen-year-old phenom hockey player than in having him be found guilty of rape. Once we'd figured out her motives, we'd looked into her past and discovered she'd done the same thing before. In Canada. When we brought it to the attention of the prosecutor, he'd dropped the case, and our eighteen-year-old hockey player was absolved of any wrongdoing.

"Thank you, Rayne. I'll take you up on the offer." I need all the help I can get.

Before everyone departs, I promise to draw up an agreement for all the lawyers to sign, and we set up August 3 as our launch date. If the space in the Crystal City office I plan to lease is not available, we can work out of my condo. It's big enough to handle everyone who's coming on board.

Later, when we're finally alone, Madrigal and I sit in the living room, sipping wine.

"You're happy," she says.

"Yes, I am." A rare emotion. I haven't had many opportunities to be truly happy in my life. My law school graduation, the phone call from Holden Gardiner offering me a position at his law firm, and every damn minute I've been with Madrigal. All I have to do is breathe the same air she does, and I'm in heaven. "You make me happy."

She laughs. "It's not just me. It's what happened here today. Your own law firm. You've been wanting this for a while."

"I have."

"So what should we do to celebrate?"

"Oh, I can think of a thing or two."

Rising to my feet, I hold out my hand to her. She takes it, and I kiss her fingers before leading her to the bedroom, where I waste no time in helping her out of her clothes.

I strip her down to her underwear, which consists of a peekaboo lacy bra and a thong. "What's this?" My voice gravels as I insinuate a finger under her bra strap.

"I went shopping on Wednesday, remember?"

"With Madison. Don't tell me you picked these out in front of her?"

"No. She found a friend at the mall. They went off to one of those infernal stores teenagers frequent. I told her I'd meet up with her later for lunch."

"And using that excuse, you bought this."

"Yes."

"It matches your eyes."

"That's why I bought it."

Her curves have always called to me. With the reverence duly due her lace peekaboo bra, I suckle her nipple right through the bra, run a knuckle down the satin of her skin. She's lovely, and young, and what she wants with me is anyone's guess. But I don't intend to ask her that question. Not ever.

She throws her head back and moans. I test her readiness through the satin of her panties. She's wet and about to get wetter. I tease one finger beneath the fabric and stroke her clit. She pants little puffs of air. "It's been too long."

"We fucked last Sunday."

Her eyes flash. "Like I said, too long."

I pick her up and lay her on the bed. Knowing what she likes, I slide the panties off her and toss them aside. Gripping her thighs, I open her and bend down to lick my way to her mons. Her pussy is dripping wet and smells like heaven itself. "You want me."

"Yes." When my tongue licks a path to her clit and I nip her, she curls her hand in my hair and yanks. "In me, Steele."

"All in good time, sweetheart."

I insert two fingers into her heat while suckling her pearl. Hips pumping, she writhes on the bed. "Now, Steele."

She's had enough teasing and, frankly, so have I. I need to be inside her, feel her heat clenched around me. I toss my jacket aside, my tie, my shirt, the rest of my clothes. I slide open the drawer, ready to roll on a condom.

"Do we really need that?"

"Yes, we do."

"I'm on the pill."

I'm not about to take chances. She's twenty-four and about to embark on her law career. She doesn't need the complications a child would bring. And the last thing I want is a kid. "Better safe than sorry," I say.

She makes a face. "I'd rather have you bare against me with nothing in the way."

Tempting, but I'm not negotiating this. I finish rolling the condom over my cock and kiss my way down to her mons again. When she's writhing on the bed once more, I plunge into her. She screams. A moment later she comes, and so do I. We rest together, finding our peace with each other. But for how long?

Chapter 16

Madrigal

"Hello, *querida*. How are you holding up?" Cristina Sanchez, my best friend from law school, asks.

I'd asked her to drop by, hoping to get her take on my parents' murder case. We'd gone through three years of law school together, lived in the same house, taken many of the same classes. By a sheer stroke of luck, we'd ended up interning in DC for the summer. She at the Department of Justice, and me at my grandfather's law firm. He'd insisted I learn the defense side of the law before I started my job as a prosecutor at the Arlington County Commonwealth's Attorney's office, which is how I'd ended up under Steele's tutelage. From him, I'd learned much more than the law.

"Fine. All things considered." I give her a rundown of Madison's situation, Mitch being charged with murder, and the status of my parents' case.

"You have your hands full, that's for sure. Still taking the Virginia bar exam?"

"In less than two weeks. I'm boning up every chance I get."

Without warning, the shadow of Hunter Stone looms over us. "Ms. Berkeley. Your sister's gone riding. I just wanted to let you know."

"Thank you, Hunter. This is my friend, Cristina Sanchez."

He nods at her. "How do you do?"

"Uh. Fine." His appearance has apparently struck Cristina deaf and dumb. As soon as he walks away, she whispers, "Who's that gorgeous bastard?"

"He's the head of Stone Security, our new security company."

"That's your bodyguard? Holy Chihuahua."

I smile. She's always reacted strongly to good-looking men. And I have to admit Hunter is drop-dead gorgeous. "One of them. We ended up with four. Round-the-clock protection."

"Wow." She glances over her shoulder at our retreating bodyguard. "Nice ass."

I laugh. "What about your boy toy from the Senate?"

She makes a face. "Oh, we're still together. He's very nice. Loves vanilla sex."

"And you like a little Rocky Road now and then."

"Yeah, with nuts on the bottom. So why did you ask me here?"

"To get your take on things." We'd taken Criminal Law I and II at Yale, and Cristina had gotten the highest grade in both classes. She can analyze cases like nobody's business and understands the intricacies of criminal jurisprudence better than anyone I know. Except for Steele, that is.

With her behind me, I stroll into our newly created evidence room and hand her a binder outlining the facts of the case. The board clearly delineates the timeline of all the known events. Charlie managed to get his hands on photos of all the players, from the two men who broke into the house to my parents to the house staff. We've pieced together what happened, what I remembered from my mother's diary, and what I recall from before that day.

After I introduce her to Charlie, who's studying the detective's file and scribbling away, Cristina taps the binder. "Can I make notes?"

"Yes. That's your copy."

It takes her an hour to review the narrative. While she reads, I jot down a couple of things I want to ask her.

Once finished, she sits back, rubs the space between her eyes. "Are you sure those two burglars didn't do it?"

"About ninety-nine percent. Neither had ever committed anything but robberies or been involved in anything violent before they broke into our house. The one that's still alive doesn't appear to have the smarts God gave him. Of course, he's a stoner, so his brain could have been fried from too many drugs. But I don't believe they killed my parents."

"Why do you think that?" she asks.

"The one I talked to liked my mother. He liked the fact that she served him food and attended to them. I don't think he had it in him to kill her, especially as horribly as . . ." I catch my breath and will away the images.

"What happened to the house you lived in? Was it sold?"

"No. My grandfather kept it, maybe for sentimental reasons. Or maybe he had another motive."

"Have you gone there?"

"No. Not since"—I wave my hand at the board—"the murders occurred. Aside from the fact my grandfather would have never approved, I couldn't make myself return."

"It won't be easy for you to visit your old home, but you know you'll need to do so, don't you?" Kindness shines from her eyes, as well as a bit of tough love.

"Yes, I do. And I will. Soon."

Rather than push me on the subject, she flips to a page in the binder. "The summary states that Madison saw your grandfather burying something in the backyard."

"That's right. She was only four at the time, though."

She tosses her head. "An unreliable witness at best."

A knock on the door interrupts us. "Come in."

My sister pokes in her head, her face bright with curiosity. "Hi."

Talk about the devil. "Back from your ride already?" I ask.

"Yeah. It's too hot out there," she says, stepping into the room. "Marigold was having a hard time with the heat. So I came back. After I hosed her down, I took a shower myself."

A braid of gold hangs down her back. Her T-shirt and jeans are crisp and neat. I'm glad she took the time to clean up before dropping in on us. Sometimes she brings the eau de stable with her. "You remember Cristina?"

"Yeah, hi." She waves at her. Even though she's been on a regular course of her meds for only a few days, she's calmer, less volatile. Still a bit restless, though.

"What are you guys doing?" she asks. Like she doesn't know.

"Cristina's helping me go over the evidence. Fresh set of eyes and all that."

"I can be a fresh set of eyes." Her eagerness tugs at my heart. She wants to help, but I'm afraid of what it might do to her. I couldn't eat for a day after looking at those photos.

"I don't know about that, Maddy."

"I can handle it, Mad. I saw those pictures, remember?"

Cristina's gaze swivels back to me. "What pictures?"

"Madison discovered photos from the crime scene at the *Washington Courier* morgue the week she interned there."

"Why aren't they up here?" Cristina points at the big whiteboard, which outlines every known fact of the case.

Recalling the bloody images, I shudder. "Too gruesome."

"I can take a look at them to see if I can spot some clues. If you don't mind, that is." Even though I will not allow Maddy to lay eyes on those pictures again, Cristina is another matter entirely. And she's right. She might see something in those images that I can't. But it's already six, and going over all of the evidence we've collected as well as the photos will take some time.

"It's kind of late to start that now. Can you stay until tomorrow?"

Her head bobs up and down. "I can stay the whole weekend. Scott's in Minnesota with his senator. They're getting ready to launch an initiative, and they want to drum up as much support as they can in her home state. Won't be back until Monday night."

I'm thrilled to hear that. Cristina's got a wicked sense of humor, so having her around will be fun. Something Maddy and I sorely need. "Great. I'll have one of the maids prepare a room for you."

After I work out the details, I head off to my bedroom, where I've kept the photos that Madison "borrowed" from the *Washington Courier* when she interned there. After Gramps's death she never resumed her internship and so didn't have the chance to put the photos back where they belong. Frankly, I don't want her to do so now. If she were caught, God only knows the kind of trouble she'd be in. Given she was asked to look for something else in the newspaper files during the one week she worked there, even someone without brains could figure out that she was the one who took the photos. So we'll have to find a way to return them. In the meantime, Cristina's right. We'll need to examine them to get a clearer picture of what happened that night.

Unlocking the file cabinet where I keep important papers, I retrieve the photos, head back downstairs, and hand them to Cristina.

While Cristina studies the images, Madison's busy inspecting the evidence board, which runs the gamut from the timeline to photos of our parents while they were alive, to accounts of the evidence she contributed the night of the murders, and to the interviews with the staff the morning my parents were found. After the maid who discovered them screamed down the house, everyone had come running—the other maid; Helga, our cook; Hans, our gardener and general jack-of-all-trades; and, of course, Olivia.

Madison turns back to me. "Sally discovered Mom and Dad?" Sally had been only eighteen at the time. To say the discovery had traumatized her and she'd needed to be calmed down is an understatement. She'd quit that day and never returned, which was just as well, since our household transferred to Gramps's mansion, complete with cook, handyman, Olivia, and us. The other maid, whose name I can't remember, had quit as well.

"Yes. You don't remember that?"

She scrunches her brow. "No. I remember Olivia waking me and telling me I had to stay in my room. I played with my dolls until Gramps came and took me away. I recall hearing a lot of people in the house, coming and going, someone sobbing."

"What did Olivia tell you?"

"That I was going to spend some time with Gramps. I wanted to say good-bye to Mom, but she wouldn't let me. On the way out, as I walked by our parents' bedroom door, the smell wasn't right. You remember how Mom always smelled of honeysuckle?"

"Yes, it was her favorite cologne."

"It didn't smell like that. It smelled strange. Like copper."

Blood. She'd smelled the blood. I shudder while mentally thanking Olivia for rushing my four-year-old sister out of the house. At least she hadn't been traumatized by the sight of that blood-drenched room.

Cristina's eyes mist at Madison's tale. She clears her throat. "Where's Trenton?"

"Setting up his new office in Crystal City. The Realtor is showing him some properties."

Her head comes up. "You're not helping him?"

"He wants to surprise me, so he won't let me see it until it's all done. He should be back by dinnertime."

"When's that?"

"Seven."

Time passes while everyone resumes their activities—Charlie continues with his inspection of the detective's file and Madison scrutinizes the board. At one point she grabs a legal pad and a pen, pulls up a chair, and starts making notes.

After a while, Cristina asks, "Does Mr. Stone come and go or is he a permanent fixture?" It's a casual question, but she doesn't fool me for a minute. She's interested in Hunter Stone.

"He comes and goes. Today he's got the evening shift from four until midnight. He'll be back tomorrow as well."

"Will he join us for dinner?"

"No. He eats in the kitchen with the staff."

"Darn."

Chapter 17

Trenton

At Friday's dinner, Rayne Adams had shown an interest in the new office location. So when she calls to find out when I'm meeting with the Realtor, I'm not surprised that she asks if she can accompany me. The three of us spend a couple of hours touring several listings. Rayne points out the weakness in one of them—the building only has tenant parking, which would make it difficult for our clients to park nearby. Another space, she says, would face the sun during the hottest time of day, which would not be a good thing during the summer. But the third location is perfect. Although the building is older, some of the build-out work has already been done.

"How big is it?" I ask.

"Five thousand square feet," says the Realtor. "A not-for-profit corporation leased the space, but halfway into the negotiations, their funding fell through, so they had to back out. The owner is eager, so he's willing to cut a deal. First year's rent is thirty-five dollars a square foot."

"This could work," I say. The building is centrally located right in the heart of Crystal City and only a block away from the Metro stop. Five large offices, three smaller ones, a kitchen/employee lounge, and a nice-sized reception area. We would share the lavatories with only one other tenant on the floor. "Okay. I'm sold."

"Not so fast," Rayne interjects. She rattles off a bunch of requirements I'd never dreamed of asking for. By the end of the conversation, I'm reasonably assured we've gotten an excellent deal.

"And the best part is you can move in right away," Rayne says over a quick lunch at an eatery across the street. "Once you sign the lease, we could go shopping for furniture, paintings, and such."

"Paintings?" An interior designer I'm not. I paid somebody to furnish my apartment.

"You need something to hang on the walls, at least in the reception area. Don't worry; I know a place. We could go look now if you want."

"Sure. No time like the present."

We spend the afternoon picking out office furniture at a warehouse and paintings and other decorative accents at an Alexandria, Virginia, antiques shop. "How do you know about these places?"

"I live down the street. I've window-shopped at this store on weekends more times than I can count. I could never afford most of the things here," Rayne says. "That painting you bought of a Virginia foxhunt is perfect. You have great taste." She's being generous. My idea of decor is a coatrack by the door. But Rayne managed to cobble together a bunch of items that I believe will lend the right tone. "Virginia country-manor chic, that's what it is."

Never heard of such a thing, but then what do I know?

"Where shall we deliver the goods, sir?" the clerk asks.

"Can you hold it in storage? Shouldn't be more than a week." I can't very well ask them to deliver to the new office before I've signed the lease.

"No problem. Just sign here." The price for the decorative items would have floored a lesser man. Thank God I can afford it.

"All these furnishings sprinkled in the reception area will instantly give the place class, you'll see." Rayne glances at her watch. "Gotta run. Have a wedding to attend. I need to go home and prepare for it."

"Thanks for the help, Rayne. Couldn't have done this without you."

"You're welcome. Hope the space is available by next weekend. All the stuff could be delivered by then. I'll help set up. You'll want to welcome new clients as soon as possible."

"The smell of sawdust and fresh paint will still be in the air."

"They'll understand. Don't worry. See you next Saturday?"

"You bet."

Being so close, I decide to stop by my Crystal City apartment and pack more clothes. I run into my maid, who's busy vacuuming.

"I put your mail on the counter, Mr. Steele."

"Thanks."

I go through the usual—sales flyers, bills, solicitations from charities, and discover one letter with no return address. Curious, I open it.

Trenton Steele,
You think you're good enough for Madrigal Berkeley? Ha.
What a laugh. You're nothing but a guido. Your father
was a fall-down drunk, your mother a whore, and your
brother a drug mule. Did you enjoy what you did with
your foster brothers in your room? I bet you did. I bet you
loved getting fucked in the ass.
You faggot.
Madrigal Berkeley is too good for the likes of you.
Stay away from her, or I'll tell her what you did the sum-
mer you were ten.

"Anything wrong, Mr. Steele?" Manuela asks.

I breathe hard before letting the air out. "No. Nothing. Just some bills, that's all. I'll be in the bedroom. Got some packing to do."

"Going somewhere?"

"I—" How do I explain what I'm doing? Temporarily moving in with my girlfriend? Madrigal is so much more than that. "Yes. Something like that."

I pull out my biggest suitcase and spend the next hour picking out suits, shirts, oxford blacks and tennis shoes, underwear. The sweats remind me I'll need to find a place close to Madrigal's house to work out. She doesn't own a single piece of gym equipment. A temporary fitness membership will do. Of course, I don't know when I'll find the time with everything that's going on.

The maid comes to the door and knocks. "I'm leaving now, Mr. Steele."

"Thanks, Manuela."

When the apartment grows quiet and I know she's gone, I head to the kitchen and pour myself some wine. My hand trembles as I stare at the goddamned letter. Who sent it? And how the fuck does he know about my past? Except for those sons of bitches who jumped me, held me down and raped me, nobody knows what went down that night. After it happened, I'd run away and hidden under a bridge. It'd been fall and bitter cold. God only knows what would have happened to me if a policeman hadn't found me huddled under a cardboard box. He'd hauled me to juvie while they straightened things out. Too ashamed to talk about what they'd done to me, I refused to talk. But two days later, one of the bastards who raped me got busted for dealing drugs and was thrown in juvie with me. I avoided him and his new buddies as much as I could. But they found me again. If it weren't for some members of a Latino gang who came to my rescue and kicked the shit out of them, they would have made me their bitch. Two days later I went to a different foster home. The boy I shared my room with was younger than me, and there were no older foster kids in the house. So I'd felt safe, at least for a little while.

The memories I've fought so hard to suppress riot loud and clear across my mind. Once again the bitter taste of blood fills my mouth. God knows I'd tried to fight back. But a ten-year-old is no match against two fourteen-year-olds. They'd punched me, almost broken my nose. Took turns raping me. One held me down while the other had a go at me. And afterward, when I'd lain torn and bleeding, they'd laughed and tossed me on the blood-soaked mattress like unwanted refuse. Other than the day I learned my brother was dead, that was the worst day of my life. And somebody knows about my shameful past. Somebody who intends to use that information to take Madrigal from me.

I grab the edge of the counter, throw back my head, and howl with anger, sorrow, and pain while hot tears rain down my face. With one arm, I sweep everything off the counter. The goblet and bottle crash to the floor, and the pungent scent of the burgundy rises up. Wrapping my arms around me, I collapse against the refrigerator door. Its cold metallic surface cools my rage. Gradually my breathing slows until the air whooshes in and out of my lungs and my heart beats in a saner rhythm.

The wine bleeds over the tile while the glass shards sparkle in the bright kitchen light. Manuela would be upset to see all her hard work gone to waste. Exhausted, I grab a mop and broom and get to work.

Chapter 18

Madrigal

"I think you should bring Hunter Stone into the investigation," Cristina says. Honestly, she doesn't give up.

"Why?" I ask.

"Fresh set of eyes, and he's an experienced investigator."

I smile. "You just want him in here so you can ogle his fine ass."

Charlie chuckles and shakes his head. He's so quiet, sometimes I forget he's here.

"Hello? Teenager in the room," Madison exclaims.

"Oh, like you've never noticed a man's ass before," Cristina tosses in her direction.

"I have." She twirls the end of her braid. "But I don't talk about it."

"Well, you've missed out on some serious girl talk. I'll have to teach you some of its finer points."

"I agree with Ms. Sanchez," Charlie pipes up.

What? "You think Hunter Stone has a fine posterior?" I ask.

Laughing, he holds up his hands. "I meant his expertise. Hunter Stone has extensive experience investigating criminal matters. I've used him a couple of times when I've run into walls."

I rub my bottom lip while I think about it.

"You are paying him," Cristina offers, "and he must be bored to tears sitting out there all by himself."

"That's the job," I say.

"It still has to be tedious as all get-out. What do you have to lose by showing him the evidence?"

"Nothing, I guess. Very well." I stand up and go looking for him. He's right where he should be, by the front door. "Hunter, I was wondering if you could help me with something."

He comes to his feet. "Of course."

"I've been investigating my parents' murders. That's why Charlie and Cristina are here."

"I heard some rumblings about it, and of course I couldn't help but overhear when Ms. Sanchez showed up."

Darn. I'll have to be more careful when I discuss the case. "Both Cristina and Charlie suggested you might be able to help us analyze the evidence. Would you mind?"

"No. Not at all. Let me get Alicia to cover the front door. She's monitoring the security equipment." Once he takes care of that detail, we head to the evidence room.

As soon as she spots him, Cristina's eyes light up. Glad I made one person happy, because once Steele finds out, he's going to be upset. No matter how much he denies it, he's a bit jealous of our security guard. And when he discovers I've brought Stone into the investigation, he's likely to go ballistic.

As soon as I firmly close the door behind Stone, I turn to Charlie. "Could you catch up Hunter on the facts of the case?"

"Sit over here, Chief," Charlie says, patting a spot next to him on the settee.

Great. He's calling Hunter "chief," the same moniker he uses for Steele. Strike two.

After handing him the binder that contains all the known information surrounding the murders, Charlie walks him through the evidence. When he gets to the gruesome details, I ask Madison to leave. I don't want her suffering nightmares again.

I'm proud of her when, without a single word of protest, she walks out of the room.

Once Hunter's caught up, we spend the next hour discussing the evidence.

"Who was at the house that night?" he asks.

"My mother and father and Madison," I answer.

"And your grandfather showed up in the middle of the night?"

"Yes."

His brow furrows. "Wasn't he on a business trip?"

"Supposedly."

"Did he return early?" He flips through the pages in the binder. "That doesn't appear to be noted here."

"He must have, because the following morning he picked me up at my friend's house where I'd stayed for a sleepover."

"You'll need to verify his whereabouts that night."

"You're right. I'll have Charlie look into it." We should have thought of it before Hunter suggested it, but with so much evidence to pore over, we hadn't zeroed in on Gramps's location that night. "For the sake of argument, let's just say Madison saw him. But why was he there? You don't drop in on someone that late at night."

"Great question," Hunter says.

"Maybe somebody who was there that night rang him up," Cristina suggests.

"It couldn't have been my mother. Not when she was being . . . abused. And my father wouldn't have done it either. Not when he was the one abusing her."

"Let me see those pictures again," Hunter demands, sticking out his arm.

Cristina hands them to him.

He organizes them into various groups. First the photos of the entire room. Then the pictures of its different areas, and finally the close-up shots of my mother and father. The ones I find difficult to view.

"How did the newspaper get these pictures?" Hunter asks.

"If I had to guess, somebody got paid off," Charlie says. "I can't imagine they would have allowed a newspaper photographer to take pictures of a crime scene."

Hunter leans over so his nose is practically buried in one of the photos. He taps it. "Your father's body was moved. See how his feet angle the bed?" He taps another. "But in this one he's parallel."

"Maybe the way the photographer took the shot made it look that way," I propose.

"Maybe, but my gut tells me differently." He pats his very tight stomach, which Cristina does not miss. "I'd bet my bottom dollar that somebody moved him."

"Why?" I ask.

"Do you have a magnifying glass, Charlie?"

The detective gives Hunter the fish eye. "Who do you think I am, Charlie Chan?"

I have to smile at him. "Olivia has a lamp she uses for her crafts," I say. "It has a magnifying glass."

"Go get it, please," Hunter says.

When I return, we all gather around Hunter while he examines the photos in question. "There!" What was not apparent to the plain eye is quite obvious under the magnifying glass. My father's body *was* shifted.

"Well, I'll be," Charlie says. "You're right. He was moved."

"Yeah, but the question is who did it and why," Hunter states.

"Could have been a crime scene investigator," Cristina suggests.

Hunter's annoyed glare drills Cristina. "You know very well, Ms. Sanchez, they're not allowed to move the bodies until everything has been photographed and evidence has been collected."

Cristina bristles. Darn. I hope they don't end up disliking each other. It would make things even more difficult than they already are.

"My grandfather. It had to have been him," I interject, hoping to defuse the tension.

"He was there the morning after the murders?" Hunter asks.

"Yes. He was the one the police called. He was the closest next of kin." Other than Maddy and me, and we were too young to be notified about the murders.

"They wouldn't have allowed him into the room," Hunter says, frowning.

"You didn't know my grandfather. If he'd wanted into the room, a team of wild horses couldn't have kept him out."

"But why would he move the body?" Cristina asks.

"Maybe he saw something that he didn't want entered into evidence," Hunter says.

"Because?" Cristina asks.

"My guess?" Hunter says. "It would put him or someone else at the scene of the crime. Someone he wanted to protect."

"But who?" I ask.

"That is the question. And once you find the answer, you'll be a lot closer to discovering your parents' murderer."

Chapter 19

Trenton

When I get to Madrigal's house, Alicia Carson, Madison's bodyguard, is posted at the door, which means Maddy must be home. I head to my room and unpack my belongings. Once I'm done, I return to the foyer in search of intel. Alicia would know Madrigal's location. "Where's Ms. Berkeley?"

"The evidence room." I'd known about it, of course, as Madrigal had described it to me Thursday night. But with everything going on, I hadn't had a chance to check it out. Eager to see her, I walk toward what was formerly the parlor.

There I find Madrigal, Cristina, Madison, Charlie . . . and Hunter Stone. *What the hell?*

Madison stands at the ready in front of one of the boards. After Charlie blurts out a few words, she scribbles madly. Cristina writes something on another one and stands back to study all of them.

Madrigal's seated in one of the settees, a coffee table in front of her with a book of some kind resting on it. But what grabs my attention is the gorgeous son of a bitch rubbing shoulders with her. Hunter Stone.

They're flipping pages, whispering about something in the book. Cozy does not begin to describe them.

"What's going on?" I ask.

Madrigal's head comes up. "Trenton. You're home."

Everyone in the room stops what they're doing to stare at me.

"It's after six. Where else would I be?"

She walks up to me, places her dainty hand on my chest, and shoves me out the door. "You can't be in here."

I allow her to exile me to the corridor. No sense making a scene in front of everyone. "Why the hell not?"

She crosses her arms across her chest in a move I've come to know very well. Whatever she's going to say, I'm not going to like. "I've decided to conduct the investigation without your help. I need to do this on my own."

I snort. "On your own? There were four people in there with you, including that bastard Stone!" I yell.

"Will you hush?" She grabs my hand and leads me toward the screened-in porch where I first proposed we move in together. Could that really have been only a week ago? So much has happened since then. But that plan's gone up in smoke, burned to cinders by Mitch's case, the need to establish my own law practice, and now Madrigal's determination to exclude me from the investigation into her parents' murders.

"Hunter's helping us with the evidence. His assistance has been incalculable. Between him and Charlie, we have a new theory of the crime."

"Such as?"

She tosses her head. "I can't tell you."

"Can't or won't?"

"Won't. I want to do this on my own, Steele. Can't you understand that?"

"You're shutting me out of your parents' murder investigation?"

"Yes, I am." I've never seen her this adamant.

"Why?"

"You ordered Charlie to keep the detective's file from me. Did you think I would never find out?"

"You've seen what's in that file. I wanted to protect you."

"I don't need protection. You knew how important that information was to me, and yet you asked him not to hand over the folder."

Time and time again, she's told me she wants to stand on her own. I took that choice away when I kept the file from her. The look on her face tells me I'm losing her, and I have no one to blame but myself. I breathe in and out. Hard. The damage to our relationship is right there in her eyes. But it's not in my nature to give up without a fight. "I can help. You know I can."

"Not going to happen. You'd be in there calling the shots. And I'd never know if the decisions came from you or me. It's important I solve this. Besides, you have enough to worry about with Mitch, setting up your new office, and getting new clients. You don't need any more on your plate. Can't you see that?"

I've been pushed aside. That's what I see. But I'm not going to make a big deal of it. She's dug in and not about to change her mind. I'll have to wait until an opportunity comes along, because I sure as hell am not ceding my spot to Hunter Stone. "Fine. When will dinner be served?"

"Half an hour or so."

"I'll be in my room." The room she assigned to me. Not the one we've been using for the past couple of nights. If I'm going to seethe, I want to do it in private. "Got some calls to make."

"Okay," she says in a pained whisper. Her decision to shut me out comes with a price. I'm hurting, but so is she.

At dinner, to which Charlie's been invited, they purposefully don't discuss her parents' case. Cristina and Madrigal share news about law school friends. Madison asks Charlie a million questions about his investigative work, and he's more than happy to answer. I'm glad to see her interested in something else besides horses. At least that handsome bastard is not seated at the table. He's gone back to his duties as guard, as well he should, since that's all he is.

After dinner, Charlie leaves, and Madison and Cristina head upstairs, which leaves Madrigal and me alone in the living room. The room exudes Southern gentility with its French doors and lacy curtains, vintage sofas and cream antique chairs. I think far enough ahead to lock the doors behind us. Madrigal waits patiently on one of the couches for me to make my move. Going by her staccato breathing, she knows what's coming.

I pull her into my arms and ravish her mouth. She doesn't protest as I take things vertical. I give thanks she's wearing a skirt as my hand rides up her bare thigh to her mons. When I circle her pearl, she moans and writhes beneath me. She knows what I'm doing, claiming her, proving she's mine in the most primitive of ways. But when things get a little too hot and heated between us, she pushes me away. "We have to stop. Anyone can see through those French doors."

She's right. Only sheer lace curtains cover the damn things.

With a groan, I come upright and head for the bar cart. "Want a drink?"

"No, thank you." Polite as always. It was one of the traits that appealed to me when I first met her. She's always been a lady. Prim and proper in public. A sex kitten in the bedroom. After dropping a couple of ice cubes and pouring two fingers of the Macallan Fine Oak into a tumbler, I turn back to her. "I'm going to put down a deposit on that nearby property."

Her eyes widen. "Do you need to do that now? You have enough on your plate, Steele."

"If I don't, somebody may snap it up."

"What will you do with it?" When we first talked about it, before everything went to hell in a handbasket, she wanted us to own the property jointly. But her question clearly signals she's changed her mind.

"Inspect the house. If it's worth saving, I will. If not, I'll tear it down and build something new."

Her eyes mist over. "I hope you won't do that unless there's good cause. I love that place."

"I'll hire an engineer and see what he has to say." I swirl the ice in the glass. "I'm thinking about selling my apartment in Crystal City."

"Why? Until your new property is habitable, you'll need somewhere to live."

In other words, I won't be living here much longer. If that doesn't spell doom for our relationship, I don't know what does. How could everything have gone so wrong so fast between us? I clear my throat and get ready to take the hit like a man. "Are you saying we're through?"

Her eyes mist over with tears. She pats the sofa cushion next to her. "Please sit."

A punch to the gut, that request. She's fallen for the gorgeous bastard, and she's about to say good-bye.

"I've been thinking about your proposal that we move in together. We can't continue as we have been in the last week. Not in the long run. That's very clear to me."

This is it. Here it comes. There's the door. Don't let it slam you on the way out. Taking the seat next to her, I drape my arm over the back of the couch and wait for the ax to fall.

"Madison and I have been talking."

Not where I thought she was going with the discussion, but okay. "About?"

"She doesn't want to commute back and forth to school. So when it's back in session, she wants to board there during the week. She'd asked Gramps, but he wouldn't allow it. Probably because he wanted to keep tabs on her. Given her medications, it makes sense."

"And you're considering this?"

"Yes. She's been taking her meds for the last several days. Well, except for the one pill she says makes her feel like a zombie. And she's doing well. She promised she would stick to her medication. She knows if anything happens at school, I'll yank her out and bring her home. She really wants this, Steele."

Is she seeking my counsel? From the look of expectation on her face, it appears so. But I don't want to overstep if she's not. "Are you asking for my opinion?"

"Yes."

Suspicion is in my nature, so I have to ask, "You're not just throwing me a bone because you shut me out of the investigation?"

Her tinkling laugh rings out. "I'm not that devious, Steele. I truly want to know what you think."

"Okay." If that's the case, I owe her the best advice I can give her. One obvious issue jumps out at me. "What about boys? Aren't you afraid she'll sneak one into her room?"

"It's an all-girls school, and Philippe will be two hours away at the University of Virginia. Too far away to drop in."

I snort. "You don't know the mind or sexual drive of a college boy. A two-hour drive is nothing to a young man in lust."

She tosses her head, which sets her dark hair dancing around her shoulders. I want to tangle my hand through that mass of curls, pull her onto me, and brand her as mine.

"They have a very good security system, Steele. And iron bars on each window."

"Now that's something that can be counted on."

"So you think it would be okay to let her do it?"

I twirl a loose curl that's fallen across her face around my finger and breathe in her scent. My cock lets me know in no uncertain terms what it wants. "You're her guardian now, so it's your decision. But if it were my younger sister, I'd at least give her a chance to prove herself."

Her limpid gaze finds me. She's not unaffected by my touch. But then I'm not playing fair.

"I thought so too. I'm going to say yes."

"Madison will be thrilled, I'm sure." Letting go of her hair, I toss back what remains of the Macallan.

"She'd come home on Saturdays and Sundays, of course. If for no other reason than to ride Marigold. I'd be home during the weekends as well. But during the week, I was wondering, could I live with you in your Crystal City apartment?"

My heart stutters. Did she just ask me if she could move in with me? The thought of having her all to myself five days a week is everything I've dreamed of. Apparently the ax is not about to fall after all. "Yes, sweetheart, you most certainly could."

"Thank you, Steele." Her smile is just as sweet as the rest of her.

"You're welcome, Madrigal." Something momentous just happened. Something that will set the course for our relationship—and yes, there will be a relationship, at least for the near future. "In the meantime . . ." I cup her face in my hands, kiss her lips, nibble at her throat.

"Not here. I know a better place."

"Your room?"

"Gramps's bedroom. I haven't been in there since he passed away. It's about time I was. But I don't want anyone to see us heading there, so we'll go up the back way."

She gets to her feet, as do I. "Back way?"

"Yes." Taking me by the hand, she leads me through the French doors and along the outside of the mansion. "I'm sorry to say that at least one of my male ancestors carried on an extramarital affair."

Happy now that the dark clouds have lifted, I laugh. "How on earth do you know such a thing?"

"He built a secret stairway that led directly to his bedroom."

At the back of the house, she points to a door. "Here. It's always locked. But the key's handy enough." She points to an old rusty hook right next to the door. "Guess it hasn't been used in quite a while," she says.

"Let me try." With a little elbow grease, I get the key to turn. Rather than put it back on the hook, I take it with me. Don't want somebody dropping in on us.

Upstairs in her grandfather's bedroom, I don't waste time in preliminaries. I turn the lock to the door we just came through as well as the one to the second-floor corridor.

"They won't hear us," she says, throwing her arms around my neck. "That's solid oak, too thick for sounds to escape. So we can make as much noise as we want."

"I'll do my best to make you scream, then." I pick her up and lay her on the big four-poster bed.

Before we get down to business, she says, "George Washington slept here, you know."

"Good for him. But we're not going to do any sleeping."

She giggles. "I hope not."

In no time flat, our clothes fall away. And soon I'm riding her to paradise and back. It takes but a few minutes to find completion. I'll need to slow it down next time.

"You're smiling," I say.

"I'm happy."

I discovered early on she's ticklish. So the devil in me goes after her, drumming my fingers up her flank, across her stomach. She laughs so hard she rolls off the bed. I catch her before her head hits the floor. But before I can pull her up, she stops me. "Wait. There's something down here."

"Where?"

"Under the bed."

I let her down easy and crouch next to her. "It's a box."

"Thank you, Captain Obvious," she says to me.

I smack her rump. "Behave. Maybe your grandfather used it for extra storage."

On all fours, she pulls out the box. And of course my cock notices her ass in the air. As soon as she's investigated the contents, I'll pull her back onto the bed and enjoy another bout of hot sex. The metal box, unlike so many ancient things in this house, appears to be brand-new. When she wrestles the lid off, she gasps. Rows of books rest inside.

"What are those?"

She glances at me. Even in the dim light, I see the moisture in her eyes. "My mother's journals. He never burned them."

Chapter 20

Cristina

After an hour of listening to Madison extolling the virtues of her boy-friend, Philippe, I was in serious need of a diversion. I searched out Madrigal and Trenton for some grown-up talk, but they were nowhere to be found. So intending to take a leisurely stroll around the mansion, I wandered outside. When I discovered the pool, nothing could keep me from stripping down to my undies and jumping into the pristine blue water.

My parents' pool in Miami was never heated, so the warmth is a pleasant surprise. After swimming back and forth to work out the kinks, I lie back and float, allowing the water to buoy not only my body but my spirits. As my mind turns inward, I recall how excited I'd been to start my internship at the Department of Justice. Catching the bad guys has always been a dream of mine. I love my work; I really do. But something's missing.

And I know just what it is. My relationship with Scott never really took off. He doesn't push my buttons the way a certain bodyguard does. After one look at Hunter Stone, I'd been ready to lick him from head to toe. My body flushes at the thought of that six-foot-something mountain of a man hovering over my body, tasting me, ravishing me.

"Enjoying yourself?" His husky voice drifts over the water, sending my senses soaring. Does he sound real in my imagination or what?

"Umm, yes," I answer.

"What on earth do you think you're doing?"

What? I open my eyes to find the object of my fantasy standing at the end of the pool with a scowl a mile wide across his face.

In a hurry, I find the pool's bottom and stand. "H-Hunter. What's wrong?"

"What's wrong?" His big, manly hands are propped on his hips. "You're out here by yourself swimming in the open. Right now, anybody could be training a rifle on you."

I wade to the shallower end of the pool. "Why would anybody do that?"

"You're approximately the same height and build as Madrigal Berkeley, and your hair's dark just like hers. You could be easily mistaken for her. And yet you're out here in the dark seemingly without a care in the world."

"She's not in danger, is she?"

"Ms. Sanchez. Why do you think she hired me?"

"I don't know. To find out who killed her grandfather?"

"To protect her, her sister, and the members of the household, which right now includes you." He swings his arm sideways. "Get out of the pool."

Darn. Here I was having such a lovely fantasy about him, and now he's ruined it. "I'm sorry. I didn't think." When I climb up the steps and out of the pool, his eyes flash with heat. No wonder. All I'm wearing are a sheer bra and panties. He can see every inch of me.

I grab my clothes from the beach chair I'd thrown them on and drape them in front of me. "Turn around so I can dress."

For a couple of seconds, his appreciative gaze takes me in from top to bottom, but then he does as I ask.

Leaning back, I jam on my shirt and button it. Wet as I am, the jeans are a lot harder to slide on. At one point I lose my balance and stumble against him. He reaches back and grabs my hip to keep me from falling. His hand lands on the edge of my panties, an inch away from paradise. If he moved his finger just a tad, he'd feel how soaked I am—and not only from the pool.

When I finally wrangle my legs into the jeans and pull up the zipper, I say. "Okay, you can turn around now."

When he does, the heat in his eyes sets me reeling. Obviously, he's not unaffected by me, but I can't start anything with him. Not now. Not when I'm still with Scott and don't know if I'm going to remain in DC or move back to Florida. If I were to start something with Hunter Stone, it wouldn't be easy to let go.

Chapter 21

Madrigal

The treasure trove we just discovered makes my heart sing. I thought we'd lost my mother's diaries to the fire, but for some reason my grandfather kept them. "I have to read them."

"It's late, Madrigal. If you start reading them, you won't stop."

"It's not *that* late. Only a little after eleven."

"You remember how the last one upset you."

"Yes, I do." I know he's trying to keep me from suffering more hurt. But after studying all the details surrounding my parents' murders, I've toughened up. I'm not the same woman who went crying to him after I read my mother's final journal. "I'll be fine, Steele."

"How far back do they go?"

"To the time she was a teenager . . . Strange."

"What?"

"The handwriting looks different than I remember."

"Stands to reason. Your handwriting changes as you get older."

This great find calls to me, but he's right. If I start reading now, I won't quit until I'm done. Tomorrow will be soon enough. I'll organize them by year. Read the most recent ones first and then work my way backward. I'll have to read all of them by myself. No one must know I've found them. "We'll have to keep this a secret."

"I can help you," he volunteers.

"Steele?" Has he forgotten about my desire to handle the investigation on my own?

"There are at least twenty of them in there."

I count them. "Twenty-four."

"And they're thick. It'll take you at least a couple of hours to read each one. You're supposed to be studying for the bar exam. How far do you think you'll get if you read your mother's journals instead?"

I make a face. "Not far."

"It will go faster if you split the journals between us. I'll skim them and let you know the important parts so you can zero in on them. Once you have time, you can read them from cover to cover."

"Fine, but leave the ones surrounding the date of her death to me. Okay?"

"Okay." He holds out his hand. "Now come back to bed. I'm not done with you yet."

He doesn't have to ask me twice, not when he has that spark in his eyes.

**

At breakfast the next morning, Madison questions our disappearance. "Where did you go last night?"

Wanting to test her reaction, I tell her the truth, or as much of the truth as can be shared in polite company. "Trenton and I went to bed."

Cristina whoops and then chuckles into her napkin while pink-cheeked Madison struggles against an outburst. It's touch and go there for a second, but finally all that emerges from my baby sister is "Oh. Okay."

Steele winks at me, which tells me he approves of how I handled that particular inquiry. Wanting to reward Madison for her newfound maturity, I ask, "Have you heard from Philippe?"

Mouth full of French toast, she takes a moment to respond. "Yes. We're Skyping in about half an hour."

The video call should cheer her up. "That's good. When will he be back?"

She sighs. "Not till August fourth."

I'll need to alert Hunter to post someone next to that tree outside Madison's window. "That's only a week away. Not that long."

"It'll seem like forever. May I be excused? I want to make sure my laptop's set up for the call."

"Sure. Say hi to Philippe. I'll invite him and his parents to dinner when they return."

Maddy squeals and throws her arms around my neck. "Thank you. Thank you. Thank you. I'll let him know." With that long-legged gait of hers, she gallops out of the room.

Hiding a grin, Steele stands up. "Will you excuse me? I have to make some phone calls before we get on with our project."

"Okay. Find me when you're done. I'll be in the evidence room," I say.

Leaning over, he kisses me. He tastes of syrup and hot, delicious man.

When I manage to get my bearings, I meet Cristina's gaze. For the first time in all the time I've known her, there's a touch of envy in her eyes. "That man loves you, *querida.*"

"You think so?"

"Uh-huh. And believe me, I know. He looks at you the same way my father looks at my mother."

"I'm not sure how I feel about that. Even if it were true. I don't need any more complications in my life. I have more than I can cope with at the moment."

She props her chin on her hands. "You handle *him* really well."

I laugh. "I don't handle Steele at all. I can barely keep my head above water around him. He's so much . . . more than I am. He's one of the top criminal lawyers in the country, infinitely more sophisticated than me and, needless to say, way better in bed."

Grabbing her fork, she twirls it in my direction. "Yeah, but you've got something he wants."

"What?" I'm not asking for vanity's sake. I'm truly curious. Maybe if I knew, I could deal better with him.

"That's something only you can determine. You fill a need in him, that much is clear." She folds her napkin and lays it on the table. "And as far as Madison is concerned, I don't think you need to worry. She's fine."

I'd shared my worry about Madison with her, so I appreciate her take on my sister. "You think so?"

"Yes. I did volunteer work at a mental health clinic while in high school, so I've seen firsthand people suffering from mental illness. She's nothing like them. She's spirited, yes, but I think she was mainly frustrated by the restraints your grandfather imposed on her. With you as her guardian, she'll blossom."

I rise from my seat and hug her. "Thanks, Cristina. I'm so glad you dropped by."

"Anytime, *querida*. I'll head back to the evidence room. I want to go over those testimonies again." Among other things, Detective Collins had sent us his notes on Helga's testimony and the other witnesses in the case. His summary is the closest thing we have to the actual trial transcript, which we can't obtain because the court files are sealed. I probably have Gramps to thank for that. No doubt he argued that the gruesome details of the case should not be made public. Stuff leaked out, of course, but the evidence never did. If it hadn't been for Charlie White's contacts and Detective Collins's file, we would be nowhere. So I'm thankful for the evidence we have, even if it's not complete.

Finished with breakfast, I head to the foyer where Hunter Stone's on duty. Does the man ever sleep? Yesterday he spent the entire day with us from ten to six. "On duty already?" I ask.

"I just checked in. I wanted to go over the details from last night with John." John Thompson's one of his operatives.

"Anything to report?"

"A fence was torn down."

"Where?"

"About fifty yards south of the stable. I told Hartley. He sent out a repair crew."

Hartley not only functions as our barn manager and horse trainer but also makes sure the fences in and around the property are in good repair. The last thing he'd want is for one of his horses to escape through a break.

"The cameras didn't catch it?"

"No." His tech guy had installed security cameras in and around the estate, but of course they couldn't capture everything, especially late at night. "With your permission, I'll post extra guards tonight."

"Thank you, Hunter." In gratitude, I pat his arm—just as Steele strides toward us.

His face pinches for a second, but then the expression vanishes. He's jealous of Hunter Stone. That much is clear. He shouldn't be. Our head of security may be gorgeous, but he does nothing for me.

"Done with your phone calls?" I ask him.

"Yes."

"Should we head up then?" Before coming down for breakfast, we'd locked the journals in the filing cabinet in my bedroom.

"Go on up. I'll meet you in five."

The air vibrates from the tension between the two men. I don't know what Steele is going to do, but I'm pretty sure I won't like it. "Steele?"

"It's fine, Madrigal. Go on."

Not much I can do except what he wants. He's hell-bent on his purpose, whatever it may be. I hope no blood's spilled. The Aubusson rug they're standing on dates back to the eighteenth century. I'd hate to see it ruined.

Chapter 22

Trenton

"Stone," I say, narrowing my gaze. He's rubbed me the wrong way since day one. Something about him sets off alarms. He's hiding something. I can feel it deep in my gut.

The son of a bitch smirks. "That would be Mister Stone to you."

I mirror his expression. Two can play at this game. "But Hunter to Madrigal?" I ask, gritting my teeth.

"She's my boss and can call me whatever she damn well pleases." The sexual undertone to that statement is hard to miss.

I'd love to tear the bastard limb from limb. But I have to keep my temper under control if I'm to have any hope of getting information from him. "Who are you?"

He snorts. "I believe we just established that."

"That's who you say you are, but that's not your real name, is it?"

All I get is a raised brow.

"I checked you out. You didn't exist before 1999. You popped up in the system when you joined the Navy SEALs. Before that? Nada."

His right shoulder hitches. "Maybe your research missed something."

"My research is the best there is." This time I bare my teeth.

"Surely you didn't ask Charlie? He vouched for me."

"I have sources other than Charlie. He's not the only one I depend on to get to the truth."

"Don't know what I can tell you, then. Obviously, somebody missed something."

"No, they didn't." I step forward right into his personal space. "I'm going to find out who you are if it's the last thing I do."

"Doubt it." The corners of his lips curl up, triggering a memory, one hidden deep in time. Son of a bitch. A glimmer of an idea shimmers to the surface. Something that can't possibly be. But it would explain a lot.

Well, there's only one way to find out. I thump his chest. "Stay away from Madrigal, you hear me?"

He slaps my hand away. "Hard to do. She's my boss, after all."

"You make any move toward her, and I'll slice off your nuts, *tu pezzo di merda*." You piece of shit.

"*Vaffanculo*." Go fuck yourself.

Hiding a smile, I turn and trot up the stairs. I've gotten what I need to know. I just have to prove it. And that is something I'm very, very good at.

I enter Madrigal's bedroom to find her frowning at the pile of books on her bed.

"What's wrong?"

"Four of the journals are missing. Last night there were twenty-four. Now there are only twenty."

I glance between her and the place where she'd tucked the diaries. "But you locked the file cabinet."

"Yes, but I left the key in my desk drawer. Anyone could have gotten it. That was so stupid of me."

"Hey, don't beat yourself up." I rub my hands up and down her arms. "Who knew where you kept the key?"

"Madison, for one. But even if she knew about them, she wouldn't take them without asking. She knows how important these journals are to the investigation. But honestly, anyone could have taken the key. All they had to do was search my desk."

"It had to be while we were at breakfast. Maybe we could dust for fingerprints? Charlie has a kit."

"It wouldn't do any good. The maids dust every day. Madison loves to snoop." Her bottom lip trembles. She's trying hard to be brave, to hide what the loss of the journals means to her.

I drop a kiss on her head and tuck her against me. "Maybe you should ask Hunter to investigate. He's got cameras throughout the house. Maybe one of them caught somebody going into your room."

"That's a good idea," she says, wrapping her arms around my waist. "I should have been more careful. Locked them up in that safe downstairs."

"What safe?"

"The one in Gramps's study."

"I didn't notice a safe."

"It's behind that hunting scene painting on the wall. I'm surprised you didn't find it."

"Guess I must have missed it. We'll need to open it and see what's inside."

"Yes." She wipes a tear from her cheek, and then a thought occurs to her. "Oh my God. What about the evidence room? Somebody could get into it."

"You have the only key to the door. But you should change the lock. I'll get Stone to do it."

She shakes her head as if she can't quite believe what I just said. "That's the second time you've mentioned him. You buddies now?"

"Not exactly. We talked. I know where he's coming from now, so I understand him better."

"Good." She strokes my chest. "Honestly, Steele, you have nothing to worry about. I barely have time for you. I wouldn't dream of adding another man to the mix. Ménage à trois is not my thing."

I could tell her she's missing out on something special. But I won't. She'd be shocked to her very core if I did. Besides, no way I'd share her with another man. I'd cut off his dick first. I curl my hand around her nape and bend down to kiss her soft lips. "Thank you for saying that, *mia bella donna.*" My beautiful lady.

Her cheeks bloom pink. "Oh, I like that."

"I'll use it more often, then." I turn over her hand and kiss her palm before I let go. "So how do you want to handle the journals?"

Over the next three hours we go over the diaries, starting with the most recent ones and working our way back. When I get to the one from 1997, I make a rude discovery. A January entry details Marlena's growing unhappiness with her husband.

January 14, 1997

He thinks I don't know, but I'm fully aware he's having an affair with his secretary. How cliché. The way they carried on at the holiday party sickened me—furtive brushes when they passed each other, longing glances across the room. What I hated most of all were the pitying looks from the staff at his lobbying firm. They all seem to know and feel sorry for me. I never loved him. I see that now. But what choice did I have but to marry him? I was pregnant with Madrigal, after all. Father would never have allowed me to have a child out of wedlock. He would have demanded an abortion. And I would never do that. No. I made the right choice. Even if my life is a living hell. I need to talk to someone, though, before I explode. It can't be any of my society friends, not as much as they love to gossip. No. It will need to be someone I can trust not to talk. Mitch Brooks. We've been friends since high school, more than friends actually. At one time, I'd imagined myself in love with him. He works for Father's law firm. I think I'll give him a call.

An entry several days later fills me with even more concern.

January 28, 1997

I met Mitch at a bar hotel. Bad idea as it turned out. After a couple of drinks, I broke down. Mitch being the perfect gentleman suggested we take our discussion somewhere private. Not wanting anyone to notice my misery, I agreed. He rented a room, and one thing led to another. God. It was so wrong. I've never cheated on Tom. And I don't intend to do it again. But it felt so good. I realize now Mitch's the man I've always loved. He's always been there for me. It's him I should have married. But it's too late now. I've made my bed and I must lie in it. When we said good-bye, I knew it'd be the last time I'd confide in him.

Had that tryst yielded consequences? Madison had been born almost nine months to the date. She resembles Mitch. How could I not have caught that? Their eyes are the same shade of brown, and they're both blond, although Madison's hair is closer to amber and Mitch's a whiter shade of gold. Madison's hair color could have been inherited from her grandfather. In his younger days, Holden's hair shone gold. Tom's eyes must have been brown, because as far as I know, he wasn't suspicious of Madison's coloring. Or maybe he found out, and that's why he abused Marlena.

"What's wrong?" Madrigal asks.

"Nothing." I rise, stretch. "I'm gonna get something to drink. Do you need anything?"

"A glass of water."

"Okay." She's so caught up in the journal she's reading, she doesn't bother to look up. Employing a sleight of hand I learned during my youth, I hide the journal in my jacket. I trot down the stairs and head for the private room she assigned to me. With my trusty penknife I cleanly cut the two pages from the journal. Her mother wrote sporadically, not following a set schedule, sometimes going as long as three weeks without making an entry. As long as she doesn't refer to her rendezvous with Mitch again, it'll be okay.

After stopping in the kitchen to grab the water, I trot back upstairs to her room. Not five minutes later, the house fire alarm goes off. We run into the hallway, where we're joined by Madison. All three of us dash down the stairs toward the source of the smoke. The kitchen. Half the staff's in there already, along with Cristina and Hunter Stone.

"What's going on?" I ask.

Hunter's retrieving a burning pan from the oven using a pair of long-handled tongs.

"Did Helga forget something in there?" Madison asks, a crestfallen expression on her face. "Hope it wasn't dinner."

Helga rushes in from the back of the room and snaps her hands to her cheeks. "Ach, my oven!"

Stone places the burning pan on top of the stove. "Where's the fire extinguisher?"

"Beneath the sink," Hans exclaims. "I'll get it." He fetches it and lets it loose on the pan. Before long, the fire's out.

What remains of the funeral pyre is clearly not food but books.

"My mother's journals." Madrigal turns a tearful face to me.

"Can they be saved, Stone?" I ask.

"Doubt it." He's right. They're too far gone. Nothing legible will emerge from them.

"Who could have done it?" Madrigal asks, tears streaming down her cheeks.

"I don't know. Did you see anyone, Stone?" The expression on the bodyguard's face mirrors his name. He's furious, although he hides it well.

"No," he says. "And the security camera won't help us. Somebody covered it up." He points to the equipment in the corner. A kitchen towel is draped over the lens.

The staff glance suspiciously at one other. Can't blame them. Someone in this room is the culprit. Someone who broke into Madrigal's filing cabinet and stole the journals. Whoever did it took quite a risk. If he'd been caught, at the very least, he'd be fired. "Mr. Stone and I will look into this. Won't we?"

"Yes, Mr. Steele, we certainly will." The look he sends me is cryptic. There's something he knows, but clearly he's not talking.

Chapter 23

Madrigal

Again I must make do with what I have. My mother's journals were a wonderful discovery that would have shed light on those important months leading up to her murder. But they've been burned beyond recognition, and only a pile of ashes remains.

So I'm forced to take extreme measures.

The house we lived in when I was a child still stands. I'd avoided going there in the last twelve years, but now? I have to, no matter the cost. I'll need someone to accompany me. The question is who. It can't be Steele, not as busy as he is setting up his new law firm and dealing with Mitch's case. Charlie is busy with that as well, and Cristina's at her internship. Madison's not an option. So my only choice is Hunter Stone.

We make the trek up I-66 to the Beltway and from there to the Arlington house I lived in until I was twelve. My grandfather never sold or rented the house, but took care of it as if my mother still lived there. The house lies empty, but the grounds have been landscaped, the grass mown, the hedges trimmed. The furniture inside is exactly as I remember.

"Where is your parents' room?" Hunter asks.

"Upstairs on the second floor. Maddy and I had our children's suite on the third. Olivia lived with us up there."

"No other bedrooms on the second floor?"

"Guest rooms. But as far as I know they were never used. Nobody stayed here other than the family. The servants had their own quarters in the back of the house."

"Strange."

"Not really. My mother and father were only children, and my grandfather had his own house. So no family members to visit."

When we get to my parents' bedroom, I take a deep breath. I haven't seen the inside of this room in over twelve years.

Sensing my distress, Hunter steps back and allows me space and time to gather my courage. Finally, I grab the knob. It turns as easily as if it's been oiled or kept in good repair all these years. Clearly, somebody's taken care of it, and the orders could have only come from one person—my grandfather.

I thrust open the door and step inside. Everything looks exactly the same. My parents' king-sized bed in the center of the room. My mother's vanity table with its tufted bench. A chest of drawers on the side, and the hope chest in front of the bed where my mother stashed the quilt at night when they slept. Now it covers the bed. Such happy colors. Turquoise and peach in a traditional wedding-ring pattern. She'd loved that quilt. So had I, thinking how well it symbolized their happy union. How very wrong I'd been.

Like the furniture in the rooms below, the furniture here is dust-free and so is the carpet beneath our feet. Not even a ghost of a bloodstain remains. Had Gramps replaced the rug? More than likely. He'd want the place to remain exactly the way it'd been before my parents were killed. I wander to the vanity table and pick up a framed photograph. The four of us smiling at Christmas. Another one of my mother and father on their wedding day. She'd been so beautiful in her wedding gown.

"You look like her," Hunter whispers over my shoulder.

"Yes."

I pick up another Christmas photo. This one includes the four of us plus Gramps and Mitch. While everyone's staring into the camera, Mitch is looking at my mother. The longing on his face takes my breath away. Clearly, he loved her. Why hadn't I figured that out? It makes perfect sense now that I think about it. She must have had some feelings for him as well since she insisted Gramps make him a co-trustee of the trusts he drew up for Madison and me.

"What about friends? Didn't you have sleepovers?"

"No. My father never allowed it." That should have been my first clue that something was wrong. My beautiful mother had gone from one control freak of a father to another in a husband. She should have married a man who truly loved her. Like Mitch. He never married. Was he happy to worship her from afar?

My stomach churns at the myriad of possibilities this discovery creates. Where was Mitch the night of my parents' murders? That question never came up as far as I know. It never seemed important back then. But now? At one time, he and my mother were close friends. Would she have turned to him, revealed her abuse? If she had, I doubt Mitch would have stood aside and allowed it to continue. He would have done something. Could he have walked in on them and found my mother dead? If he had, would he have killed my father? Seeing how the alarm had been turned off, he could have simply entered the house. Is that why Gramps manipulated Helga's testimony? Because he knew Mitch had killed my father? Or maybe Gramps killed him himself?

God, so many possibilities. I don't dare mention this to Steele. Not with him having to deal with Mitch's case right now. He's bound to have a jaundiced view. I'll need to figure things out on my own. And there's only one way. To go directly to Mitch and ask him point-blank.

As the thoughts whirl around in my head, I sway on my feet. My vision starts to waver.

"Whoa!" Stone says, catching me by my elbow. "Are you okay? You look pale. Here. Sit. Put your head between your legs. I'll get you some water."

I wait on the stuffed aquamarine chair in the corner of the room until he returns with a cold bottle of water.

"How did you manage that?"

"I keep a cooler in the back of my car. Before we left the house, I put the bottles and some ice packs inside." He waits until I take a couple of sips before saying, "I think we should go." His eyes register nothing but kindness and concern.

"No. I'm not done yet." Coming slowly to my feet, I test my ability to stand. When my knees support my weight, I walk toward the hallway, make a right, and climb the stairs to the third floor where my room and Maddy's were located. Her tiny bed's still there. It will never be slept on again. At least not by her. At some point, I'll call Goodwill or the Salvation Army and donate most of the furniture. But only when I'm through with my investigation.

I head toward the wall where Mom marked our heights. I find the one that recorded Madison's at different ages. The mark for four shows she was forty inches tall. With Hunter trailing, I retrace our steps and walk to the hallway window that faces the backyard. It was there Madison spotted Gramps digging up Scruffy's grave.

"How tall would you have to be to reach the bottom of that window?"

Hunter pulls out the tape I'd asked him to bring and measures the distance. "Forty inches."

"Could someone forty inches tall see into the backyard?"

"No. Only the top of her head would reach the bottom of the window. She would have had to use a step stool."

We had one. She'd used it to open chest drawers too high for her. But when she told us about Gramps digging in the backyard the night of our parents' murders, she'd never mentioned that detail. It's entirely possible she forgot. Or maybe, just maybe, she dreamed the whole thing up.

Chapter 24

Trenton

"Why did you leave the firm, Mitch?" I've come to the Loudoun County Detention Center to interview Mitch, but he's not cooperating and stares stone-faced at me.

"Do you want to be found guilty of first degree murder?" I ask.

He relaxes into his chair, seemingly without a care in the world. "That's not going to happen."

"How do you know?"

His gaze reminds me of the one he used when I said something incredibly stupid during my youth. "They have to prove me guilty beyond a reasonable doubt."

"And you think they won't be able to do that? You had means and opportunity!" I yell.

"But no motive." In contrast to my excited voice, his is a soft whisper.

"How do you figure that, Mitch? You argued with Holden that very afternoon. He threw you out of his house. And that night? You were there to rescue Madrigal after he locked her in. How on earth is that not motive?"

"First of all, I was with you most of that time. You jumped the fence to get inside. Not being as nimble as you, I remained outside. You'd taken very few steps before the shots went off. One wounded you. The other killed Holden. How on earth could I have traveled that distance and gotten into the house without you seeing me?"

He's right, damn it. It doesn't make sense. But then it doesn't make sense that he was charged with Holden's murder either. The prosecution has something up their sleeve, and I don't have a clue what it is. And Mitch stubbornly refuses to cooperate. Maybe if I take another tack, he'll let something slip. "I saw somebody running toward the wall and climb the fence."

"And you think that was me? With my bad knee?" When he was younger, he'd injured his knee playing tennis. He'd undergone surgery to repair it, but it had never healed right. "Besides, he was running away from the house, and you yourself said the shots came almost on top of each other. So whoever that runner was, he didn't kill Holden."

"You could have hired somebody to do it."

He comes upright, rattles the handcuffs chained to the table. "I wouldn't—I'd never do such a thing."

No. If he ever killed somebody, he'd do it himself, not pay someone to do it. Or would he? The more he stonewalls me, the more I think I don't know him as well as I do.

Regardless, I have to keep his trust in me if I'm to have any hope of getting the truth out of him. "I know you wouldn't. But they can sell that theory to a jury."

"They can't just throw out accusations without something to back it up. They'd need proof, which they won't be able to get because I never did such a thing." For a couple of seconds, air bellows in and out of his lungs, but gradually he gets his breathing under control. "How are the girls?"

So he wants to change the subject. Okay. We'll take a break from my interrogation. And even though he's my own client, it is an interrogation. "Fine." I fill him in on Madison's doctor visit. "Madrigal's handling her meds now. She seems pleased with Madison's progress."

"There's nothing wrong with Madison." A rattle tells me he resents being handcuffed. If I were in his shoes, so would I. "Holden used drugs to control the women in his life."

"What do you mean?"

"He used them on Marlena whenever she disobeyed him, used them on his wife too. He liked his women docile."

"How do you know this, Mitch?"

"Marlena told me. He'd slip drugs into his wife's tea whenever she 'stepped out of line.' His phrasing."

God. The man was a monster. "And Marlena never reported him?"

"Who would she report him to? She was fifteen. Nobody would believe her."

"He seems to have taken the same tack with Madrigal and Madison." After her mother's death, Madrigal suffered a breakdown, so he'd placed her in a mental health care facility for an entire year. With Madison he took a different direction. He'd asked his friend, Dr. Holcomb, to put Madison on a drug regimen for God only knew how long. "Madrigal is working with this new doctor to find out if Madison really needs all those pills."

"My guess is she doesn't. It's something Holden favored. And as long as he had his friend prescribing pills and no one objecting to it, everything was fine. The bastard. I'm glad the son of a bitch is dead. If he were still alive, I'd—"

"Mitch, for God's sake, keep your voice down."

"Why? You're my attorney," he tosses out. "Nobody should be listening in."

"True. But I'd just as soon not take any chances."

His head droops as despair seems to flow over him. "Damn his black soul," he whispers. "I hope he's burning in hell. How could he do that to his own daughter and granddaughters?"

"The man had an ego the size of Texas. He never could stand anyone going against his wishes, and he needed to be in control."

"He wasn't infallible. The decisions he made ultimately cost him his daughter's life."

"What are you talking about?"

"Marlena's marriage to Tom Berkeley. Holden picked him out. Dangled him in front of her every chance he got the summer after her junior year in college. God. She hated those damned company picnics. But found it impossible to say no to her father. She was terrified of him. And then when she went back to college, Tom was always around. It got to the point she couldn't go anywhere without him following her."

"How do you know all this?"

Lost in his narrative, he continues almost as if I'm not there. "She'd tell me. I wanted to do something, but I was at Harvard and she was at William & Mary. I told her to hang on. That college would be over soon. And then I would take her away from her father, from Tom. But then one day she called to tell me she was pregnant and Tom was the father." When he looks up, tears shimmer in his eyes.

"She was pregnant with Madrigal."

"Yes. I wanted to propose after graduation. I thought getting my Harvard degree would make me worthy of her, but I waited just a shade too long."

"And then you had another opportunity when she came to you."

His head jerks up. "What do you mean?" Fear lurks in his gaze.

And I know why. He's afraid I know the truth. But I'm not ready to reveal that to him. When the proper opportunity arises, I'll use it to find out why he left the firm. But for now, I'll play dumb. "She came to you a couple of months before she died, asking for your help. You said so yourself."

His tension eases. "Yes, she did."

"If everything had gone according to your plans, she would have run away with you. It would have been you, her, and the girls."

"And it would have been perfect. I'd have made sure of that."

"I know you would have, my friend."

There's a knock at the door. With a rattle of keys, the guard enters. "Time's up."

I come to my feet. "I'll see you soon. Anything you need?"

"No. Just tell the girls I love them."

I squeeze his shoulder on the way out. After I retrieve my belongings from the locker, I wander out to my Jag. It's one of those hellacious summer days. A storm's brewing on the horizon. Soon it will arrive. And then all hell will break loose.

Chapter 25

Madrigal

"Thanks for seeing me, Uncle Mitch." He looks the same and yet different. The orange prison uniform suits his blond coloring, but in only a few days, he's lost some weight. Shadows darken the skin below his eyes, and that special vivacity he always had has gone missing. I sense surrender in him. Like he's fought the good fight and is resigned to his fate, which doesn't make any sense. He's always fought for what he felt was right. Why, look at how he took on Gramps. When it came to championing Madison and me, he'd always been fierce. But now? It's like he's given up. I hate to see him like this. "How are you, Uncle Mitch?"

"As fine as can be expected under the circumstances. How's Madison?"

"She's . . . content. Goes riding every day."

"Of course." He bows his head.

"She misses her boyfriend."

His head jerks up at that. "She has a boyfriend?"

"Yes." Of course he doesn't know. The whole episode with the boyfriend happened after he'd been thrown in jail. "His name's Philippe.

She met him at a steeplechase race." I tell him as much as I know about the young man, leaving out the details about Philippe sneaking into Madison's bedroom. Uncle Mitch would just get upset if he knew.

"She's growing up."

"Yes, she is. She wants to board at school during the fall. I think I'll allow it."

"Holden kept her on a pretty tight rein. At times he took extreme measures to curtail her freedom."

"You knew about the drugs?"

"Yes."

"How did you find out?"

"She had a fall from her horse and ended up in the hospital. She called me on her cell in tears because Holden was threatening to put down her mount. Apparently, she'd been on some heavy-duty meds and had refused to take them. Holden ascribed her wild behavior to not following her regimen."

"You didn't know before that?"

"No. I didn't know he'd gone that far. She slept in the stable for an entire week, petrified that he'd follow through on his threat. I interceded as best I could, but Holden flat out told me it was none of my business. That Madison was his granddaughter and he'd do what he thought was best for her."

"Yes, I can see Gramps saying that. He could be pretty stubborn."

Something about my words causes him to frown. "He didn't force you to take meds as well, did he?"

"No. But he did lock me in my room on a couple of occasions when I sneaked out of the house."

"I didn't know. I'm sorry you went through all that. I asked Olivia to keep tabs on the situation and let me know if Holden became too dictatorial, but she never did."

"She was afraid of him, I think. Or afraid he'd fire her and she'd never see us again. She'd grown attached to us."

"Thank God she was there. She acted as the buffer between Holden and you. Otherwise, God knows what he would have done."

"Was he that way with my mother?"

He nods. "Growing up, Marlena was terrified of him. He imposed strict curfews on her time away from home and didn't approve of most of her friendships."

"But he approved of you."

"Not really. I don't think he realized the extent of my friendship with your mother. I didn't count. I was a charity case at her high school, there on a scholarship. So he couldn't envision her choosing me as a confidant. And then there was the fact I was a boy. Unlike most teenagers, Marlena was singularly uninterested in boys."

"But you did become friends."

"Yes, close friends. Very close friends."

I reach out and cover his handcuffed hands with my own. "You loved her."

He heaves out a sigh. "Yes, I did. But I was foolish and proud. My vanity got in the way. I wanted to offer her something more than a poor man with no prospects. I waited until after graduation from Harvard to propose to her. But by then it was too late. She'd fallen in love with your father. Right after she graduated from college, they married."

My lips bow into a smile of sorts. "She was pregnant with me."

"You know?"

"Of course. I can do basic math, Uncle Mitch. I was born in September, and they got married in June. It stands to reason she was carrying me."

"Yes. Nothing I could do at that point."

The guard who escorted me into the room appears. "Time's up."

My lips twist. "I'll come back. I promise. Do you need anything?"

"It'd be nice to have a photo of your mother and the two of you."

"I'll bring it with me next time."

"Just the photo. They don't allow us to have frames."

Probably so the prisoners can't use them to fashion weapons.

"I understand. Until next time."

"Say hello to Madison." His heart is in his eyes. His eyes. They're Madison's eyes.

My breath shorts. Could he be Madison's father? Is that why he cares so much about her? How did I not see this before? I was too close to him, to Madison. That's how. But now the murder investigation has opened up my eyes to this new possibility. And it's something I must seriously consider. Well, there's one sure way to find out. Compare their DNA. I'll have to find a way to get something from him. A hairbrush would do. I can get it from his house.

"I will. Is there something you'd like from home?"

"There is. A picture of your mother and me when we were teenagers. It's on my dresser. Trenton has the key to my house. He can let you in."

"Sure, I'll bring it. Take care, Uncle Mitch." Bending down, I kiss him on the cheek.

He tugs on my ponytail the way he's done since I was five. "You too."

As I walk out of the jail, I debate the best way to tell Steele about our meeting. I never told him I'd be visiting Mitch. And seeing how Mitch is his client, he's bound to object.

Chapter 26

Trenton

Tuesday morning I head toward my new offices in Crystal City. After a discussion with the building's owner, I'd hired the same crew that had done the earlier construction. By the time I arrive, they're hard at work. After a short conversation with the foreman to make sure everything is proceeding smoothly, I drive to my apartment. Since I'll be working with Charlie the rest of the day and we'll need food, I make a pit stop at the grocery store and pick up a couple of things. When I arrive at my building, he's waiting for me in the lobby, sipping a Starbucks coffee. He's addicted to that stuff. Good thing there's one on the ground floor.

As soon as he sees me, he stands, battered briefcase by his side. "Hey, Chief."

I nod at him. "Thanks for coming. Sorry to keep you waiting. Got your favorite bagels plus some ham, cheese, and chips to get us through lunch." I fish out my elevator key card, insert it into the slot, and press "PH."

"How is the office coming along?" he asks.

"As well as can be expected. They won't be finished by Friday, that's for sure. But my private office will be in good shape."

"And your staff? When will they arrive?" he asks, taking a sip of coffee.

"Our target date is August third. According to Marcus, the Gardiner firm is complaining that the mass exodus will leave their criminal law practice group shorthanded. But if their employees want to leave, there's nothing they can do about it. Others are interested in jumping ship as well, but I can't take on any more employees until I get some clients." Right now all I have is Mitch, and I certainly won't be charging him for my time.

"Serves the bastards right for letting you go. They didn't think that move through, if you ask me."

"Dick Slayton was never good at people management or making decisions. Holden had Joss to smooth things out, but Slayton won't, because I wouldn't be surprised if she left as well. Nothing to keep her there with Holden gone."

After I put away the groceries and guzzle down a glass of water, I check the mail. Thankfully I don't find another nasty letter. I'd debated whether to hand the envelope over to Charlie and have him investigate, but I don't want him to take on one more thing, not with all the other work he's doing for Madrigal and me. More importantly, I don't want him to know I was raped. Irrational as it is, I'll have to live with that shame for the rest of my life.

I plop down a plate of fresh-baked bagels and muffins from the corner bakery and a container of cream cheese. After we serve ourselves, we get to work.

"So what did you find out about Mitch?"

"Nothing that you don't already know. He has a pretty good-sized bank account. I suspect you had something to do with that."

I shrug. "He taught me the art of trading in the stock market. I invested some of his money. We both came out ahead."

He retrieves a notebook from his briefcase and plops it open on the table. "He graduated from Harvard, both undergrad and law school.

After graduation, he went to work for Gardiner and stayed there until he jumped ship for the SEC. He owns a home in Loudoun County, a beach house in Bethany Beach, and another place in the Florida Keys."

"Really?" I ask, biting down on a bagel. "I didn't know about the Florida Keys."

"Apparently, he likes to go deep-sea fishing. Some primo spots down there." He guzzles back the last of his Starbucks and tosses the cup in the trash before he opens the refrigerator and grabs a water bottle.

"Anything else?"

"He's never been married, but has had several relationships. None lasted longer than a year."

"Come on, Charlie, I know all that stuff. I want to know his sins, his dark underbelly."

"Sorry, Chief." He snaps shut the notebook. "Nothing popped up other than he's an alcoholic, but you already know that."

"Yeah. He hasn't touched a drop in I don't know how many years." Leaning back in the chair, I rest my head against my hands. "Fuck. I was hoping you'd find something shady."

"The man's a damn Boy Scout," he says, grabbing a muffin.

I bounce forward, pull my laptop toward me. "Well, it is what it is. Let's brainstorm, then." For the next few hours, we work on several theories of the crime as well as list the names of those who were there the night Holden was killed. Charlie will need to investigate them, including Madrigal and Madison. Nobody is exempt.

"I'll need to get the names of all the staff."

"Hunter has those. I'll get them from him."

He cocks a brow. "Hunter, huh? You guys best buds now?"

I laugh.

"What's so funny?"

"Those are the exact words Madrigal used."

"Well, are you?"

"Not best buds, no. Let's just say we understand where we're both coming from. As long as he doesn't make a move toward Madrigal, we'll get along."

Charlie chokes out a laugh.

"What?"

"He's got zero interest in your girl. It's Cristina Sanchez who gets his motor running."

"Cristina. Really? She has a boyfriend."

"Yeah, like that's going to stop a man like Hunter Stone. If he wants her bad enough, he'll go after her."

"Huh. Didn't pick her as his type. Now about the murder . . ."

The rest of the day we go over likely scenarios. We don't have anything concrete, but we do have possible avenues of investigation. Finally at three o'clock, I call it. He's beat, and so am I.

"I guess I'll see you Saturday?"

"Actually, I'll be at the mansion tomorrow. I have some news for Ms. Berkeley."

"What news?"

He clams up.

I chuckle. "Oh boy. Okay, fine." I open my arms wide. "I had to take a shot."

"Yeah, Chief," he chuckles back. "You did."

The drive to Madrigal's house is brutal. An overturned trailer blocks I-66, and it takes me two hours to get there. Not only that, but the AC in the Jag picks today of all days to shut down on me. By the time I arrive at her house, all I want is a shower and a cold drink. I'm tossing my suit into my dry cleaning bag when she walks in, looking fresh as a cucumber.

"You're here."

"Yeah, I arrived a minute ago," I say, sealing the bag.

"I have to tell you something you're not going to like."

I prop my hands on my hips and catch a whiff of me. God, I reek. "What?"

"I visited Mitch."

"You what?"

She takes a step back. "Don't yell. I did nothing wrong."

"Okay. I'm sorry." I wave a hand in the air. "Who gave you permission?"

"He did."

"You should have asked me." I tap my chest. "He's my client."

"I'm sorry. I didn't think you'd object. Why are you objecting?"

I peel off my shirt, toss it into the dirty clothes hamper. Those pit stains are not coming out. And that's a $600 shirt too. "Because I like to know who he's seeing."

Her chin jerks up. "I'm taking Madison with me next time. He wants to see her."

"Fine. But please limit yourself to one visit a week."

"Why?"

"Because Charlie and I need to talk to him as well, and he may not be available to us at the same time. You do understand the case takes priority over a social visit."

"Stop talking to me as if I'm a child, Steele. Of course I understand."

"I'm sorry. I shouldn't." I sit on the lid of the commode and drop my head in my hands. Fuck. This is not how I wanted our meeting to go. I glance up and plead, "Can we start all over again?"

Her lips quirk up. "Of course."

I gaze at the beautiful picture she makes in her sleeveless flowered dress, and the tension flows out of me. "Hi, honey. I'm home."

"I'm so happy you are. Would you like a drink, darling?"

"Not right now, sweetheart. Maybe later."

She walks up to me, and even though I'm hot and sweaty and pretty sure I smell like a three-day-dead skunk, she kisses me. "I'll be sure to make your favorite. What is your favorite, by the way?"

I shrug. "Anything with alcohol in it."

She drops the 1950s saccharine-sweet housewife act, which I have to admit I kinda like. "Come on, Steele. I really want to know."

"Do you?" I grab her by the waist, plop her on my lap, and my cock gets its hopes up.

"We're not doing it while you're sitting on the toilet."

"In the shower, then?"

"Can't. Helga is waiting for me downstairs. She wants to know whether you prefer mashed potatoes or baked potatoes with filet mignon."

"Baked and dripping with butter"—I kiss her—"and sour cream"— I kiss her again—"and smothered with bacon." I devour her mouth, which tastes of peppermint.

She wriggles free. "I'll let her know. See you in a few." I swat her bottom before she leaves.

That night I'm sitting up in bed with my hands folded behind my head, and she's lying cuddled up against me when I decide to bring up her meeting with my client. Might learn something after all. "So what did you and Mitch talk about?"

"Oh, this and that. I caught him up on everything that's been going on with Madison."

"You didn't tell him about Philippe?"

"I mentioned she had a boyfriend, that's all. He wants me to bring him a photo from his bedroom and a couple of books to read."

"Let me know what the books are, and I'll stop at his place tomorrow."

"That would be silly. He lives off Route 15. That's out of your way. You shouldn't have to make a special trip. Besides, I want to do it."

"Why?"

When she sits up and plumps her pillow, I instantly miss her warmth. "Because he asked me, Steele, not you. If he'd wanted you to do it, he would have asked you."

"He probably didn't think of it."

She grabs a bottle of her lavender-rose lotion and spreads some on her hands. "Or you never asked him. I want to do this for him."

I'd offered to bring Mitch anything he needed, but he just didn't ask. "Please, Steele."

She knows what those *pleases* do to me, the witch. I tweak her chin. "Very well. The key's in my apartment. I'll bring it back with me tomorrow, unless you want to meet at his house?"

"Why don't I follow you into Crystal City in the morning and get the key from you then? The Arlington Commonwealth's Attorney's office wants to meet with me. I need to provide them with some documentation and security details before I start working for them. Might as well kill two birds with one stone."

"Sounds like a plan. Now hand over that lotion."

She bites down on her lip. "What are you going to do?"

"Rub it all over your beautiful skin, among other things."

Her eyes round with wonder as she hands the bottle to me.

Chapter 27

Madrigal

"Thank you for coming, Charlie. You called to say you have news." He'd rung me up the day before to request a meeting. When I'd prompted him, he'd told me it'd be better if we discussed the information in person. Since then, I've fretted, wondering what the heck he has to relate.

"Yes. I didn't want to trust this to the telephone. Never know who might be listening. Can we go to the evidence room to talk?" He points in the general direction of the converted parlor he's come to know so well.

"Of course." As soon as we step inside and close the door, I ask, "What's wrong?"

He sits in his usual spot, the chintz floral love seat, and pulls out a folder from his briefcase. "You asked me to look into your stay at the Meadowlark Mental Health Facility the year after your parents' deaths."

"Yes."

He props open the folder on the cream-colored coffee table in front of him. "Well, according to their records, you were never there."

"What? That can't be. I spent an entire year in the facility as Dr. Holcomb's patient."

"I know, but there are no official records of that. After spreading some money around, I finally got a nurse to talk. Apparently, some patients stay there without records being created. Either the families don't want anyone to know, or for some other reason."

I jab my hand at the air. "Why would they conceal my time there?"

He rubs his chin while contemplating my question. "I don't know. What do you remember about your stay?"

Wrapping my hands across my waist, I pace up and down the room. "My bedroom was pretty. I remember that. Blue wallpaper with little flowers on it. Yellow primroses, I think."

He makes a note of that.

"The same nurse would come in every morning, take my temperature and blood pressure. She'd give me my morning pills. Then an orderly would roll in my breakfast on a cart."

"You didn't have breakfast in the common room with the other patients?"

"No. Never."

He makes a note in the folder. "And then what?"

"I'd be escorted to the shower room."

"You didn't have one in your room?"

"No. Only a toilet and a sink. After my shower, I was escorted to Dr. Holcomb. He would talk to me, ask me questions." Jagged memories of my time at Meadowlark crash into my mind like birds against glass. I'd been petrified of what they'd do to me, of never seeing Maddy again. I'd buried those memories long ago, but recalling them is one more painful step I must take to get to the truth of my parents' deaths. God, will it ever stop?

After taking more notes, Charlie asks, "What did you discuss?"

"How I felt. At the beginning, my grief over my parents' deaths overwhelmed me. Sometimes I'd cry; other times I would sit there and stare at the wall. When I became agitated, he'd inject me with something. Things got fuzzy after that. Then it would be lunch. If the weather was nice, they'd serve it on a private balcony, adjacent to my room. If it was raining or cold, I'd eat indoors. After lunch, I usually napped or read depending on whether I could stay awake. I'd take daily walks on the grounds, again if the weather cooperated."

"By yourself?"

"A nurse would hover over me. I never saw anyone else. It was a pretty place filled with flowers in the garden."

He jots something down. "And then what?"

"In the evening after dinner, they'd wheel in a television set. I'd watch shows from seven to nine, and then it was lights out. Next day I'd do it all over again."

"And you did this for an entire year?"

"Yes. The routine never varied. At first I accepted it, but as time went on, I balked at the pills, the injections. That's when they strapped me down and forced the medicine down my throat. I learned to acquiesce after that. I'd take them and hide them under my tongue, but then the nurse caught on, and I went back to being force-fed the pills. If they couldn't get them down my throat, they would give me an injection, which made me stupid."

"Did your grandfather ever visit?"

"Every Sunday afternoon for exactly one hour. I begged him to let me come home. But he said Dr. Holcomb wouldn't approve. Finally, after a year, I was allowed to go home, except of course it wasn't home but Gramps's house. Terrified I'd be sent back to Meadowlark, I didn't step a toe out of line. At least for the next couple of years. Gramps relaxed when he witnessed my good behavior, but he imposed strict curfews on me, just like he'd done with my mother. When I turned fifteen, I rebelled. One day I decided to go shopping with my friends after school. When I arrived home, my grandfather punished me by locking me into my room. If it hadn't been for Olivia, who threatened to call the police, I wouldn't have been given any food for the entire weekend."

Charlie mumbles something under his breath. The only word I catch is *bastard*. He waves his pen in the air. "Did your grandfather keep a diary?"

"If he did, I haven't found it. I searched his room and study."

"Could he have kept one on his computer?"

"No. He was old-school, wrote everything down." Just like Charlie.

He puts down his pen, shuts his trusty notebook. "He's the key to solving your parents' murders. His actions were too arbitrary, both the night of their deaths and when he committed you to the mental health facility. It was like he was afraid of something coming out."

"But what could it possibly be?"

"I don't know, but if we want to figure out who killed your parents, we're going to have to find out. Is there someone he could have confided in?"

"Yes, Joss Stanton."

"Talk to her. See what she says." He pauses a moment before he proceeds. "If I may suggest something, Ms. Berkeley?"

"Please do."

"You're keeping Trenton Steele out of the loop because you want to handle this yourself."

My shoulders tense. I swallow hard. "That's not the only reason. He's got enough on his plate with setting up his new practice and Mitch's case."

"I think you're making a mistake. You need to bring him in. Everything in your case keeps circling back to your grandfather. Something tells me the two are related. Solve your parents' murder case and you may find out who killed your grandfather."

He may have a point. Am I letting my pride get in the way of solving my parents' murders by shutting out Steele? Would his assistance help me get to the truth? "I'll consider your advice, Charlie. Thank you."

"One more thing I wanted to mention. I looked into Dr. Holcomb's finances. He's close to bankruptcy. Too many expenses and not enough income. His mental health facility doesn't bring in the patients it once did. In my opinion, desperate men are dangerous, so I'd keep my distance from him."

"He was my grandfather's friend, not mine. Never mine, not after what he did to me." He'd also been Madison's doctor. But he won't be anymore.

"Weren't you almost engaged to his son?"

"He proposed. I didn't accept."

"Well, he might come calling again given the family's financial straits."

"I'll instruct Hunter to refuse entrance to both father and son."

"That would be wise."

I'd been so worried about what he had to report that I'd failed to offer him the usual tea and biscuits. Seeking to remedy my sad lack of manners, I ask, "Would you like to stay for dinner?"

"Regrettably, no. I got some work to do for Steele."

"I'll see you over the weekend, then? We'll need to put this information on the boards and discuss it with the team."

"Of course." He thrusts his notebook into his briefcase and stands. "I'll be here."

No sooner does he leave than Dr. Durham calls. "I received Madison's records from Dr. Holcomb. According to him, your sister suffers from a form of delusion referred to as confabulation."

"What does that mean?" I ask, confused.

"It's a memory disturbance, the product of fabricated, distorted, or misinterpreted memories without the conscious intent to deceive." After a pause, she continues, "Did you verify your sister's story about running away with the people she mentioned?"

"Yes, I did. Madison was telling the truth."

"Hmph." She sounds frustrated. No, more than that, disgusted. "Frankly, Ms. Berkeley, I saw no evidence of mental illness in your sister. She seems pretty grounded in reality. I'm quite concerned about the medication and the high dosages she was prescribed. It makes no sense to me."

Yeah, I don't think my sister is delusional either. Which begs the question: Why did Dr. Holcomb prescribe that medication for such a long time? Was he just incompetent or did he have some other motive?

Chapter 28

Trenton

Despite filing a change of address with the court and the Loudoun County Commonwealth's Attorney's office, a court document in Mitch's case gets sent to my ex–law firm. By the time I get it straightened out and have the legal document delivered to me, I've lost two days.

The misdirected document sets the date for the preliminary hearing. At that time, the Commonwealth's Attorney must show that probable cause exists that Mitch murdered Holden. The preliminary hearing is the first step before a full-blown trial. If the judge finds probable cause, he or she will certify the case to a grand jury. It will be up to them to issue an indictment. And Beauregard Jefferson intends for Mitch to be indicted for capital murder.

What circumstances could he be relying upon to support such a claim? Only the death of a police officer, a pregnant woman, or a murder-for-hire scheme would support such a charge. The first two clearly do not apply. Does Beauregard Jefferson have evidence that Mitch hired someone to murder Holden?

Eager to find out what evidence they have, I call the Commonwealth's Attorney's office. I'm transferred to an assistant attorney who gives me the runaround, claiming Beauregard Jefferson's tied up in a meeting. Is this more posturing by the Commonwealth's Attorney in his bid for a congressional seat? Or does he have some evidence to back up the charges?

I call Charlie to see if he can pick up some scuttlebutt from his contacts at Loudoun County. I don't have long to wait.

"They're wet-their-pants excited," Charlie says when he returns the call.

Fuck. "About?"

"Don't know, Chief, but they seem to think they have a slam dunk."

"They'll have to show their hand at the preliminary hearing. But it will be two weeks before that happens. In the meantime, Mitch's in jail when he should be free."

"Face it, Chief. He's in jail for the duration. No matter what you do."

Much as I hate to admit it, he's right. "See what else you can find out. I'm at my new place. Furniture's being delivered today. Once it is, we'll set up an evidence room." At one point or another, we'll have to pull an all-nighter.

While I'm on the phone with him, someone buzzes to get into my new suite. Charlie promises to keep digging until he finds something while I walk up to the glass office door. Rayne Adams stands on the other side, holding a pizza box and a couple of bottles of pop.

"You're here," I say with a forced cheerfulness I'm not feeling in the least.

She cocks her head to the side as if she can't believe my obvious statement. "Yes. I took half a day off. Thought I'd come by to help you set things up. Brought sustenance." She points to the pizza box. "Hope you like mushrooms and pepperoni."

"I do. Thank you."

Having nowhere to sit, we camp cross-legged on the rug. I devour half of the pizza in nothing flat, while she limits her share to one slice.

I point to the box. "Is that all you're going to eat?"

"Watching my girlie figure," she says, patting her stomach.

The gesture focuses my attention on her. With her mocha-shaded skin and lustrous brown eyes, she's strikingly beautiful. If it weren't for my obsession with a certain brunette and her pansy-colored gaze, I might be interested. But Madrigal's the only woman I want in my bed. Or in this instance, her bed. Coming to my feet, I offer my hand to help her up. "Thanks. I needed that."

"My pleasure," she says.

Within the hour, the office furniture arrives. Slowly but surely the space comes to life as the movers arrange the desks, chairs, and credenzas in the private offices, and sofas and chairs around the reception area.

"You'll need a sign over the receptionist's desk with the firm's name," Rayne points out.

"I'll need a logo as well."

"You can work on that later. What's important is the name."

"Trenton Steele and Associates. It has a nice ring to it, don't you think?"

Laughing, she gestures to the telephone console now resting on the receptionist's desk. "I see they installed the phones."

"This morning. Now all we need are clients."

Almost as if the gods heard me, my cell phone rings. I don't recognize the number, but I pick up. "Trenton Steele."

"Hello, Mr. Steele. My name is Bernard Bates."

The name sounds familiar, but I can't quite place it. "What can I do for you, Mr. Bates?"

"I'm the general manager of the Washington Stars. One of our players is in trouble, and I heard you were the go-to guy."

"Which player?"

"Mikhail Robinson, one of our rookies." As he rattles off the details behind the arrest, I gesture for a pad and pencil to Rayne. She fishes out what I need from her briefcase and hands them to me. Taking a seat at the receptionist's desk, I jot down the details. A wide receiver caught with drugs at a club. Arrested last night but freed on his own recognizance. Makes sense they let him go. A football player about to attend training camp is not going anywhere.

"Can you help him?" Bates asks.

"Of course. Where is he?"

"He's at our Ashburn training facility. He's scared shitless. Done nothing wrong his whole life. If he were found guilty, it would totally devastate him and his family. They're as straight as they come."

I recall reading something about the young man's background when he was picked up by the Stars. Religious family, strict parents. Of course, that could all have been PR spin. Guess I'll find out. "I'll be there in an hour."

After I hang up, I turn to Rayne. "Looks like we have a client."

Her face lights up with a smile. "Congratulations."

"I have to go. Can you stay and sign for the rest of the stuff? Those things you picked out in Alexandria are due to arrive this afternoon."

"Of course. Don't worry about it. By the time you get back, everything will be set up."

Three hours later, after my interview with Mikhail Robinson, I return to find a totally transformed office. Paintings hang on the walls, area rugs cover the floors. All those things Rayne chose now adorn every room in the place. I arrive to find her arranging flowers in the reception area vases. The lobby appears cozy and classy at the same time. "This looks fantastic. Where did you get the flowers?"

She flushes a little at my praise. "From the florist shop downstairs. It doesn't look bad, does it? I called the rest of the team. They'll be here tomorrow to set up their offices. How did it go with Robinson?"

"Great. He was definitely set up by someone trying to make him look bad."

"Who?"

"A groupie. On the way back, I stopped at the DA's office. Once I explained about the groupie, they promised to look into it. Pretty sure I can get the charges dismissed. They're not eager to enrage the Washington Stars' fan base by dragging their number-one draft pick through the mud at the start of the season." I pop open the bottle of bubbly I picked up from the liquor store downstairs and pour it into the two plastic glasses I grabbed as well. "To our first client."

"May there be many more." We clink, spilling a little of the champagne. Just as we do, the doorbell buzzes. "Maybe it's another client."

But it's not. It's Madrigal.

"Hi. Glad you stopped by." I buss her on the cheek and then point to my valuable assistant. "You remember Rayne?"

"Yes, of course." They shake hands.

"I stopped at Pietro's and got a couple of dishes to celebrate your new office. I'm sure we can stretch it to three servings." Her tight smile tells me she'd rather not.

"Oh, no." Rayne waves her hands. "I have to go. Got a . . . thing tonight." Her hesitation tells me she has no plans. But she's doing the right thing by leaving us alone. Madrigal does not appear too happy about her being here.

After Rayne leaves, we set out the food in the kitchen.

"So, your furniture arrived."

"Yes. They even delivered the water cooler." I point to the contraption in the corner.

"And you asked Rayne to help?"

"No. She just showed up. Took half a day off. Nice of her to stop by. Don't know what I would have done without her."

Her lips twist. "You could have called me. I would have loved to help."

"You have enough going on, Madrigal. How's the bar studying going? That's next week."

"Don't." She spears me with her glance.

"Don't what?" I ask, all innocent.

"Don't change the subject."

"We have a subject?" I ask, trying to lighten the mood.

She folds her arms across her chest. "Don't get cute, Steele. It doesn't suit you."

"You're upset."

"Yes."

"About Rayne."

"What clued you in?"

"The smoke coming out of your ears and that little green monster sitting right there." I brush my hand across her right shoulder.

She bops me on my shoulder.

I pull her into my lap. "You got nothing to worry about. She doesn't do a thing for me."

She pushes back. "Stop paraphrasing my words."

"Seriously? You're jealous?"

"Why wouldn't I be? She's gorgeous, smart, and infinitely more stylish than me. Just look at that gorgeous dress she was wearing. And here I am in blue jeans and a shirt."

"I like you in blue jeans and a shirt. I like you even more out of them." Pulling on her shirt, I inch it out of her jeans.

She stands up. "We're not going to screw here, Steele."

"Why not?"

"Because. Now eat your dinner like a good boy and then show me around."

"I've never been a good boy."

"Oh, I don't know. I think you're pretty good at some things."

"Like what?"

"Lawyering."

"And?"

"I'll tell you after you show me around," she says, dancing out of reach with a smile.

Chapter 29

Madrigal

I've spent the weekend studying for the bar, and now Steele is taking me out to a hot new restaurant in Leesburg as a welcome distraction. But just as I'm getting dressed, Cristina calls. In tears. "What happened?" I ask.

"That son of a bitch."

"Who?"

"Scott. Did you catch the news?"

"No. I've had my nose buried in study guides the entire weekend."

"He's been screwing his boss this whole time," she says through a sob. "All those weekends he's been campaigning were spent under the sheets. The scandal just broke. It's all over the news. She's a married woman, for heaven's sake."

Well, there goes her career. And his.

"You want me to come over?" As much as I hate to break my date with Steele, I have to be there for my friend.

"No. I don't want to inflict my misery on you. And now I've got to find a new place to live. I moved in with everything I owned. And since I subleased my place in Georgetown, I don't have anywhere to go. Damn him."

"You can stay here with us until you find a new place. Steele lives in Scott's building. We're coming over to help you pack."

As soon as I hang up, I turn to Steele. "Change of plans."

"What?"

"Cristina's boyfriend, Scott McCarthy? He's been cheating on her with his boss. Apparently, it's all over the news." I fire up my laptop that I'd purposely turned off so I wouldn't be tempted to surf the web. It takes no time to find the gossip item, with pictures to boot. The two of them doing the nasty in some hotel room. Yeah, the senator's not making a comeback from this. And she's a Republican too. "You'd think they'd know to draw the curtains."

Steele taps the screen. "Look at the angle. Those pictures were taken from inside the room. Probably somebody hiding in a closet."

"Ugh. Who would do such a thing?"

"Lots of private investigators. My guess is the husband probably suspected she was two-timing him and hired someone to prove it."

"That cheating bastard. Cristina's a mess, and she's got no place to go since she subleased her place. I told her she could crash here." I glance up at him to gauge his mood. "You don't mind, do you?"

He shrugs. "Why should I mind? It's your home."

"I know, but it's yet another person in the house."

"It's a big house." He captures my hips and grinds against me. "And we can be private in here."

Who would have thought my grandfather's bedroom would become our refuge? "We have to go help her move her things."

"Um, about that. I have a better plan. Why don't we ask Hunter to go with us? After she's packed, he can drive her here and we"—he kisses the tip of my nose—"can enjoy dinner at Pietro's and spend the night in my apartment."

"Are we going to fuck or make love?"

He grins crookedly at me. "Lady's choice."

We drive to Crystal City in separate cars. Steele and me in his Jag, Hunter in his Grand Cherokee. After Cristina lets us in, she takes one look at Hunter and wails. "Why did you bring him?"

Too late I realize I should have warned her. "He's here to help you move. Just how much stuff do you have?"

She points to several boxes, plus oodles of clothes and shoes draped over the couch and chairs. Knowing Cristina's penchant for fashion, I'd brought two huge suitcases. In no time at all, we've got everything packed.

"Is that it?" I ask.

"Yes."

Hunter picks up several boxes while Steele drags the suitcases toward the door.

"Wait." She fishes a key card from her purse and hands it to Steele. "You'll need it for the elevator." The key cards only work for specific floors, so we couldn't use Steele's to gain access to Scott's apartment. When we arrived, she had to buzz us in.

After Hunter and Steele head out with her things, she bursts into tears. I wrap my arms around her.

"You shouldn't have brought Hunter. I don't want him to see me like this. Mascara running, sniveling nose. I look like hell." She dabs at her face while more tears course down her cheeks.

She's making it worse, so I take a wipe from my purse and gently repair the damage. "You didn't really love Scott, did you?" I ask once I remove most of the heartbreak evidence.

"No. But I hate that men seem to think it's all right to do this to me. I really do. I'm never dating again."

Yeah, sure. That will last until the next gorgeous man catches her eye. Come to think of it. One already has. And he's helping her move. "Okay. I think that's for the best."

She laughs and wipes the tears from her face. "I ruined your evening, didn't I?"

"Why do you say that?"

"Look at you." She gestures at me. "You never get dressed up."

"We're going out to dinner. At Pietro's. Hunter's driving you home."

She juts out her chin. "I don't need him driving me. I have my own car."

"You're upset. You shouldn't be driving. He'll come back and get your car in the morning. Now wash your face and brush your hair."

She takes but a couple of minutes to fix her face. When she comes back, she looks more like her usual self.

"I'll need to return Scott's key card to him."

"Mail it to the bastard so you don't have to see him again."

"Okay."

The doorbell rings, and I open the door to find Steele and Hunter on the other side. Standing next to each other, their resemblance strikes me. They have the same build and coloring, except where Steele's eyes are slate gray, Stone's are midnight blue.

"Is that all?" Hunter asks. "Or is there more?"

Cristina takes a look around. "Just those two boxes."

Stone picks them up and heads toward the door.

I hug her again. "I'll stop by your room when we get home tonight, okay?"

"Don't. I'll probably be asleep by then. But I'll see you in the morning."

"Yeah." I kiss her. "Hunter will take good care of you."

"Right."

"Shall we?" Steele nods to the door.

We say good-bye in the lobby. We'll walk to the restaurant, which is just around the corner, while they take the elevator down to the parking lot.

"Have a great time," she says.

"We will." I hate to see her so sad. She's such a good person. But she has the worst luck in men I've ever seen. As I stroll down the side-walk, happy to be holding hands with Steele, I have no way of knowing how the events of that night will come back to haunt us in the months ahead.

Chapter 30

Cristina

"Have you had anything to eat?" Hunter asks after we slip into his *mucho* macho SUV. So many men drive big cars to make up for their sexual inadequacies. Doubt Hunter Stone has any problems in the bedroom department, though. Everything about him is big. His hands, his arms. I can imagine what else.

"Dinner, you mean? No."

"Want to stop somewhere? I know a place."

"I'm not dressed—"

"It's a diner. Nothing fancy."

"Okay."

The place, next to a budget motel, is close to a dive. But going by the crowded parking lot, it must serve great food.

It takes us a few minutes to be seated. The waiting area's so tiny, people jostle us as they scoot to the front to give the hostess their names. And I end up being thrust against Hunter. God. He's hard all over and smells of some yummy cologne.

"So are you taking the Virginia bar or the DC one?" He'd heard Madrigal talking in the evidence room, so no surprise he knows about it.

"Neither. I'm taking the Florida bar. I'm flying to Tampa tomorrow to take the test on Tuesday and Wednesday. Afterward, I'll head to Miami to spend a couple of days with my family before coming back."

"Why aren't you taking the DC bar? You're working for the Justice Department."

"It's just a summer internship. At the end of the summer, I may be offered a permanent position or not. So I'm keeping my options open. This way I can work in DC or Florida."

His name is called, and we follow the hostess to a booth. As soon as we're seated, a harried waitress rushes over with our menus.

"Anything to drink?" she asks, pen poised over her pad.

He orders coffee and water; I ask for iced tea to combat the heat and humidity of the summer night.

"So how does that work?" he asks once she leaves.

With my mind occupied by the train wreck of my life, I've lost track of the conversation. "How does what work?"

"How does taking the bar in Florida keep your options open?" He leans back, spreading a massive arm over the top of the booth.

I gulp at the sight of his bulging bicep just as the waitress arrives with our drinks.

"What would you like to eat?" she asks.

I haven't bothered to look at the menu, but like every other diner in the free world, it has to have one thing. "I'll take a cheeseburger, medium well, and fries."

Hunter orders the same but with bacon.

Enthralled by his powerful hand, I watch, mesmerized, as he pours cream and sugar into the coffee and stirs slowly.

"Options?" he asks, bringing me back to our conversation.

"Your test scores from another jurisdiction can qualify you to practice law in the District of Columbia. But the reverse is not true."

"Really?"

"Think about it. How would knowledge of DC law help someone practice in Florida? State-based lawyers usually handle wills, domestic relations, or other issues particular to that jurisdiction. Most of the attorneys working in DC deal with federal agencies, such as the IRS, the Department of Justice, the Securities and Exchange Commission, Congress."

"Makes sense. But do you want to stay in DC?"

"I did before"—I slash the air—"this happened. Now I don't know."

I gaze into my tea as if the answer is to be found there to keep him from seeing my tears. I hate it when I cry, especially over a good-for-nothing bastard.

"Hey." He reaches across the table and wipes the moisture from my cheeks. "Are you really going to let one man's betrayal drive you away from a career you love?"

I toss back my head. "No."

The waitress arrives with our food, which gives me time to get myself together. When we pass the ketchup and mustard back and forth, our hands inadvertently brush against each other. Something zings through me—lust. I gaze at him as a wild thought pops into my head.

"It's good," he says of his bacon cheeseburger after he's chomped down half of it. "How's yours?"

"Same."

He smiles. "How would you know? You haven't taken a bite." He pushes the plate closer to me. "Eat. Carbs are good for a broken heart."

"My heart's not broken. It's pissed off," I say, chewing on my burger.

"Good to know." He swallows, and I'm fascinated by the bob of his Adam's apple.

Angry with myself, with Scott, with the predicament I find myself in, I snap at him, "Stop being so damn agreeable."

Although he doesn't say a word, his raised brow speaks volumes.

And I'm instantly contrite. "I'm sorry. I shouldn't be yelling at you. It's just you're so—" I bite my tongue before I blurt out something I shouldn't.

"So?"

"So male, okay?"

He laughs. "And that's bad?"

"No. Of course not. It's just. Here you sit a foot away. Gorgeous, stacked, and I imagine well hung."

He sputters, coughs.

"Are you okay?"

He holds up a finger while he gets his breathing under control. Once he does, he takes a sip of his coffee. Planting both elbows on the table and folding his hands, he stares at me, not in anger but in wonderment. "Do you always blurt out every thought in your head?"

"If I'm upset or excited, yes, I do."

"At work as well?"

"No, strangely enough. When it comes to the legal stuff, I'm very logical and unemotional. But then I'm a Gemini, which explains the dual sides of me."

He picks up a French fry and swirls it in the mound of ketchup he built.

"Do you have a girlfriend?"

He takes the time to chew before he answers. "No. Too busy with my business, plus I travel quite a bit. And I have absolutely no desire to settle down."

We spend the next few minutes finishing our food. When the waitress shows up to clear our plates, I ask for a slice of lemon meringue pie for dessert. He goes for the apple pie à la mode.

While we wait, I glance at him over my glass of iced tea. "You see that motel over there?" I point my chin toward the budget inn on the other side of the parking lot.

His head swivels between the motel and me. "Yes. Planning on spending the night there?" he asks, all scrunched brow.

"No. Not the night. Just a couple of hours."

His left brow arches as his gaze roams over me. I may look like hell, but the spark in his eyes tells me he's interested.

The waitress interrupts with our desserts, but as soon as she leaves, he says, "Are you asking what I think you're asking?"

"If you think I'm asking for a hookup, you're right."

He jams a forkful of the apple pie into his mouth. "Is this revenge sex? He screws his boss. You fuck another man?"

I should be offended by his crude language, but I'm not. Tonight, such words seem entirely appropriate. "Yes. And no. I've been attracted to you since the moment I first saw you."

"Yeah," he says, finishing up the last piece of his dessert, "especially my ass."

"You noticed?"

"Of course. It's my job to notice things."

"That's not the only thing I like about you."

"Oh?" He leans his elbows once more on the table and folds his hands. A lopsided smile quirks his lips. "So tell me, Ms. Sanchez, what else do you like about me?"

He's challenging me. He thinks I won't tell him. Well, he's got another think coming. "You're smart, polite, dedicated to your job. You know how to issue orders."

"You like that, do you? When a man bosses you around?"

"Depends on the man and what he's asking. You also know when to take direction, even when it comes from a woman."

"Ms. Berkeley is my boss. She pays me to obey her orders. Anything else?"

"You're strong, kind, patient."

"I'm a veritable saint."

"You're very good at hiding your emotions, but every once in a while your temper slips through."

"How did you figure that out?"

"A raised brow, a clenched fist."

"You're good at reading body language."

I give him my most sexy pout. "Aha. Took a whole semester of it in college."

"Well, that certainly explains it."

"There's only one thing I don't know about you, Hunter."

His tongue darts out to lick his lower lip. "Only one?"

"How good you are in bed."

He hisses in a breath. "And you'd like to find out."

"Yes. It's a onetime offer, good only for tonight."

"And what happens afterward?" he asks, stealing the last morsel of my lemon meringue pie from my plate.

"You go your way and I'll go mine. No strings attached."

He brings the lemon meringue to my lips. I open my mouth, swallow. When I lick the remnants from my lips, his eyes spark with blue fire.

He folds the napkin on the table, pushes it forward a little. "All right."

Really? "Really?"

"Yes. I could use a tune-up." After tossing the tip on the table, he grabs the check and stands up. His other hand he holds out to me.

I shimmy from the booth in my tight skirt. Without letting go of me, he fishes out enough money from his jeans pocket to pay the bill at the cash register.

Outside, he leads me to the SUV and opens the passenger door. I slide in. "Don't go anywhere."

Where on earth would I go? We're just off the interstate. The only buildings nearby are the motel and the diner.

While I wait in the Cherokee, he checks us into the hotel. The room's on the second floor, so the climb up gives me time to rethink the situation. Do I really want to do this? Have sex with this man? I shiver. Yes. Yes, I do.

He takes his time inserting the key card into the slot. Turns on the light. "This okay?"

"Yes," I say breathlessly. I've never propositioned a man before. I fully expected him to say no. But it's too late to back out now. "You do have condoms."

He closes the door behind us and pats his pants pocket. "Always carry some with me."

"Do you want to shower?"

"No, Cristina." He hauls me to him. "I want to fuck," he says before lowering his mouth to mine. I expect power and heat, but he's amazingly gentle, tasting me, exploring me, licking the seam of my lips.

Wanting to return the favor, I whimper with frustration. My hands are caught against the steel of his chest so there's no chance to trail my hands over his arms, his abs, his cock.

He stops the kissing to sweep his tongue over his lips. "You taste sweet."

"It's the pie."

His sensuous mouth curves into a grin. "And you." Putting distance between us, he unbuttons his shirt, tosses it over a chair. His chest is a thing of beauty, all chiseled abs and sculpted pecs, along with a scar or two. An especially nasty one lies low on his stomach. And what looks like burn marks pucker his arms.

"What happened there?" I brush my hand across the blemished skin on his abdomen.

"Didn't move fast enough."

"And here?" I touch one of the scars on his arm.

"An explosion."

I gasp. "You've led a dangerous life."

"You don't know the half of it." He steps back and stares at me. "Take off your blouse."

"Don't you want to do it?"

"No. I want you to strip. Don't stop until I say so."

He's not making this easy, but then I did ask for it. If a striptease is what he wants, I'm going to do my damndest to give it to him. Screwing up my courage, my hand goes to the top button of my blouse, the second, all the way down. Once they're all unfastened, I tug slowly until the blouse is free. I take it off and throw it at him.

Catching it, he takes a whiff, and his eyes turn a stormy blue.

I tug down my skirt zipper, shimmy the garment off me. All I have on beneath is a thong. I squat on my haunches, come back up, turn around, bend so my tush is pushed right against him. He's so damned tall, though, all I'm brushing against are his legs. Nowhere near the Promised Land.

With my back to him, I straighten up and roll down the straps, unclasp the bra. Holding it against my unfettered breasts, I turn back around.

"Lose the damn bra," he growls through clenched teeth.

I shake my head, and my curls come loose, tumbling down my back.

He steps close, picks me up by my ass, and grinds against me while he devours my mouth. I wrap my legs around him. While holding me to him, he rips off my bra and slings it halfway across the room. Then he walks us to the bed and tosses me on it.

I come up on my elbows and watch him loosen his belt buckle and snap it free. His hand goes to his button fly, and one by one he slips them open while keeping his hot gaze on me. He steps out of his jeans, and I swallow hard. He's got nothing on underneath.

A little drool escapes the corner of my mouth as I gaze at the most magnificent erection I've ever seen. The ruddy color of the head, the size and girth. He's more than fine. The damn thing curls almost all the way up to his belly button.

"Condom?" I breathe out.

He opens his hand, and there it is, a foil packet he tears open with his teeth. He rolls it over him while keeping his gaze on me. And then he kneels on the bed.

"How do you want it? Hard and fast? Or slow and tender?"

"Hard." I gulp. "And hard."

He chuckles. "Whatever the lady wants."

One-handed, he grabs my ass and pulls me under him. When he works my clit, I almost come from his touch alone.

"Ready?" his deep voice asks.

I nod. I don't think I have enough spit in my mouth to speak.

With one hand he notches his cock in my entrance. With the other he traps both of mine and raises them above my head. "I like to be in control. You understand?"

I bob my chin up and down again and let him do what he will with me.

***

We arrive at Madrigal's house after midnight. Good thing he's the head of security; no boss to question what took so long. The guard on duty buzzes us in. Once we're inside, he communicates which room has been assigned to me. I grab the one suitcase I'll need for tonight and leave the rest of the things in the SUV. My flight for Tampa doesn't leave until the afternoon, so there'll be plenty of time in the morning to retrieve and stash the rest of my things.

When we say good-night at the door to my room, Hunter brushes his thumb over my mouth, and I bite the tip. He brings it to his mouth and licks away the hurt. I want him to kiss me one last time, but without a word of good-bye, he pivots military-style and walks away from me.

Chapter 31

Madrigal

The trip back from Roanoke where the bar examination took place will take approximately three hours along I-81. Two hours into the trip, I make a pit stop to pee and grab a bottle of cold water from a mini-mart. Just as I'm getting back in my car, my cell rings. Steele. Odd. I called him before I left to let him know about my estimated time of arrival. Is he getting antsy about my return?

"Hi," I say. "Miss me?"

"Yes. How soon will you be home?"

"In an hour or so."

"Okay." He sounds a bit tense.

"Anything wrong?"

"No. I just wanted to hear your voice, that's all. See you soon?"

"Okay."

"Madrigal?" he says just a beat before I hang up.

"Yes."

"I love you."

"What?" He blurts this out now? When I'm nowhere near him?

"You heard me. Bye." And he's gone.

Did he really say he loves me? I giggle. Yeah, he did. My heart flutters. I've always known he cares for me, so his declaration of love makes sense. How do I feel about him? I love the way he treats me, the things we do in bed. He's smart and protective. Sometimes a little too much. But his heart's in the right place. I don't know if the way I feel about him amounts to love, though. He's older and wiser, knows what he wants. But there's so much about him I don't know. He shuts down whenever I bring up his childhood, his past, only sharing what he wants. I'll need more than that from him, a lot more, if I'm to trust him with my love. Sliding back behind the steering wheel, I start the car and point it toward the highway. Time enough after I get home to discuss what he just said.

When I arrive home an hour later, a dozen vehicles block the driveway, some of them police cruisers, one an EMT transport. What on earth's going on? My first thought is of Madison, the second of Steele. His voice had sounded strange on the phone. Has something happened? I practically fall out of my SUV in my hurry to climb down and race up the driveway, past the myriad of uniformed police.

But before I get to the house, one of them blocks my way. "You can't go inside, ma'am."

"Of course I can. It's my home."

"You're Madrigal Berkeley?"

"Yes. What's wrong?"

"Please come with me." Taking me by the elbow, he leads me through the throng. As we pass them, one and all stare at me with concern in their eyes.

"Please tell me. What's wrong? Is my sister hurt?"

"Your questions will be answered in a moment, ma'am."

There's a commotion by the front door, and then Steele is standing in front of me.

I grab him by the lapels of his jacket, my surety in a world gone topsy-turvy. "What's going on?"

He clamps his hands on my arms. "Madison's been kidnapped."

My knees wobble, and he wraps his arm around me to keep me from dropping to the ground. "Who took her? When did this happen?"

"Let's step inside so we can talk."

The officer who brought me this far pushes people aside to give us a clear path to the foyer. On the way, I pelt Steele with questions. "How could this be? Wasn't Alicia Carson with her?"

"Yes, they went shopping." Men and women crowd the inside of my home, some in uniforms, others in suits. I don't know a single one of them.

A blond man in a dark jacket steps forward. "Ms. Berkeley?"

"Yes."

He flashes an ID with "FBI" stamped on it. "I'm Agent Riley O'Connor. Can we talk?"

"In a minute," Steele says, pulling me into the living room. As soon as we step through, he locks the French doors behind us. After he leads me to the couch and orders me to sit, he steps to the drink cart and pours scotch into a tumbler. When he returns, he pushes it toward me. "Drink."

"I hate that stuff."

"I know. Drink it anyway."

Knowing better than to argue with him, I knock it back in one gulp and slam down the glass. "Talk."

"Madison wanted to buy a present for Philippe, some riding trinket she'd seen at a Tysons Corner shop. An hour ago, we got a phone call from the police. Alicia Carson was shot and Madison kidnapped. Alicia's been taken to the ER at Fairfax Hospital."

"Is she okay?"

"She's in surgery right now. We'll know in a couple of hours. After the kidnapper shot Alicia, he pushed Madison into his car and, wheels squealing, took off. Nobody got the license plate number. They only caught a Virginia tag." He waves toward the French doors. On the other side, Agent O'Connor, among others, is blatantly staring into the room. "As you can see, Fairfax and Loudoun County police are here. So is the FBI's Child Abduction Rapid Deployment Team. They've questioned the staff, but they need to talk to you."

My heart's in my throat. Is Madison hurt? In pain? I refuse to consider anything more than that. "Who could have taken her? And why?"

"They have no idea. They're looking at footage from security cameras, but so far they've found nothing."

"How could that be? That's a busy mall."

"I don't know. I wish to God I did." He rakes a hand through his hair. It's only now I notice his disheveled appearance. He's normally so well dressed, but his tie is crooked and his jacket's buttoned up wrong.

"I can't imagine Madison going quietly. She's strong."

"Yes, she is." He kneels in front of me, tucks my cold hands between his. I crave his warmth, his strength, with every ounce of me. "She's not hurt, Madrigal. You have to believe that. He took her for a reason."

"Such as?"

"My guess would be money. Your grandfather's murder has been in the news, and photos of you and Madison have been splattered all over the media. Somebody figured out how to make a quick buck by grabbing her and demanding ransom. You'll see."

A sob escapes me.

"Madison has spirit. She's a brave girl. She'll get through this."

"*Will* she get through this?"

"Yes, she will. You must believe this."

"I can't lose her. Not now."

Steele wraps his arms around me. I lean against him to draw from his strength.

"You need to talk to Agent O'Connor," he says. "Should I let him in?"

"I need a minute."

"You don't have one, sweetheart. The sooner they piece together the facts, the faster they'll find Madison."

I sit up, brush back my hair, take a deep breath. "Okay."

Steele opens the door and motions Agent O'Connor into the room. No sooner does he do that than my cell phone chirps. It's Brad Holcomb. I debate letting it go to voice mail, but some sixth sense tells me to answer the call. "Brad, I can't talk to you right now. My sister's missing."

"I know. Dad took her."

I gesture wildly to the two men in the room and turn on the speakerphone. "Dr. Holcomb took her? Why?"

"Money. What else? He asked me to call you. He wants three million dollars deposited into a Cayman offshore account. You have twenty-four hours to do so. The minute he gets the confirmation the money is there, he'll let Madison go."

"He won't get away with this, Brad. The FBI is looking for him."

"I know that. Don't you think I know that? But he's not thinking clearly. Not when he's about to lose everything he owns. You got something to write with? He wants me to give you the bank information."

Charlie had called it. A desperate man will take desperate measures.

Agent O'Connor retrieves a pad and pen from the inside of his jacket. Pen poised over the pad, he nods.

"Go ahead," I say into the phone. Once Brad rattles off the details, Agent O'Connor holds the pad in front of me so I can read the bank information back to Brad. A glance at my watch tells me it's after closing hours at the bank. "It's past five. Banks won't open again until tomorrow. I won't be able to do anything until then."

"As long as the money's in his bank account by close of business tomorrow, everything will be fine. If not, I don't know what he'll do. He's not kidding around, Madrigal."

"I'll take care of it. But if he hurts one hair on Madison's head—"

"He won't if you wire the money. Just remember, he's a doctor with access to drugs. He can give her a lethal injection and walk away."

Gorge rises in my throat. "He wouldn't do that."

"He's already done it."

I clutch the cell so tight my fingers hurt. "What are you talking about?"

"His medical facility? Families use it to get rid of rich relatives who've lived just a little too long. He admits those poor souls, and they end up dead. No one complains. Least of all the family members. That's how he kept us afloat all these years. I think he's planning to go somewhere with the three million and start over again."

"The police will find him and bring him back."

"Not if he ends up in a country with no extradition treaty with the United States."

"How do you know all of this?"

"He's been planning an escape for years. I convinced him to wait. That's why I proposed to you. We were going to use your money to pay off the debts we've racked up. But when you turned me down, he moved up his timetable."

"So he always planned to kidnap Madison?"

"If you didn't agree to marry me. Yes."

"He's insane."

"I know, but he's my father. And I don't want him to die."

When the police catch up with him, and I have to believe they will, I wouldn't put odds on his father making it out alive. "Let me hang up so I can arrange for the money."

"Okay."

"What's his address?" Agent O'Connor asks as soon as I end the call.

I rattle off the location that's only a few miles from us.

"I'll arrange for a team to head there now."

"Okay."

O'Connor steps out of the room, closing the door behind him.

Wrapping my arms around my waist, I pace up and down the rug. "I don't know what to do!"

"About the money?" Steele asks.

"Yes. Even if I pay him, he may still kill Madison."

He walks up to me, throws his arms around me, drops a kiss on my head. "He won't. Kidnapping her is bad enough, but if he harms her, he's done for. He's not dumb. He knows the consequences of such an action."

"Yes, but he's desperate." Think, Madrigal, think. I take a deep breath, let it out. The money. I need to take care of that first. "The bank manager. His number is in Gramps's study, in the bottom drawer with his business papers. Please go get it."

"Are you sure?"

"Yes. I have to believe he'll let her live as long as I pay him."

As soon as he leaves, the FBI operative steps back in. "I have someone tracking the GPS in Dr. Holcomb's car. We'll find him, Ms. Berkeley, don't worry. We'll be leaving for his house in five minutes."

"I want to go with you."

"I'm not sure that's wise."

"I know Brad. He was my boyfriend at one time."

Steele overhears this as he steps back into the room. His frown intensifies. "Here," he says, handing me a piece of paper with a name and a phone number.

Something chirps in Agent O'Connor's jacket. His cell. He retrieves it and reads the message. "We've tracked the GPS in his car as far as the Potomac River. A team's been dispatched to the location. While we wait for their report, I'm headed out."

"Where are you going?" Steele asks.

"To Brad Holcomb's home."

"I'm coming with you," I say.

"No," Agent O'Connor says.

I stuff the piece of paper Steele handed me into a pocket as a different scheme flits into my head. "You won't get anything out of Brad. He'll see you as a threat to his father. But I can get him to talk."

Agent O'Connor mulls that over for a couple of seconds.

I grab Steele's hand. "And he's coming with me." If Brad refuses to talk, I'll set Steele loose on him.

O'Connor's gaze bounces between Steele and me. Hands clasped, we stand ramrod straight like soldiers.

"Fine," O'Connor says. "But you'll need to stay out of the way and let me do the talking."

"Okay," I say. Steele promises no such thing.

On the way to Brad's home, the police report in. They found Dr. Holcomb's car abandoned, and there are tracks from another car nearby. They don't know whose.

"Could he have rented a car?" I ask.

"No record of that," O'Connor clips out. "He must have bought one. In cash. Or stolen it from somebody. Tell me about Brad Holcomb."

I give him a rundown. "I doubt his father would trust him with any details. Dr. Holcomb did not have a high opinion of Brad. He thought his son was weak."

"You never know. Holcomb owns several properties. We have teams headed to all of them. He's bound to make a mistake. As soon as he does, we'll grab him."

The memory of a conversation I overheard between Gramps and Holcomb pops into my mind. "He has a place that might not be on a list of his properties."

"Where?" O'Connor and Steele ask in unison.

"In West Virginia, near Bear Rock Lakes."

Agent O'Connor checks something on his phone. "You're right. It's not there."

"It wouldn't be. I heard him and my grandfather talking about it one day. It's nothing but a trailer with a porch hanging off the side. They stayed there when they hunted."

"That doesn't exactly narrow it down," O'Connor says.

"The son has to know where it is," Steele jumps in.

"Let me talk to Brad. I'll get him to tell me."

When we arrive, I'm surprised to see Hunter Stone jump out from one of the FBI vehicles. How did he talk them into letting him come?

Agent O'Connor pounds on the door. Brad looks shit-in-his-pants terrified, but he lets us in. Mrs. Holcomb looks like hell swaying back and forth in a rocking chair. Although I feel sorry for her, I don't have time for sympathy, not when my sister's life is on the line.

"We have some questions," Agent O'Connor says to Brad.

"You mind if we use the study? My mother has Alzheimer's. She's confused over what my father did. I'd just as soon not cause her more upset."

"Lead the way."

Once we arrive at the study and Brad shuts the door, he turns to us. "I don't know where he's keeping Madison. He didn't say."

"Ms. Berkeley mentioned he had a trailer at Bear Rock Lakes, West Virginia," O'Connor says.

"Yeah, he does. It's the kind of place men go to drink beer, fart, and scratch their balls without anyone thinking anything of it. He never took me there."

"You don't know the location?"

"No."

"Gentlemen," I say, addressing not only O'Connor but the other agents present. "If I could have the room, please. I'd like to talk to Brad alone."

O'Connor appears ready to balk, but something makes him change his mind. Maybe it's the way Brad's looking at me, like I'm his last hope of salvation.

The FBI agents leave, but Steele remains with his arms crossed, legs spread wide. "I'm not going."

We haven't discussed our approach, but he knows what I'd like from him. "Fine by me," I say.

Brad's shaking in his boots. What a sniveling coward he is. I don't know how I ever allowed this sorry excuse of a man to talk me into having sex with him. But right now, that's not important. Madison is.

"Brad, you know where this place is, don't you?"

"I knew about it, but my father never took me. I never enjoyed hunting. All that blood." He shivers.

"Go stand by the door," Steele says to me.

"What are you going to do?" I whisper.

"What do you think?" One-handed, he picks Brad up by his shirt. "You're going to tell me where that camp is, you little prick, or I'm going to beat you so hard your eyes will swell up. You won't be able to see. You'll be eating soup through what remains of your teeth. Have you ever had your kidneys punched? I have. You'll pee blood for a week."

"Don't hit me!" Brad screams. "I don't know. I honestly don't know."

Somebody pounds on the door. "What's going on in there?"

I open the door a crack. O'Connor is standing on the other side. "Nothing. We haven't laid a finger on him."

"We don't condone violence," O'Connor says, but I can tell by the look in his eyes he's hoping Steele beats the shit out of the little bastard.

"I understand." I calmly shut the door and just as calmly say, "Hit him, Steele, hit him as hard as you can."

Steele pulls back his arm. When he does, Brad pees his pants. The stain spreads down his khakis. The stench is disgusting.

"Wait. Wait," Brad begs, holding up his hands. He's crying; snot streams from his nose. Ugh. "I can tell you how to find him. My father's watch."

"What about it?" Steele asks.

"He uses it when he goes hiking and hunting. He linked it to his desktop computer so he could keep track of his stats. It has a GPS tracker."

"So we can find out where he is," Steele says. "Do you know the computer password?"

"Yes. He changes it weekly, but he writes it down in his little black notebook."

"Where is the notebook?" I ask.

Brad pries his shirt from Steele's hand and stumbles toward his father's desk. He searches underneath the center drawer and comes up with a small notebook. "He thinks he's so smart, but he's not. He jots down all his accounts and passwords in this one little book where anybody could find it."

"Why the hell didn't you tell this to the FBI?" Steele asks.

"Because if I'd told them, they would have gone after him and killed him, that's why. He may have done bad things, but he's still my father, and I don't want him to die." Stepping away from the computer, he walks in my direction. Under the eagle eye of Steele, he stops in front of me and clasps my hands. "I want him brought back alive. It would kill my mother to find out he's dead."

God. I actually feel sorry for the worm. "I can't control what the FBI will do, Brad. Surely you see that. At the very least they'll capture him, and he'll go to jail. How's your mom going to handle that?"

"I'll take care of her. If God's merciful, in a couple of years, she'll forget all about him."

There's some humanity in the worm after all.

I pry my hands from his sweaty grasp. "I'll do my best to see him brought back alive. But if it comes to a choice between him and Madison, all bets are off."

Chapter 32

Trenton

Madrigal hands over the watch details to O'Connor and relates what Bradley revealed.

The agent barks out a name, and a guy who appears to be about seventeen walks up to him. "Find the GPS location off this." In less than a minute, the tech returns with a piece of paper that has the location on it.

"Where is that?" O'Connor asks staring at the numbers on the note.

"Bear Rock Lakes in West Virginia."

So what Bradley said was true. His father is holed up there with Madison as his hostage. Son of a bitch.

Within seconds, O'Connor starts issuing orders. "We need a helicopter and a team in the air in less than fifteen minutes."

"I'm going," Madrigal says.

"Ma'am. The mission's bound to be dangerous. You would just get in the way."

"I was Dr. Holcomb's patient for over a year. I know how he thinks, his tells. I can talk him into turning over Madison without spilling blood."

O'Connor shakes his head. "Sorry, ma'am. Not this time."

She raises her voice. "I will not be left behind, not when my sister's life is on the line. If you leave without us, I'll figure out a way to get there. Leesburg has an airport. I'm sure I can find a helicopter to fly us to those coordinates."

"You'd screw up the mission to save your sister?"

"I won't if you let me come along."

"I'm going as well," I say. No way is she getting on that helicopter without me.

"God help me," O'Connor exclaims.

"I'll do exactly what you tell me to do," Madrigal says. "But I have to be there. She's my baby sister, my only living relative. I can't lose her."

"Very well. You'll need dark clothes, hiking boots, all of you."

"Where are we leaving from?"

"Right out there." Agent O'Connor points to the terrain behind Brad's house. There's enough clearance back there for a helicopter to land.

Madrigal calls Hartley. After she tells him what we both need, she asks him to drive it over to the Holcomb estate. "You need to be here in fifteen minutes."

Hartley must have broken every speed record, because he arrives just as the helicopter lands outside.

"Take off all your jewelry," O'Connor says. "Don't bring anything, and I mean anything, that reflects light. And whoever is coming along better keep his or her mouth shut."

Madrigal and I step into a side room to change. We walk out to find O'Connor and Stone headed for the helicopter.

"How did you snag a ride?" I ask Stone.

"I'm a trained sniper. Ex–Navy SEAL." The weapon he's carrying looks awfully comfortable in his hand.

The four of us—O'Connor, Hunter, Madrigal, and I—jump in the back. We're each given headphones to protect our hearing from the noise of the rotor blades.

After we're strapped in, the helicopter pilot yells back, "The Special Forces team's already taken off from Quantico. We should be landing in about fifteen minutes about a mile from the GPS location. It will be lights out all the way."

Madrigal hangs tough through the helicopter ride. Not by a bat of an eyelash does she betray any emotion. But she's wound up so tight she may snap.

O'Connor hands blankets all around. I tuck one around her without saying a word.

Hunter brought a thermos filled with coffee. He pours some into the cap and hands it to her. "It's got a bit of a kick to it."

She takes a sip and makes a face. "What's in here?"

"Bourbon."

"Thanks." She takes another sip. Maybe it's the liquor, or the blanket, or my body warmth, but after a few minutes, she relaxes. Thank the fuck.

We barely breathe, much less talk, during the fifteen minutes to the site. We land in an open spot next to the helicopter that arrived ahead of us.

"You'll have to stay here," O'Connor says.

"You've got to be kidding," Madrigal protests.

"The trailer is a mile away. You're not going to move as fast as these men. They're trained for this."

"I used to run track in high school and college. I can do this."

"Did you really?" I ask when O'Connor's back is turned.

"No. But he doesn't know, does he?"

Once he's done conferring with his compadres, O'Connor turns back to us. "I will not be held responsible if something happens to you. Do you understand?"

"Yes."

Everybody moves out. The swish of the men in uniform leading the way. The terrain is rough to say the least. A hill lies in front of us, but Madrigal attacks it with fervor and a will I've never seen in her before. The other side is worse. Rocks, bushes. She stumbles once, and I catch her, but she manages the rest on her own.

The soldiers beat us to the bottom. They're communicating via hand gestures. The leader signals to Hunter, who nods in acknowledgment.

I know better than to speak or move as the soldiers head out single file. They're wearing night goggles so they can see the terrain. On Hunter's wordless command, we follow. Our boots are sturdy but cumbersome. Hopefully, we won't trip over something.

There's a full moon tonight, which works both against and for us. The light helps us see the land ahead, but then it makes us more visible as well. When the soldiers reach a rock formation, the team leader signals again. Again Hunter acknowledges his command. Apparently, we're to crouch behind the rocks while they move forward toward the trailer that sits about fifty yards away.

Suddenly an alarm goes off, and the lights around the trailer snap on.

"Son of a bitch," Hunter exclaims. "He must have set a trip wire."

Dr. Holcomb steps out of the trailer. He has Madison in a choke hold while his other hand presses a gun to her head. "Don't come any closer or she's dead."

Her blonde hair shines in the light. Because she's tall and he's of average height, her body's very effective as a shield. Her head's slumped; she appears to be out of it. The bastard must have drugged her.

There are only three soldiers in front of us where before there were six. Where did the other three go?

"I only want my money," Holcomb yells. "Give it to me, and I'll let her go."

Before I can stop her, Madrigal circles the rock formation to stand in front of it. "Dr. Holcomb, it's Madrigal."

"Mad!" Madison's cry is slurred, as if her mouth can't quite form the word.

I start to go after Madrigal, but Hunter tackles me to the ground. "Don't be an idiot. You don't want that crazy old man to get an itchy finger and pull the trigger."

"What if he shoots Madrigal?"

"He'd have to aim the gun at her instead of Madison. He's got seven weapons trained on him. The soldiers won't miss."

"What are you doing here? You're supposed to be home, getting my money!" Holcomb yells.

"I came to get my sister back."

"You shouldn't have brought them." He nods toward the agents.

"I didn't have a choice. They overheard the conversation I had with your son."

"That little weasel," Holcomb mutters. "He couldn't have told you about this place. I never brought him here. He's nothing but a weakling who hates the sight of blood. A doctor's son who gets queasy from a blood kill. Can you imagine?"

"Please let Madison go. She's only sixteen."

"You were younger than that when I treated you. You remember, don't you?"

"Yes, I do."

"You were in my clinic for an entire year. Your grandfather asked me to hold you there."

"Why?"

"Because you knew too much, and so did she."

"She knew nothing. She was just a baby."

"You knew more when you came to me. A lot more, but I made you forget. Made her forget too."

"What are you talking about?"

"She saw things that night. Things she shouldn't have seen. We had to drug her to get her to calm down. Kept her that way for twelve years, and then you had to go and take her to a new doctor. She started asking questions. She questioned the drugs I put your sister on. I couldn't have that come out. If it did, they would investigate me, the clinic, and then everyone would know."

"Know what?"

"What I did there. You think you were the only patients I was paid to handle? Think again. There are plenty of people who want to get rid of a troublesome relative. I took care of that for them. And everything worked fine until you had to go and stir it up. That's why I need the money, to get away and start fresh somewhere else."

The missing agents are sneaking up behind him. He's so into his mad rant he doesn't hear them.

"Maddy! Drop!" Madrigal yells.

Her sister falls to the ground. Unprepared for the dead weight, Holcomb loses his hold on her, which gives the sharpshooters the opportunity they need. The rat-a-tat of guns going off fills the glade, and Holcomb falls. Probably dead before he hits the ground.

One of the agents kicks away his gun while Madrigal runs toward Madison, with Hunter and me close behind. Madrigal tries to lift her, but Madison's dead weight is too much for her.

"Here." I gather her sister in my arms and lift her.

"Mad?" Madison whispers weakly. "You came."

"Of course I came, sweetheart. You're my sister. I'd walk to the ends of the earth for you."

A weak smile is all she gets in return before Madison's head lolls to the side.

Hunter steps forward to feel her pulse. "She's fainted, that's all. He probably drugged her to keep her quiet. We'll need to get her to a hospital and have her checked out."

"You're okay, sweetheart. You're fine," Madrigal says, brushing Madison's hair away from her forehead.

"Dr. Holcomb?" Madison mumbles, coming back to life.

"He's dead, sweetheart. He can't hurt you anymore."

Within less than a minute, the helicopter lands in the clearing, and we're bundled into it.

"Leesburg Hospital's the closest one with a landing pad. Should be there in fifteen minutes," Riley O'Connor says.

And then we're flying east over Pennsylvania before turning south to Virginia and home.

Chapter 33

Madrigal

As soon as the helicopter lands at Leesburg Hospital, Madison's rushed to the emergency care unit. O'Connor and Hunter accompany us while the second helicopter returns to Quantico.

"Coffee?" Hunter pours more of the bourbon-laden coffee into my cup. Without a single protest, I slug it back. I'm beginning to get a taste for it. While we wait for the doctors to examine Maddy, interminable minutes pass. Finally, a nurse asks us to accompany her to a private room that contains a serviceable couch, a couple of chairs, and a coffee table. This is the room they use to give people the bad news. I clutch Steele while he wraps his arms around me.

A couple of minutes later, a doctor enters.

"How is she?" I ask.

"Fine. Her urine sample shows she's been given a very strong sedative."

Steele curses.

"She wasn't sexually abused."

"Thank God." I break down and cry in Steele's arms.

"She's okay, sweetheart. That's the important thing."

"We're giving her oxygen to counteract her reduced respiratory rate. We also gave her activated charcoal to absorb the drug. But she's strong and healthy. She'll be up and about in a couple of days. We'd like to keep her until then."

"Of course. Whatever she needs. Thank you, Dr.—" Somehow, I missed his name.

"Young."

"Thank you, Dr. Young."

"The nurse will bring you back in a few minutes so you can see her before she's moved to a regular room."

"I'd like to spend the night."

"Of course."

After she's settled in, Steele and I bunk in Madison's room, cuddling in the bed next to hers. She sleeps; we don't. We spend the night checking on her to make sure she's still breathing.

In the morning, Steele volunteers to go to the cafeteria and bring back some much-needed coffee and something to eat. Neither of us has eaten anything since yesterday's lunch. Before he returns, Madison wakes up with no apparent lasting effects from her ordeal. Great. She looks fine. I resemble roadkill.

"What happened to you?" Madison asks.

I stretch, and something creaks in my back. "Couldn't sleep. Worried about you."

"I'm fine. My stomach's a little sore, that's all."

No sooner does she say that than a nurse arrives to take her vitals. "You're looking good."

"Feeling good."

"Um. The doctor may send you home today after all."

"I hope so. I hate hospitals."

I yell "Maddy!" but the nurse just chuckles.

"Nothing I haven't heard before. Now if you would kindly step out of the room," she says to me. "I need to check her urine output."

"Eww," Madison says.

"Serves you right for being so rude."

I step into the corridor in time to see Steele return with two cups of coffee and Danishes. I gobble mine down and am thinking about sending him back for more when a cry erupts from the room.

I rush in. "What happened?"

"I removed her catheter," the nurse says calmly.

"That hurt." Maddy's expression is priceless.

We hang out at the hospital, but it's pretty clear Madison's getting antsy. An hour later the doctor shows up and examines her. Pleased with her progress, he announces she can go home.

"Yippee," Madison yells.

Not long afterward she's wheeled out to the front where Hunter waits for us in the SUV. After Madison's settled in the back next to me, we head away from the hospital toward Route 7 and home.

"So does this mean I can finally stop taking all those pills?" Madison asks.

"More than likely, but you can't quit cold turkey. I'll call Dr. Durham and explain what Dr. Holcomb said. She'll figure out the safest way to reduce the dosage."

"Just so you know, the press is camped out in front of the estate," Hunter says.

"Really?" Madison cheers up.

"They want a quote or two."

"I'll handle it," Steele says. "You take them inside. Neither of you should be on camera."

"Why not?" Madison asks.

I stare at her. "Haven't you learned anything from your ordeal? What if another crackpot gets it into his head to kidnap you? I can't go through this again, Maddy." Tears roll down my face.

"Hey, I'm sorry. You're right. I'll keep a low profile over the next couple of days. I won't even go horseback riding."

"You can't. Alicia's been shot, remember?"

"It all happened so fast. One second she was standing next to me; the next she had blood pouring from her shoulder. It was horrible. Is she going to be okay?" Her former bravado has disappeared. All that's left behind is a scared little girl.

"Yes," Hunter says from the front. "She'll be out of commission for a little while, but if I know her, and I do, she'll be back in a couple of weeks. In the meantime, I'll try to find someone else to go horseback riding with you."

"Philippe can ride with me."

"Philippe's not a bodyguard, Maddy. You don't want to expose him to danger."

Hunter joins our conversation. "If she's up to it, Agent O'Connor needs to interview her as soon as she gets home. He'll need the details of her ordeal."

"How do you feel about that, Maddy?" Madrigal asks.

"Okay, I guess," Madison says. Subdued, she stares out the window. Maybe she's finally beginning to understand how serious this is. From what she shared in the hospital, she was kept drugged most of the time, so she remembers very little, which is a blessing, really. If she can't remember, she won't be traumatized by the event.

When we get home, Hunter drops off Steele at the gate where the press is camped out. I probably should accompany him. I am the head of the family, after all. But all I want is to help Maddy through the FBI interview, put her to bed, get something to eat, and take a nap. But first I gotta take a bath.

No sooner do I get out of the bathroom than Cristina calls. "*Querida*. I just saw the news. Is Madison all right? Are you all right?"

"She's fine. Hungry as usual. Scarfing down her lunch. Philippe's back, so she invited him to dinner tomorrow night. That will give her something to look forward to." After I give her the brief version of last night's events, I say, "Honestly, I think I'm more upset than she is."

"I'm in Miami with my folks, but I can be on the next plane if you need me."

"No. We're fine. Steele's talking to the press, and Hunter is handling security."

"Look, with everything going on, you don't want me under your feet. I'll find a place as soon as I can."

"Please don't. I like having you around the house. With all the craziness, you're a bit of normal."

"Well, to tell the truth, I like being there. Are you *sure* it's not too much of an imposition?"

"Of course not. When are you coming back?"

"Tomorrow night. My flight arrives at Dulles around five."

"Great. You can join us for dinner then. Should I send Hunter to pick you up? You can enjoy his fine ass on the way here."

"He's more than a fine ass, Madrigal."

Uh-oh, she sounds offended. Where did that come from? "I didn't mean to make fun of him. I know what a great guy he is. He helped with Madison's rescue."

"No. I'm sorry. I shouldn't have snapped. It's just—never mind. We'll talk tomorrow. I'll text you the flight details."

"Great. See you then." After I hang up, I wonder about her reaction. I thought she'd enjoy my comment, but maybe after Scott's betrayal, she's touchy about men. I shake my head. Too much to worry about at the moment to deal with that as well.

After I get dressed, I check in with Madison. Instead of resting, she's Skyping with a friend. She's been warned not to share any details, so I remind her of that before heading down to the kitchen to grab something to eat. A ham sandwich and a glass of milk should fill the hole in my stomach just fine. I reach the kitchen to find Olivia talking to Helga.

"You're back!" I hug her. It's nice to see her again. Maybe her arrival will bring back a sense of normalcy to our lives.

"Yes. Returned this morning."

"How did you enjoy your time with your sister?"

"It was good to catch up."

I fill her in on the events of the last week, especially last night's.

"My poor lamb. Should I check on her?"

"No. Better leave her alone. She needs to get back to her usual routine." Unfortunately, as future events would unfold, normal would become a thing of the past.

Chapter 34

Trenton

Since Madison needs to be debriefed after we get home, Madrigal allows the FBI to question her. A half hour later after Madrigal arranges for a meal to be brought to her, she bundles Madison upstairs for a much-needed hot bath and sleep.

Finally, the house quiets. After the harried hours of the night before, it's a welcome change. Once I make sure Madrigal's asleep, I head to Hunter's room. He offered to move in, claiming he could provide more effective protection if he was available round the clock. Madrigal was more than happy to agree. I can't blame her. Not with the three-ring circus going on outside the main gate to the estate. Between Hunter and me, we can play interference for her.

I knock on the door to his room.

"Come in."

"Did I disturb you?" I ask, stepping in. He's lounging on the bed, reading something on his phone.

"Not at all," he says, sitting up. "I'm too wired to sleep. I called in an extra operative to replace Alicia. She'll be here at eight. She doesn't ride horses, so Madison will need to remain indoors."

"I don't think she'll object. At least for a day or two."

"I'll find someone else to accompany her. Shouldn't take longer than that."

I tuck my hands into my pockets and fix my gaze on him. "Are you going to tell me the truth?"

"About?"

"Your real identity."

Staring down at the floor, he clutches the side of the bed so hard his knuckles turn white. "I can't. Lives other than mine are at stake. If I told you, I'd put them in danger."

"Would it help if I told you I already know?"

His head comes up at that. "You can't possibly."

"You think I don't know my own brother?"

"I'm not," he chokes out.

"Don't." I hold up a hand to stop him. "You had work done on your face. Probably on your body as well. More than likely, the authorities put out the story that you died to save you. And then they relocated you somewhere. Maybe to another state. How am I doing so far?"

His lips quirk. "You always were a smart son of a bitch."

"We weren't together that long."

He comes to his feet. "Six years. But I always remembered you. I never forgot."

"Neither did I." I grab him by the neck, pull him toward me as hot tears roll down my cheeks.

As he squeezes me back and tucks his head against my neck, I can feel the hot moisture on his face. "You can't tell anybody, not even Madrigal."

"I won't."

Coming upright again, he wipes his face. "I'm serious."

"I know you are." I cup his cheek. Last time I saw him, he was six. And now he's a grown man with whiskers on his face. "Will I find out the truth one day?"

"Maybe when things clear up."

"You're not just a bodyguard, are you?"

All I get is silence.

"Fine. If you ever need anything, anything at all, let me know. I have money, millions."

"How'd you do that?"

"Playing the stock market. I have Mitch to thank for that."

His face takes on a dark tone.

"Does Mitch have anything to do with whatever you're investigating?"

"I can't talk about it," he says.

"Damn." Figures that I just find my brother and he's investigating Mitch, or at least it seems like he is.

"Well, I better go to bed. For what remains of the night anyway."

"Wait. Cristina Sanchez?"

"What about her?"

"Nothing."

"You're not interested in her, are you?"

"No. Nothing like that."

I squint my eyes. "Okay. Well, good-night." I hug him again.

"Night."

I jump in the shower before climbing into bed with Madrigal. When I do, she rolls to my side. "Where were you?"

"Talking to Ree—Hunter."

"About?"

"Getting his take on things."

"What things?"

"What Holcomb blurted out about making you and Madison forget, about killing patients. I asked him to investigate." I'll have to remember to talk to him about it in the morning.

"Charlie's investigating as well. We'll put both of them on the job. See what they can find out."

"Yes, but that's for tomorrow and the day beyond. Let's go to sleep. A new day's dawning. I'd like to get at least some rest."

But the hours roll by with thoughts of my brother and Mitch. Fuck. As if I didn't have enough to worry about, something else may blindside me as far as Mitch's concerned. I've put it off as long as possible. But I can't. Not anymore. I'll have to investigate Mitch. See what he's been up to. Only then will I get to the truth.

Chapter 35

Madrigal

"I'm so happy to see you!" I exclaim as soon as Cristina walks through the door with Hunter trailing after her. "How was your flight?"

"Uneventful," she says, hugging me back. "The same can't be said for the ride here."

"Yeah, rush-hour traffic on Route 50 can be a bear. Take a load off and freshen up. Cocktails will be served in half an hour and dinner in an hour."

"Great. I'll just take a quick shower."

"You want me to take your suitcase up to your room, Ms. Sanchez?"

She scrunches up her face. "Honestly, Hunter, you can call me Cristina."

Stone-faced, he replies, "Very well."

"Yes, please. I'll see you later, *tesoro*." She climbs the stairs, swishing her rump all the way. She's pissed. It doesn't take a rocket scientist to know it has something to do with Hunter.

What's going on between those two? I never did get the story about why it took them so long to get here after she walked out on Scott. They should have beaten Steele and me back to the house. Knowing

Cristina, she'll spill the beans sooner or later. She never could keep the deets about her dealings with men to herself.

A door opens and closes upstairs, but Hunter does not return. Well, well, well. I turn with a grin on my face and bump into Steele. "Oops."

"What put that smile on your face?"

"Nothing." I throw my arms around his neck. "You're home."

"Yes."

"I'm glad." Pulling him down to me, I suckle his lip. "Mmm. You taste good."

"Not in front of the children, dear."

"Good evening, Trenton," Madison says, passing us by.

"Good evening."

Without a glance back, she heads for the kitchen, probably in need of a snack before dinner.

"She seems to be doing well," he says.

"Yes. Amazing, given everything she's gone through."

"I told you she's strong and resilient," Steele says.

"And happy. Philippe's coming to dinner."

"Do I have time for a quick shower?"

"Of course." He wraps an arm around me, and together we climb the stairs. As we pass Cristina's room, the sounds of an argument reach us.

"Cristina's back?" he asks.

"Yes."

"Who's in there with her?"

"I'll give you one guess."

"Hunter?"

"Yep. There's something going on between those two."

"I didn't think she was his type—or he hers, for that matter. I thought she liked her men more sophisticated."

"So did I, but apparently she's developed a liking for a more primitive male."

A harried-looking Hunter opens the door and steps out. His eyes widen when he spots us. "Good evening."

Trying hard to keep from laughing, Steele asks, "Anything wrong?"

"No. Nothing," he says, closing the door. "Why do you ask?"

Something smashes against the wood. Oh, dear. I hope it's not one of the antiques.

"No particular reason," Steele says.

"Will you join us for dinner, Hunter?" I ask, trying to ignore the obvious tension in the air.

"Are you sure that's for the best?" he asks.

"Yes, I do. I'd like to thank you for the help you provided during the rescue. I don't think of you as hired help anymore, but as a friend."

"Thank you for that." He nods. "Yes, I'd love to join you for dinner."

"Great. Cocktails in"—I glance at my watch—"twenty minutes."

"I'll be there." And then he proceeds down the hall to the stairs, where he disappears from sight.

"Well, I'd say there's definitely something going on between those two."

"Great bit of deduction, Mr. Steele. No wonder you have such a great reputation."

"Are you sassing me?"

"No," I say innocently.

"Yes, you are."

He gets this spark in his eyes, and I run toward our bedroom.

I hold up my hands, trying to keep him back. Not that it does any good when he pulls me against him. "You can't start anything. We don't have time. Besides, I'm all dressed, and I don't want you to muss me up."

"Fine," he says, unknotting his tie and tossing it on the bed. "But after dinner, there will be plenty of mussing up."

"Looking forward to it, Mr. Steele."

***

"So how was France, Philippe?"

"Fine. We visited our family in Paris and Lorraine."

"I want to go to Paris someday," Madison exclaims.

Of course she does. "After you graduate from high school next year, we'll go for the summer," I say.

"So how are things with you, Cristina?" Steele asks.

"I was offered a permanent job with the Department of Justice."

"You were?" I ask. "Why didn't you say so?"

"I just found out. My boss e-mailed me. It's the informal offer. The formal one will come in the mail. I hope you don't mind that I gave him this address."

"Of course I don't mind, silly." I pat her hand.

"Which division?" Steele asks.

"White collar."

"What crimes are those?" Madison asks. She seems to be getting her curiosity back. Maybe she'll turn into a journalist after all.

"Fraud committed by business and government professionals, ranging from insurance to corporate to financial institutions to securities and commodities."

"Bor-ing," Madison says singsong-style.

"Maddy, hush," I command.

"Actually, there's nothing boring about it," Cristina says. "It requires a great deal of investigation. Some people abuse their power and steal money from companies, investors, employees. Millions of dollars are usually involved. It's the Department of Justice's responsibility to prosecute them."

"What about your plans to practice in Florida?" Hunter asks. "Isn't that why you took the Florida bar?"

"Like I told you, I did that to keep my options open, but I'd prefer to work here in DC at the DOJ."

By the look in her eye, Cristina doesn't wish to pursue the subject. Maybe after a visit with her family, she's rethinking working at the DOJ, or maybe Scott's betrayal has soured her on DC. Taking the hint, Hunter, who's gazing at her with regret and hunger, drops the discussion.

After dinner, Maddy asks permission to stroll through the garden with Philippe. Clearly, she wants to be alone with him. But since the purpose of his visit is for us to become acquainted with him, I offer an alternate plan. "How about we go bowling?"

"Bowling?" Trenton asks.

"That's a bit too public, Madrigal," Hunter says.

"Not really. We have a bowling alley in the basement. Gramps built it a million years ago. Remember, Maddy?"

Maddy groans. "That thing is hideous. It was built in the sixties."

"Oh, come on. It'll be fun," I say.

After dessert, I lead the five of them down to "Lucky Strike." Like everything else in the house, the place has been kept in good condition. The lights work, and so does the bowling lane.

"There's only the one, so we'll need to take turns." When I flip a couple of switches, lights flash at the end of the lane, and Elvis Presley's "Hound Dog" comes on over the speakers.

Madison makes a face while Cristina claps her hands. "This is totally rad."

I dig up the old scoring supplies from beneath the cabinet on the far side of the room. The sheets are a trifle musty, but the tiny pencils are still sharp.

"On rainy nights and in the winter, Gramps used to bring us down here to bowl." He did have his nice moments, although they were few and far in between.

I decree that the women choose their partners. Rather than go for the obvious choice, I pick Philippe. Maddy reciprocates by taking Steele, which leaves Hunter and Cristina to partner up. We spend the next two hours bowling strikes, spares, and gutter balls. Surprisingly, Philippe's a natural, Hunter's not.

"I never played," he says in his defense.

"You're good at other things, Hunter," I say.

"Yeah, he is," Cristina pipes up.

The look Hunter sends her would incinerate entire villages.

At the end of the evening, Philippe and I are declared the winners, and we retire upstairs for a nightcap. Well, the adults have cocktails, except for Hunter, who's on duty. Philippe and Maddy enjoy glasses of sweet tea.

When it's time for Philippe to leave, I suggest Maddy walk him to his car. They'll be watched the entire time by Hunter, but at least it will give them a semblance of privacy.

"Well, I better turn in. It's been a long day," Cristina says, yawning.

"What about you?" Steele says as soon as she leaves. "Are you tired?"

"Not really, but I am a little sore from the bowling." I rub my hip.

"How about a massage?"

"You read my mind."

Chapter 36

Trenton

Today Judge Marjorie Sutton must decide whether there is probable cause to believe that Mitch killed Holden Gardiner on the night of July 5. The prosecution only needs to submit sufficient evidence for the judge to determine if there is a fair probability that Mitch committed the crime. If she determines probable cause exists, a trial date will be set.

Yesterday, when I met with Mitch, I reminded him that the preliminary hearing does not determine his guilt or innocence. I will be allowed to question the witnesses and place their answers on the record. If later on they decide to recant, they can't do so, because it would mean they perjured themselves. But I'll do no such thing. It's the prosecution's case to prove, and I don't want my questions to alert the prosecution as to my defense.

The courtroom quiets as a handcuffed and shackled Mitch enters. It pains me to see my proud mentor brought down so low. Once they remove his restraints, I shake hands and pat him on the back after he takes a seat.

The prosecution calls the medical examiner to the stand. He testifies that the victim, Holden Gardiner, was killed by a bullet from a

.22-caliber pistol. During the autopsy, he'd retrieved the bullet from Holden Gardiner and turned it over for evidence. He found no gunshot residue on the victim's hands; therefore, it's his expert opinion that the victim did not commit suicide but was murdered.

After the forensic scientist declares that the bullet was fired from the .22-caliber pistol found next to the body, a police technician relates that the pistol belonged to Mitch Brooks.

Once all the technical details have been taken care of, Detective Broynihan's sworn in. He testifies that on the evening of July 5 he was called to the scene of the crime, where he found an eighty-year-old male slumped over his desk, blood spattered across the ink blotter, and a .22-caliber pistol in his hand. After securing the scene and notifying the forensic team, he interviewed several witnesses, including the victim's granddaughter, Madrigal Berkeley, several members of the staff, and Trenton Steele.

"This Trenton Steele? The defense attorney in the case?"

"Yes."

"Anyone else present there that night?"

"Yes, sir. Mitchell Brooks."

"Do you see him in this courtroom?"

"Yes, sir. He's right there." He points to Mitch. Nothing like pointing to a person sitting at the defense table. But there's power in that gesture, as I have cause to know.

"What was he doing there?"

"Rescuing Madrigal Berkeley. His words."

"Rescuing her? What do you mean?"

"Ms. Berkeley had been locked into her room by her grandfather." A swell of murmurs sweeps across the room. "She called Trenton Steele to tell him about it. He and Mitchell Brooks devised a plan to remove Ms. Berkeley from her grandfather's care."

"So it's fair to say that Mitchell Brooks and the victim were at odds over his treatment of his granddaughter."

I come to my feet. "Objection. Calls for speculation on the part of the witness."

"Sustained," Judge Sutton says. "Please rephrase your question, Counselor."

"Actually, Your Honor, I believe we may get to the truth of this matter by calling another witness—Ms. Madrigal Berkeley."

"Very well," Judge Sutton says. "You are dismissed, Detective Broynihan."

Madrigal is escorted into the courtroom by the bailiff. She seems to be taking her appearance in stride. Even though this can't be easy for her, she put some thought into her outfit. She's wearing a business suit, pearls adorn her ears, and her hair's swept back from her face.

After she's sworn in, Jefferson lobs a softball question. "I understand that you recently graduated from law school."

"Yes, from Yale."

"One of the finest law schools in the land. I studied at William & Mary myself."

Where the hell is he going with this? Probably putting her at ease, the bastard, so he can move in for the kill.

"So you understand the purpose of this proceeding?"

"Yes, I do."

I stand. "Is Mr. Jefferson going to get to an actual question that has to do with the case?"

The bastard tosses me a glance filled with derision. "Just laying the groundwork, Counselor."

"Get on with it, Mr. Jefferson," the judge says.

"So, Ms. Berkeley, can you tell us what happened on July fifth?"

"A lot happened. Any particular time you'd like me to zero in on?"

Good girl.

"Oh, let's start with the afternoon."

"Things were kind of tense at home."

"Why?"

"Earlier in the day, my sister, Madison, and grandfather argued, and Madison ran away."

"What did you do?"

"I called St—Mr. Steele."

"This Mr. Steele? The defense attorney?"

"Yes."

If he asks her about our relationship, I'll murder the son of a bitch.

He glances at me for a moment while he lets that tidbit sink in. "And what did you tell Mr. Steele?"

"That Madison had run away and I was worried about her."

"And what did he do?"

"He came over."

"Was he the only one who came over?"

"No. Uncle Mitch came over as well." When she fiddles with her ring, I sense she's nervous. But other than that, she doesn't let on that the questions are getting to her.

"Uncle Mitch meaning the accused, Mitchell Brooks."

"Yes."

"And what did Mr. Brooks do?"

"He tried to talk some sense into Gramps. He'd refused to notify the police about Madison's disappearance."

"And that's all they did? Talk?"

"No. They were—they yelled at each other."

"And what happened after that?"

"Mr. Steele and I searched for Madison. We found her and brought her home. She wasn't hysterical or anything, but my grandfather was upset at what she'd done."

"And?"

"I confronted Gramps. Blamed him for some things."

"And how did he react?"

"He ordered me to my room and asked Mitch and St—Mr. Steele to leave and never come back."

"So he threw both of them out of the house?"

"Yes." Her chin wobbles. I want to tell her everything will be all right. But I can't promise that. Not now when everything's looking so bleak.

"And what happened then?"

"Gramps called Madison's doctor."

I stand. "Objection. Hearsay. Witness has no knowledge of who her grandfather called since she was not present when he made the call."

"Sustained."

"Very well," Jefferson says. "So what happened later on that evening?"

"Dr. Holcomb arrived."

Before I can object, Jefferson asks, "You saw him?"

"Yes. He went into Maddy's bedroom. When I heard them arguing, I tried to get in, but the door was locked. Ten minutes later, he led her out. Her eyes were unfocused, and she stumbled on the way down the stairs. She appeared to be drugged."

"What happened after that?"

"Dr. Holcomb took her to his mental health facility."

Another wave of murmurs sweeps around the room.

Once the noise dies down, Jefferson asks, "And how did you feel about that?"

She bites down on her lip. "I was upset. When I was twelve, Gramps did that to me, and he kept me there for a year. I was afraid he'd do the same to Madison."

"So what did you do?"

"I argued with my grandfather over his treatment of Madison. He told me to go to my room and stay there. As soon as I stepped in, he locked the door. So I called Mr. Steele and told him what Gramps had done."

"And what happened then?"

"He and Uncle Mitch—"

"The accused."

"Yes. He told me they'd come around midnight to rescue me."

"And did they do that?"

"Yes."

"And when they did, that's when your grandfather was shot."

"Yes. But Uncle Mitch didn't do it. I know he didn't."

"Thank you, Ms. Berkeley. That will be all."

On visibly shaking knees, she steps down from the witness stand, but then she firms up her spine and, head held high, walks out of the courtroom.

"We call Joss Stanton to the stand." Not entirely unexpected, but a surprise nonetheless. I would have saved Joss for the actual trial. Wonder what information she has that Beauregard Jefferson needs to prove probable cause.

"Please state for the record your name and occupation," he asks her once she's seated on the witness stand.

"My name is Jocelyn Stanton. I'm a partner at Gardiner, Ashburn & Strickland."

"The law firm the victim, Holden Gardiner, founded?"

"Yes."

"How well did you know Holden Gardiner?"

"Very well. We were . . . friends as well as partners."

Jefferson's steely stare drills Joss. "Come, Ms. Stanton, you were more than friends, weren't you?"

Her breath shorts, and her caramel-colored skin flushes. I can only imagine her struggle. She's such a private person. Although it was an open secret that she and Holden were lovers, it was never acknowledged in public. I have a feeling that's about to change.

"Yes."

"As a matter of fact, didn't you have intimate relations with Holden Gardiner?"

Gasps and a couple of squeals erupt in the courtroom.

Judge Sutton bangs the gavel on her desk. "Order in the court."

I wait until the room quiets before I come to my feet. "Objection, Your Honor. The prosecution is leading the witness."

"Sustained. Mr. Jefferson, please rephrase your question in an appropriate manner."

"Beg your pardon, Your Honor. So, Ms. Stanton, what was the nature of your relationship with Holden Gardiner?"

"As I told you, we were friends."

"Casual friends or more than that?"

Joss heaves out a heavy breath. "We were lovers."

The place erupts in pandemonium. The media will have a field day with this. Nothing like a scandal to perk things up in the news.

More gavel banging from Judge Sutton. "Order. Order in the court." This time it takes a bit longer for things to calm down. But finally it does.

"So, Ms. Stanton," Jefferson asks, "did Holden Gardiner confide in you?"

"Sometimes he did, yes."

Glancing back to where Olivia and Madison are sitting, I nod toward the exit, hoping Olivia will get the message to remove Madison from the courtroom. She whispers something to her and grabs her arm, but Madison, stubborn to the last, shakes her head and refuses to leave.

"You're familiar with the defendant, Mitchell Brooks?" Jefferson asks Joss.

"Yes, I am. He was a partner at the firm."

"Was?"

"Yes. He left to take a position at the Securities and Exchange Commission."

"What position does he have there?"

"Head of the Investment Management Division."

"That would be quite a step down in pay, I imagine."

"I wouldn't know."

"When exactly did he leave the firm?"

"About three years ago. April 2011, I believe."

"Were you aware Holden Gardiner had two granddaughters?"

"Yes, of course."

"What are their names and ages?"

"Madrigal is twenty-four and Madison is sixteen."

"Do you recall what happened to Madison in late March 2011?"

"Yes. She was thrown from a horse. She suffered a slight concussion and was taken to the hospital."

I come to my feet. "Your Honor. I'm not sure where Mr. Jefferson is going with this line of questioning. As far as I can tell, it has no bearing on the case."

"It goes to motive, Your Honor."

"I'll allow it, Counselor, but get to the point."

"Very well. Do you know if the hospital contacted Holden Gardiner?"

"Yes, they did. They needed his permission to perform a procedure on Madison."

"And did they get his permission?"

"He couldn't be reached. He'd gone on a hunting trip to some god-forsaken island in the middle of nowhere. So they contacted Mitchell Brooks."

"Why would they do that?"

"Because Holden had given him power of attorney over the girls in case of a medical emergency."

"Which certainly this was."

"Yes. He gave them what they needed, of course, and went to the hospital to make sure Madison was okay."

"And was she?"

"Yes. She came through with flying colors."

"How do you know?"

"I went to the hospital with him. I was worried about her myself."

"What happened when you got there?"

"They were reviewing the list of medications Madison was taking. When Mitch learned what Madison was on, he became rather agitated."

"Why?"

"She was being given antipsychotics."

"And this upset him."

"Yes. He was quite concerned."

"To your knowledge, did he ever take up this subject with Holden Gardiner?"

"Yes, he did."

Mitch jerks up. His eyes widen and his breathing shorts. I don't know what Joss is about to reveal, but Mitch not only suspects, he knows.

"When did this occur?"

"The day Holden returned from his hunting trip. I was in his office reporting to him about a management committee meeting when Mitch called to talk to him. I'd warned Holden about Mitch's reaction, so he was expecting the call."

"What did you do?"

"Holden asked me to wait in his private restroom until he was done. I would have preferred to leave, but he was adamant. So I complied with his wishes."

"Were you able to hear their discussion?"

"Yes. It would have been hard to miss. They were both yelling at the top of their lungs. Mitch demanded that Holden stop Madison's meds because she was perfectly fine. That there was nothing wrong with her. He accused Holden of doing the same thing to Marlena, the girl's mother. He'd drugged her as well to keep her in line."

"And what did Holden have to say to that?"

"He told Mitch he had no say in Madison's upbringing. That he, Holden, was her guardian, not him."

"And what did Mitchell Brooks have to say to that?"

"He said—" She glances at Mitch, whose face has gone white as a sheet. "He said that he had every right because Madison was his daughter."

"Noooooo!" A young girl's scream rings out as the media stampedes from the room, no doubt to beat everyone else to the news.

Tears running down his face, Mitch glances back at Madison. "I'm sorry. I'm sorry."

"Get her out of here!" I yell over the commotion.

With Cristina on one side of Madison and Olivia on the other, they fight their way out of the courtroom.

It's a foregone conclusion how the judge will rule. Not only has Jefferson given means and opportunity, but a hell of a motive as well. Once the prosecution finishes presenting its case, the judge finds probable cause that Mitchell Brooks killed Holden Gardiner the night of July 5, 2014.

"Take care of them," Mitch says before he's led away.

What else can I say but "I will."

Chapter 37

Madrigal

The mass exodus from the courtroom alarms me. What on earth is going on? Did the judge issue a ruling? The swarm of activity buzzes all around as photographers set up their cameras and reporters prop themselves up in front of them. But it's only when a couple of them catch sight of me that I panic.

"There she is." A blonde, hard-looking woman rushes over with a microphone in her hand. "Ms. Berkeley, how do you feel about what Joss Stanton just revealed?"

"What did she reveal?" I wasn't in there. As a witness, I had to remain outside until the bailiff fetched me.

"That Mitchell Brooks is your sister's father."

I'd suspected it, of course, but hadn't yet confirmed it.

The doors behind me burst open, and a sobbing Madison emerges, held up between Cristina and Olivia. Cameras click-click-click all around us.

One of the reporters shoves a recorder in her face. "Did you know Mitchell Brooks was your father?"

Jumping into the fray, Hunter shoves the reporter away from Madison. "Get behind me, all of you." He doesn't have to tell us twice, and in the next few seconds we line up behind him like a bunch of baby chicks. With him as our battering ram, we make our way through the madness that is the Loudoun County courthouse. Not giving a damn whom he knocks over, he pushes through the throng of reporters, cameramen, and lookie-loos. Unfortunately, it doesn't end there. Our SUV is parked several blocks away. Relentless reporters chase us all the way to the vehicle, yelling out questions, none of which we answer. It's one of those infernally hot summer days, and by the time we reach the parking garage, most of us are out of breath and perspiring heavily. Olivia, Madison, and I scramble into the back of the SUV, while Cristina and Hunter climb in the front. Soon we're flying through the garage, tires squealing. It's only when we're on the road that I'm able to relax.

"What happened in there?" I ask once I catch my breath.

"The prosecution put Joss on the stand," Cristina answers. "She testified to a conversation she overheard between Holden and Mitch in which Mitch admitted to being Madison's father."

"Sweetheart." I hug Madison to me.

"How could he not tell me?"

"He probably didn't want you to know. And I imagine he thought you were better off with Gramps."

"Even after he found out about all the drugs forced on me?"

Between Cristina and Madison, the whole sorry tale emerges. Mitch discovering the drugs Madison was taking when she fell off her horse. The argument over the medications and Mitch quitting the law firm.

"What I don't get," Cristina says, "is why he didn't sue for custody at the time. I would have if I knew my child was being medicated as Madison was. Something's not right."

Maybe I'm too close to Madison and Mitch, but I don't get what she's saying. "What do you mean?"

"As Madison's father, he would have rights of visitation, if nothing else."

"He was welcome in our home at any time. Gramps didn't deny him entrance until that last day."

"But he knew about the drugs Madison was being given."

"Maybe he didn't want her to know he was her father."

"Why not?" Madison asks. "I'd rather have lived with him than Gramps."

"Gramps would not have allowed it, you know that. He would have ruined Mitch most probably. He had a lot of pull in the legal community."

"So Uncle Mitch gave up because he thought Gramps would ruin him?"

"I don't know, Madison. I really don't."

She juts out her chin. "I want to talk to him."

"It will have to be arranged, and he'll have to agree to it."

"Why wouldn't he? Doesn't he want me?" Tears shimmer in her eyes.

"Oh, honey." But Cristina's right. There's something we don't know. Mitch has been hiding things, but maybe Joss is hiding something as well. If I know her, she's trying to protect Gramps. And whatever she's hiding, she'll take that secret to the grave.

After we get home, I head upstairs with Madison and help her settle down. Predictably, she doesn't want to talk to anybody. "What about Philippe?"

"Not yet. I have to get my head straight first. Right now I just want to veg out."

"Okay. If you need anything, let me know." I barely make it to the door before she yells my name. "Mad?"

"Yes, sweetheart."

"I love you."

I smile at her. "I love you too."

She hugs Blue, her stuffed bear, and lies back on the covers. My heart aches for her. She's gone through so much in such a short period of time. "Can I get you anything?"

"No. Oh, wait. Some chocolate pudding would be nice."

"You got it. I'll bring some right up."

"Thanks, Mad."

"Anytime, squirt."

After I deliver the treat to Madison, I head back downstairs and run into Steele. "You're back."

"Yes. How is she?"

"Hurting, but I think she'll be okay. She asked for chocolate pudding."

His lopsided grin tells me he understands its significance.

"Did you know about Mitch being her father?" I ask.

"I suspected it. Not that he ever admitted it."

"So what happens now?"

"With Mitch's case?"

"Yes and Madison. I don't want to be separated from her." That fear has seized my heart and won't let go.

He curls his hands around my shoulders. "He's not going to take her away from you, Madrigal. You're the best thing that's ever happened to her."

I fiddle with the buttons of his shirt. "What if she wants to go live with him?" I ask in a small voice.

He chuckles at the notion. "And where would she stable Marigold? In Mitch's garage? She'd never leave her horse behind."

"Good to know her horse ranks higher than I do."

He tweaks my chin. "It doesn't, and you know it."

"So what do you think Mitch will do?"

"They'll have to find their way to each other. He'd need to establish paternity first, of course. So there's no doubt in anyone's mind that she's his daughter."

"I suspected it as well." Chewing on my lip, I glance up at him.

"Oh?"

"I took a hairbrush from his house and a toothbrush from Madison and sent them in for analysis. The results should be back in a few days."

His frown tells me what he thinks of my initiative. "You did all this without telling me?"

"I was waiting until I was sure. No sense in talking about it until it was verified. Besides, you suspected it as well and didn't share it with me."

"I couldn't since it's part and parcel of the case."

"So what happens next with Mitch?"

"The case will go to the grand jury. The prosecutor will present the evidence, and they'll issue an indictment."

"When?"

"In the next month or two. All the prosecution has is circumstantial evidence. There's no proof Mitch pulled the trigger. But the evidence against him is quite damning. They have the means, motive, and opportunity. The perfect trifecta in a criminal case."

"We'll need to find out who did it."

"Yes. Otherwise . . ." He combs his fingers through his hair. "At the very least he'll end up in jail for the next twenty years."

"And at the very worst?"

His expression turns bleak. "The unthinkable."

I shudder. "You won't let that happen to him. You'll find a way. You'll see."

He drops a kiss on my lips and hugs me. "Wish I could be that sure."

I have to take his mind off this. Otherwise, he'll brood. "Dinner won't be ready for an hour. Want to take a shower?"

His lips curl up in a wicked grin. "If you join me."

"I think I may do just that."

Chapter 38

Cristina

I'm lying on my bed feeling sorry for myself when there's a knock on the door.

"Coming." Wiping the tears from my face, I throw the door open.

Hunter stands on the other side. Since dinner a week ago, we've observed a state of détente. As long as he doesn't lob a salvo, I'm willing to keep the peace between us. "Oh. It's you." I can't stand the wistful tone to my voice.

"It's me. You got a letter from the Justice Department. It's probably that job offer you've been waiting for." He holds out the envelope, and I take it from him.

"Thanks." I plop down on the bed and tear it open. Sure enough, it's my offer of employment. All I have to do is sign the document and return it in the envelope they very kindly provided. I toss the whole thing on the bed like it's nothing important.

His brow scrunches. "I thought that's what you wanted."

"It is."

"What's wrong?"

I glance at him. "I don't know. I wish I did."

Sitting next to me, he stretches his long legs on the carpet. "Talk to me."

I breathe out a sigh. "My whole life I've wanted nothing but to be a lawyer and fight for justice."

He taps the envelope. "You got that."

"Yeah, I did." I rest my head against his shoulder and breathe him in. He smells of clean sweat and that scent that's uniquely him. The combination of those two makes me mad with longing, wishing for things I can't possibly have. "I've come to realize it's not enough."

"So what would be enough?"

Sitting upright, I let out a sigh. "I'll let you know when I figure it out."

He laughs and brushes his thumb across my cheek. The air heats between us, and he leans down to lick my bottom lip. I moan, which gives him all the permission he needs to devour me. He tilts my head so he can get a better angle, sinks his tongue into my mouth, and explores every inch of it.

No. This can't happen. I'm in enough trouble as it is. I put my hand on his chest and push him away. "We shouldn't. Not here."

"Somewhere else, then?" he asks hopefully.

I laugh. "You're horrible. No. Not here. Not anywhere. I don't need complications. And you are most definitely a complication."

"Just once, for old time's sake."

"What old time's sake? We only did it the once."

Groucho Marx–style, his brows hitch up and down. "We did it several times as I recall."

Why, oh, why does he have to have a sense of humor too? A man who can make me laugh is my Kryptonite. "Please don't tempt me. Not in my weakened state."

Crooking two fingers beneath my chin, he kisses me so very sweetly. Who knew he had that in him? Before I'm ready for it to end, he lets me go. "Very well. If that is what you wish."

He comes to his feet and heads to the door, but I don't let him get there. "Stop."

Turning around, he waits for my next words.

"Do you have condoms?"

He pats his pocket.

"Lock the door."

He does and walks back to the bed. By the time he gets to me, I'm already tossing my T-shirt over the side, unclasping my bra.

Going by his heated gaze, he definitely approves. "I didn't get to see you clearly that night. This time I mean to explore every inch of you."

Falling back on the mattress, I spread my arms wide. "Explore away, Mr. Stone."

"With pleasure, Ms. Sanchez."

I sit upright when he goes for his belt. With one foot on the floor and the other on the bed, I push his hands away. "Wait, let me do it." I unclasp the buckle, snap the belt loose.

His breathing stutters as I stroke the outside of his slacks. When I measure his length, he hisses in a breath. "Witch." Tangling a hand through my hair, he pulls back my head. Off-kilter as I am, I lose my balance and bump into the night table. A figurine crashes to the floor and breaks.

"Damn. That's an antique," I say. "Madrigal is going to kill me."

He gets this queer look on his face as he stares down at the broken pieces. One by one, he picks them up. "No. It's not. See." He shows me the bottom with "Made in China" stamped on it.

"What is that inside?" I point to a metal contraption stuck to one of the pieces.

His mouth twists. "A fucking bug. Someone planted it in your room and used it to record you."

"Why would anybody do that?"

"To gather information. What else?" He throws on his shirt, slaps on his belt. I hurry to get dressed, but the bra clasp is tricky, and he throws open the door before I'm done.

Just as I snap the clasp, Madison appears in her doorway on the other side of the hall. She takes one look at Hunter and me and does the math. "Great. Everyone's having sex but me." Her gaze bounces from Hunter to me and back again. "What's going on?" Obviously, she's noticed the worried look on our faces.

"We found a bug in my room."

"Ooh, disgusting. What was it? Did you kill it?"

"Not that kind of bug," I say. "A listening device."

"Do you know where your sister and Steele are?" Hunter asks.

"In there." She points to the room at the end of the hallway and makes a face. "They're probably doing it right now too, so I wouldn't interrupt if I were you."

She's got sex on the brain, this girl. But who am I to judge when I do as well?

Hunter pounds on the door she pointed out. "Steele, Madrigal!"

When nobody answers, he turns back to Madison. "Are you sure they're in there?"

She throws open her arms. "Where else would they be?"

Hunter raises his fist to pound on the door again, but before he can do that, it opens. A definitely pissed off Steele stands on the other side wearing only a pair of boxer shorts. "Is the house on fire?"

"No."

"Is anybody hurt?"

"Not as far as I know."

Steele almost slams the door shut in Stone's face, but Stone slaps a hand against the wood, stopping him. "We found a listening device in Cristina's room."

"What?" Madrigal appears with a robe belted around her. Her hair's wet, and so is Steele's. Obviously, they were both in the shower. It doesn't take a rocket scientist to figure out what they were doing.

"Get dressed, both of you," Hunter orders. "We're going hunting for bugs."

That's when I look down and realize I'm wearing only a bra and panties.

Dinner is pushed back while the five of us, including Madison, look for listening devices. By the end of an hour, we've searched every room in the house and found fourteen. All of them identical.

"These weren't here when I first came to work for you," Hunter says. "I swept every room at that time and found nothing."

"So they've been installed since then," Steele returns.

"Yes."

"Which means it's an inside job."

"Yes."

"Someone from the staff planted those bugs. Someone I trusted," Madrigal says.

"And more than likely that someone is connected to Holden's death," Steele says.

Chapter 39

Trenton

Unable to believe she's been betrayed by someone she trusts, Madrigal cried herself to sleep. But the sad truth is she doesn't suspect the cruelest betrayer of all. It's two in the morning, and everyone's asleep. I roll out of bed and silently make my way through the house to the room she first assigned to me, the room to which I have the only key.

I nod to the guard on duty and, without saying a word, slip into the bedchamber. He won't think anything of it. He knows I use the space as my home office. In truth, it's so much more than that.

The safe her grandfather owned sits in one corner. A second one he hid behind one of the bookcases. Every once in a while, the knowledge I learned in my miserable youth comes in handy. So with very little effort, I'd figured out its combination. Holden's secrets lie within, secrets he never wanted to see light. Now it guards mine as well.

Her mother's journals, the ones that supposedly got burned.

I retrieve the diaries, the ones that cover the last four months of Marlena Berkeley's life. They're the keepers of her sins, the things she did, the lies she told. In truth, I should have burned them, but something kept me from obliterating those last few months of her existence.

I substituted her mother's journals. The ones that perched in the sitting room, unread, unloved. No one noticed they've gone missing. Those are the ones I set on fire that day.

The diaries provide ample witness of the scheme Marlena and Mitch dreamed up. A scheme that went sadly awry the night of April 8, 2002, the night she died. The journals point the way to her killer. But they also plunge a lethal injection into Mitch's arm.

I have a choice. Reveal them and damn him to eternity or hide them and risk losing the love of my life.

My choice is made. But really, it is no choice at all.

ACKNOWLEDGMENTS

First and foremost, thanks to the superb Montlake Romance team, especially Maria Gomez, editor extraordinaire; Melody Guy, for her outstanding editorial skills; and Jessica Poore, main fire-putter-outer for her unflagging energy and great cheer. Their commitment to excellence embodies everything that is great about Amazon Publishing.

A heartfelt thanks to the Crit Divas—Loni Lynne, Andy Palmer, and Teresa Quill—for your wonderful critiques. Your insightful comments pushed me to make *Shattered Trust* the best it could be.

Thanks to my fans. I love your e-mails, posts, and answers to my silly questions. I love having you in my life.

Last but not least, to my wonderful son, Juan, his beautiful wife, Melinda, and the kids, Derek, Alicia, and Skylar. Your love and support mean the world to me.

ABOUT THE AUTHOR

Photo © Renee Hollingshead 2014

Magda Alexander loves piña coladas and walking in the rain. Okay, enough of that. Rewind.

Magda loves reading steamy romances, which she's been doing since she was ten. So when it came time to write a book, guess what she wrote. A no-brainer, right?

Magda, a lifelong learner, graduated from the University of Maryland, where she majored in business administration (because her family had to eat) and minored in English (because she needed to dream). She's lived in Maryland most of her life and now resides close to the Catoctin Mountains in a city whose history dates back to colonial times.

Visit Magda on Facebook at www.facebook.com/MagdaAlexander RomanceAuthor or at her website: www.magdaalexander.com. To find out about her newest release, sign up for her mailing list at www.magda alexander.com/mailing-list.

Magda loves to hear from her fans. You may reach her at magda alexander@gmail.com.